MAKE ME

MANHATTAN MAFIA - BOOK TWO

paige press

MANHATTAN MAFIA - BOOK TWO

New York Times Bestselling Author
CD REISS

ALSO BY CD REISS

THE DILUSTRO ARRANGEMENT

Some girls dream of marrying a prince. I was sold to a king.

Mafia Bride | Mafia King | Mafia Queen

THE GAMES DUET

Adam Steinbeck will give his wife a divorce on one condition. She join him in a remote cabin for 30 days, submitting to his sexual dominance.

Marriage Games | Separation Games

THE EDGE SERIES

Rough Edge | On The Edge | Broken Edge | Over the Edge

THE SUBMISSION SERIES

One Night With Him | One Year With Him | One Life With Him

Paige Press
Leander, TX 78641

PAPERBACK ISBN: 978-1-957647-20-3

EBOOK ISBN: 978-1-957647-19-7

CHAPTER 1

DARIO

ST. NICHOLAS STREET STATION

It's after midnight, before sunrise. Baker's hours. The middle of the night watchman's shift, and the start of the day for morning radio hosts and garbage men.

Now is the time for sleepless men to meet so they can lie, and betray, and find vengeance.

We're just two guys on a subway platform in the middle of the night. We have no history. No murder, kidnapping, or revenge between us.

Massimo, with the mid-brown hair and hazel eyes of a long-forgotten invader, could pass for an overworked yuppie.

I know what I look like—a swarthy, dark-eyed monster with ready fists.

We meet at the northernmost end, past the stairs to 147th and St. Nicholas Street.

We do not shake hands when I approach.

"Those your dad's shoes?" I ask. "They look big."

"You going to make some crack about walking crooked in them or nah?"

I shake my head and look down the tracks as if I'm waiting for the train. Mocking his father's club foot is too cheap a shot. The deformity never stopped him from running the family with an iron fist. It didn't stop him from committing a horror that will scar Sarah forever.

"Thanks for meeting me," I say.

He looks away. The platform's nearly empty at this hour, but I follow his gaze anyway—and find a late-night commuter reading the morning newspaper.

That's not a garbage man with yesterday's *Post*. My brother-in-law didn't come alone.

"Fucking pleasure," he says, seeing that I've spotted his man.

I should have expected him to bring backup, since I didn't follow the rules either.

"Your message was received," I say. "If you get Sarah back, you're going to mutilate her and sell her for meat. Got it."

"You've seen all the messages I've sent my sister. I had nothing to do with..." He doesn't want to think about what was done to show me the threat to Sarah. The hollowing. The stitching. The dress. He'd rather talk about anything else. "What do you want?"

I hate asking for this, even as a path to something bigger and better. It's humiliating.

"Peace." I spit the word I can't digest.

"What the fuck?" Massimo shakes his head, looking around as if he can't meet my eyes. "You can't be serious."

"I am."

"For what?"

"For Sarah."

So much has happened since they found my greenhouse. Since Sarah met Willa. Since I started to think about a future that's not soaked in blood.

I clear my throat to pivot from dick-swinging threats. I shake my watch down and glance at it, trying to look disinterested in the hardest conversation I've ever had.

"I want the Colonia to find something else to do with their energy." When I put down my arm, I still don't know what time it is. "I'll do the same."

"You're really talking about a truce?"

"Call it what you want."

"Fucking hell." He laughs to himself. "You aren't the same guy since you took my sister."

I'm not. The Dario Lucari who lived the hour before he took Sarah had sold his soul to destroy the Colonia. This is my last chance to buy it back for her.

"I'm offering an end to all of this."

"You started this war, and now you're offering to stop it? Like it's a bargain? And my sister? Remember her? She's part of the deal."

I expected him to try this trade, but it still pisses me off. "We'll disappear. We'll leave New York. That's all you get out of me."

"Why would we do that?" He looks into the tunnel. The light is dim yellow and the air curls unpredictably, catching wrappers and plastic bags in looping whirlwinds—only to casually drop them on the tracks. "For what? We don't want

CD REISS

peace. That's not some prize. We want you strung up like a side of beef, and we want Sarah back."

"She's better off with me and you know it." I wasn't sure if he knew that until I see his reaction. He knows. He just doesn't care. "You want to fight for her, you're going to have a fight. But then what? Drag her home? To do what with her? Turn her out like a whore? Or slice her up and sell her?"

His flinch is slight and as fast as a blink, but it tells me there are things the Colonia do that he doesn't like thinking about. He was born human and raised to be an animal. Now he's trying hard to die an animal. But the real him—the human—keeps slipping out. He's a soft touch, a reformer, and too much of a coward to change anything before his father is out of the picture.

"We can't let you live." His voice is partially drowned out by a warm wind from behind him. A nearly empty train arrives on the opposite platform. "Your deal is bullshit, and it sucks."

We say nothing for a moment, while the doors open. He hides his anxiety. I hide my regrets.

Say you want peace, Massimo. All you have to do is want it.

Mr. *Post* doesn't get on the train.

Revenge is exhausting. It takes up too much mental real estate. Too much time. Too much love. I need all of it for something else.

The conductor's voice gurgles, and with a double beep, the doors slap closed.

We're just two men talking.

Wind gusts from behind me. Train on our side.

"I'm not coming to you with another deal." I shrug, offering to clean up a mess I made.

Massimo's sneer tells me the discount on salvation won't result in a sale. "Without Sarah, there's no deal."

"You can't have her. Ever. She's mine."

"Our women aren't your trophies."

He's getting mad. This doesn't amuse me the way it might have before.

"You think you can still live in your house while it's burning down," I argue. "You're pissing in corners and convincing yourself you got a hose. You're gonna climb out the window or I'm putting out the fire. Those are your choices."

He shakes his head, looking behind me. This conversation is over. I turn to leave.

"Get my sister out of the way," he calls, compelling me to face him again. "Because we're coming, and when we find you, she better not be where she's gonna get hurt. And you know now what's gonna happen if we get her alive and prove she's a traitor."

What they do to traitors makes my blood hot while my fingertips go cold. My vision is a tunnel, and his threat is the light at the end of it.

"Did you just threaten her?"

The train rattles and rumbles behind me, and the horn blasts with the hollowness of a stuffed-up nose.

"I'll take care of her." He goes from threatening her to pacifying me. "She'll be all right if you send her back and she comes willingly."

He's sincere. He'll try to protect her, but in the end, he can't push against generations of traditions and win without destroying his own family. He's a fool. All his promise does is illustrate the risk to her, and I don't have the vision to see past that.

"And if she doesn't?"

He blinks slowly. Looks away for a moment, then back at me. "I can't protect her then."

I take him by the lapels and swing him to the edge of the platform. He grabs my forearms to keep from falling onto the tracks.

"What good are you?" I ask through my teeth. "I might as well kill you first. Move up the line until you surrender."

Light shines against the tiles. The train's coming around the corner. The driver won't see in time to stop. A coward or a child would concede Sarah.

Massimo surprises me by being neither.

"No deal without her. No peace."

He strains against my hold. I do not react. Reacting too quickly is death, even with a train barreling down the tunnel. Massimo follows the same rulebook, meeting my gaze as the train hoots and the light shines brighter on his face.

I could let the train cut him in two and disappear into the tunnel.

Sarah would never forgive me, and that's why I lose my nerve and pull him onto the platform.

Movement in the corner of my eye. Sounds at the edges of perception. The flick of a newspaper. The jerk of an open coat. Massimo's wide eyes. The way his mouth makes an O. The roar of the train drowning out his voice.

There's no pain.

Only the blur of the world.

And falling so far.

Farther than the floor.

Flying, almost, into a certain hell.

The ringing in my ears and the rumble of the train against my chest.

My face pressed against filth.

Dario.

She's calling. Urgently.

The train is coming.

I am on the tracks.

Dario. It's me. I'm over here.

Is she? There's only darkness.

Here. Here. Here. Come to me here.

I turn my head toward her voice.

The light on the tracks turns to shadow.

The train is here.

CHAPTER 2

DARIO

TWELVE DAYS BEFORE

Nico didn't show for his meeting, which is either a disaster or nothing. Oria's still in the small conference room, losing her mind over it, and I'm with Oliver and Tamara, watching a bank of security monitors. It all looks normal. Calm. Boring. The precursor to everything happening at once. Oliver just reported an uptick in SWAT team calls. Sheriff, not the police. All the buildings have a greenhouse on the roof.

"Audio doesn't match the feed." Tamara's looking into the middle distance, one fingertip touching her headphone to push it tighter to her ear. "It's got a code added."

She scribbles in a notebook. I lean over her to read the scanner. Oliver stands with his thick arms crossed, boyish face set into mature concern.

I'd thought I was hiring him, and she was gravy. When did I realize that, between them, she's the one in charge?

Just now. That's when I realized.

"How would they know there's a greenhouse on our roof?" I ask. "Do we have a mole?"

My mind runs through a list of names. Santino's guys? Oria? We planted one with them. They could have done the same.

Why did Nico miss his meeting?

"A mole would have given up our address," Oliver says.

"Google Maps," Tamara adds, switching to satellite view, revealing the tightly packed roofs of Manhattan. Water towers. HVAC units. The occasional greenhouse, legal and otherwise, built by residents desperate for a bit of outdoor space. "They're playing darts with a blindfold."

I may be the target, but Sarah's the bull's-eye. If they get me, they get her, and she's mine. They can't have her.

We're going to have to postpone Sarah's freedom. No more jaunts out to buy soup until I destroy her family.

"They know too damn much." I jab my finger at the scanner feed as robberies and car accidents scroll past.

"We're cloaked," Tamara says. "No breaches. I checked."

"The only time the two spaces were directly connected was the wedding and the video call. Which one was it?"

Tamara's as unflappable as any man. "Let me pull up the video."

I know exactly which video she means.

Where I made her strip naked.

And kneel.

And beg for water.

And take off the one bit of clothing she begged to keep.

The greenhouse comes up. I lean over the keyboard, fast

forwarding so I don't have to confirm what a monster I am with an unwilling woman kneeling into my crotch.

Did I leave her there, sobbing, then fuck my hand the next day with the memory of it?

You bet I did.

The camera had been carefully set to keep the frame generic. No windows. Just the wall. No detritus, no furniture, no gardening supplies were inside it. But at one point, the clouds move, and in the corner of the frame, for one second, the moonlight leaves a grid-shaped shadow. I freeze it there.

"Shit," Tamara says. "She threw her shoe at the camera. We couldn't recalibrate until after." She looks back at me. "I'm sorry."

I don't need an apology. I need a solution. "If they come here and find Sarah, they're going to deliver her back to them."

"We'll move her," Oliver says. "Get her somewhere secure."

Easily done, but it's not enough. I can't send her away and stay behind to wait to defend my territory. If she goes, I go, and if I go, everyone goes.

"How much time do we have?" I ask.

"I'm checking dispatch now." Tamara presses a button on her headphones. The dispatcher's mechanical voice comes over the speakers. Some of it is code. Some plain English. She scribbles shorthand on a spiral pad. She's going so fast I can't catch any of it—then she stops. "I think I got it. The code."

"And?"

"Packing up from 42 Crosby. Waiting for next hit."

There's no defense against the authorities. Not if I want to stay under the radar. When they get here, they have to find nothing but an empty greenhouse and an abandoned office.

No team. No high-level security. No guns, and especially no Sarah Colonia.

They'll think it's another missed shot and move on. We'll return after they've turned their backs, more anonymous for being inspected and discarded.

Now that I have a plan for Sarah's safety, I'm relieved. "Everyone needs to be ready to get out of here. Go bags. Hard drives. Burners. Everything."

"Should we set up the car for you?" Oliver asks.

"I'll take Sarah in the ghost. Call Benny. Tell him to prep for us."

As I leave the office to get her, the job is done in my mind. I have a safe house an hour out of town. Nice grounds. Excellent security. Plenty of places to fuck.

I don't find her in the suite, making me noodles. She's in the hallway between with a rolling suitcase. As if she's going somewhere, and Willa's a thousand miles away from where she's supposed to be, when all I need is a minute or less to talk to Sarah.

I need Willa to go away.

I need Oria to back me up.

I need it all to happen before someone says something stupid.

Then Willa calls me baby, and herself my wife, and I'm stuck between the truth of the moment and the lies of the past.

"What didn't you tell me?" Sarah's red-faced, dug in, monolithic in confused rage.

Willa's shaking her head like a school principal with a recalcitrant student opposite her desk, and Oria looks as if she wants to turn the color of paint and disappear into the wall.

"Sarah." Do I sound too stern? Is she open to a command? "You need to go sit down, and I'll take care of this."

"Am I your wife?" She answers my unspoken questions. It doesn't matter if I sound stern. She's not open to being told what to do, and she's not going into my apartment without a fight in front of people. "Yes or no, Dario."

I lock my eyes on hers as if I can use that connection to tell her it's okay, that I adore her and she's the only woman I want. But that's too stupid to even be a wish.

"Jesus," Oria mumbles like some disgusted and shocked innocent who doesn't know a goddamn thing. She knew everything from jump. Everyone knew but Sarah because that was how it had to be.

"Yes or no!"

How do I explain this, and why the fuck do I have to right now?

"Yes or no!" Sarah's fists are balled, white-knuckled, tight enough to crack walnuts. I taught her to expect something from me, and now here I am, betraying her in front of Oria and Willa.

How did I end up surrounded by so many women?

"Yes and no," I say. "Now give me a god *damn fucking* second to explain."

Less than a second passes.

"No." She moves for the elevator, but I block her way. "I'm tired of your explanations. They're just piled on top of lies and excuses."

"You're my wife." Truth weighs my voice. "You."

Willa scoffs, and suddenly, I'm nothing. The wedge of fact will not be used to displace the stone of truth.

"What have you done?" Willa asks. "What did you become while I was gone?"

"He's a monster," Sarah answers. "It's what he's always been."

She slips away to the only exit I'll allow, walking into the suite at the end of the hall. I bark her name like a sergeant who expects obedience and discipline, but she doesn't even look at me before closing the door. I rush to it, but as I push against the wood, the latch snaps.

"Let me in!" I pound my fist against the door, expecting her to open it because obedience is the rule, along with truth and loyalty. But the lock snaps with a gentle crack. "Do you think this door's going to stop me? This is my door. I own it. I can open it any time I want."

"Leave her be," Willa says from a mile down the hall. "She's traumatized, and all you're doing is making it worse."

"Open up." Cheek and shoulder to the wood, I smack the door. "I can get in, Sarah. I have every code and key to every lock in this building. I don't want to do that. You need to let me in because you want to."

My ears are ringing, but I can just hear the sound of something heavy against the floor. A piece of furniture being moved. She's barricading herself in. I punch the code, but it's too late. The door won't budge.

Willa lets out a half chuckle that turns into a scoff.

I turn away from the door. Life in the Caribbean sun has made Willa's skin darker. Richer. Her light brown eyes are as clear and incisive as ever—taking no bullshit from me or anyone.

Good. I have no bullshit to offer.

"Who called you here?" I ask.

Willa answers by turning to Oria.

"She wasn't going to St. Eustatius on her own." Oria's bent into a curve of regret, shifting her body and gaze like a defendant who never bothered to plead innocent. "Not with you doing..." She waves in my general direction.

"Doing what?" Willa asks.

My wife of the law came here for Sarah, my wife of scars and blood. Willa does not like having her time wasted. Messes are dealt with. Glitches are stamped out like roaches.

We had this in common, and I appreciated it. Now I'm the hiccup in the plan. If she tries to brush me aside or wipe me out I'm going to regret hurting her, but I'm not sure I'll have any choice.

"Your apartment's empty," I say. "If you need a new key—"

"I have it, but I—"

There's a deep scrape, then a thud from the other side of Sarah's door. Furniture.

"When I need you, I'll call you." I rap on Sarah's door, speaking sweetly enough to attract a swarm of bees. "Let me in."

Silence. I can't sense her. How is that possible? How can I not know what she's feeling at this very moment? How can she be so quiet when the noise in my head is so loud?

There are too many distractions. The questions and the

looks. The intonations in what's said and the clarity of what's unsaid.

"What is wrong with you?" Willa's brow twists in confusion. She's living the reality of weeks ago, when we agreed to take certain risks and not others. I can't pretend she's not there.

"Sarah Colonia is staying with me. Period. You can get on a plane now or you can go downstairs, to your studio, and rest first. You can eat raw meat and spit nickels for all I care. Just get out of this hallway."

"Give her time," Willa says.

"Fuck off," I murmur when I can't shout.

Oria rests one hand on Willa's arm and hits the elevator button with the other. "I'll fill you in."

The elevator slides open. I want them to get sucked into it and be gone. I want to be left here waiting for a sign that I'm not alone. None comes. It's just me, this door, this hall, and the inaccessible woman close enough to touch.

"It's not what you think." My fingertips stroke the wood as if it's her skin, and my forehead leans against it as if I'm sharing my mind with her. "Willa is... she was..."

The wall next to me rattles and hisses as if a nest of snakes is trapped behind the plaster.

It's the pipes.

She's in the shower.

I'm talking to a slab of wood, not a woman.

My forehead's pressed to the door as I consider whether I should saw off the knob, pry away the jamb piece by piece, or go down to the garage and grab the chainsaw in the storage cage. I don't think it has any gas in it, but I have cars I can siphon from.

Sarah now knows what I've pretended wasn't true. She's not my wife and never was. I started out fooling her and ended up fooling myself.

I close my eyes and replay the moments before Willa walked out of the elevator. Tamara is worried about the NYSD swatting greenhouses, and Oria's worried about Nico. I'm worried about both, but I can't think around this. Fucking. Door.

With Oria and Willa gone, I am left alone—worshipping an unseen goddess, waiting for a sign.

And it comes.

Tamara opens the door on the other end of the hall, and that sign arrives with the whistling speed of a missile.

CHAPTER 3

SARAH

I don't know how I had the strength to move the armoire, but no one's getting in until I move it again. It's turned the long way so that it's wedged between the door and the wall of the front closet.

My prison.

This shower. This suite. This building.

My prison is only a prison because I believe I'm married, which I'm not.

Without the marriage, the suite is a residence and the building is a shelter. Dario can hold my body, but my heart and mind are free.

But... no. I keep thinking with the facts of the past. There are new facts now.

He has no claim to my body. He belongs to a woman with an aura of conviction and a voice that can't possibly waver or sound unsure.

Of course, he married her out of choice. Who wouldn't? She's magnificent. Confident. Whole. Unbroken. She exudes a kind of competence that I've associated with men. I can't compete with someone so beautiful and strong. I'm her exact opposite. Weak. Ignorant. Compliant.

Under lukewarm water, with my clothes sticking to me, Dario feels like the source of my terror. I've been deeply betrayed by someone I'm sure I love. I am torn to pieces, set on fire, ashes blown to the winds.

What's left?

Dario.

I can smell him on my skin. It's a scorched memory of his touch. I hear his voice. Feel that first kiss. His smile, so elusive and hard-won. His story—not the events, but the telling of it on a trip to the south and east.

I want him so badly it hurts. Another minute of thinking of his sweet cruelty and I'll crack. But what will I do to stay whole? What's the story of the next hours? The coming days? How long can I guard my heart?

Can I imagine a future without him?

I can't, but that's because I was never allowed to imagine a future for myself.

I don't want to be Schiava, or *principessa*. I don't want to be a Colonia or a Lucari.

I want to choose and be chosen.

I want to be Willa.

The ash of who I was may be in the wind, but Dario Lucari is still deep inside me. All the water in the world won't wash him off.

Willa is the best thing that could have happened to me. If she's his wife, then I'm just a woman.

Just a woman.

Not the princess of Colonia—an asset to trade for territory. I am not hindered, owned, promised, or betrothed.

I get out of his shower, dry off with his towel, dress in the clothes he chose for me, and sit on the bed he bought for the women he valued.

The wood box of art supplies sits on my dresser. Did I almost forget it? He got it to please me—and that makes it the only thing I own that's truly mine.

I am not his. I never was. It was always all a lie.

And since I'm not Dario's wife, I have no obligation to him. I do not have to please him, or obey him, or split my loyalties. There are no more rules. No more boundaries. No more husband.

I'm just me, alone, floating unanchored in a nameless void. The feeling of being his wife was terrifying. Not being connected to him is scary, but something in me has changed. Under the fear is a current of possibility. Hope. But for what?

At the kitchen counter, I eat with the art box at my side and a pencil in my hand. I draw landscapes and skylines. What's in the window and what I imagine beyond it. The boundaries of the copy paper frustrate the expanse of what's in my mind.

Dario's in my mind.

I can't see past him. He's too close to me and this paper is too small to contain him.

Asking for something bigger is out of the question. Everything I need is right here, and when it's not—when this space runs out of necessities—I'll have to leave knowing who I am or die like a branch cut from a tree.

So I move the couch away from the wall, revealing a

lighter space. I move the end tables away, leaving one close enough to hold my supplies... and I draw.

Mountains. Seas. Boats. Clouds full of rain and lined in silver. My arms are too short for a single line, so I walk along the wall. I stand on a chair to find the upper edges of my dreams.

They're not defined in words, but I find them—and yet I find myself lost in small things.

His chin and lips at a mountain's peak.

His hand on me.

The outer edge of his eye.

What I see when I kiss him. His sliced-off ear, the back curve of his neck.

I love this shape. This scar.

No. I won't break for him again.

But what will I do instead of crack? What's the story of the next hours? The coming days? How long can I stay in this suite?

Can I imagine a future without him?

I can't, but that's because I was never allowed to imagine a future for myself.

He's lied to me and betrayed me. He's worse in my eyes today than he was the first time he pointed a gun at me. I thought more of him when he put dirt in a water glass and made me drink it.

All that disdain will go away in time, and I'll fold under the pressure of his touch. I'll forgive him and I'll come out... maybe in that order... or maybe not. But I'll make peace with him on my terms, in my time.

These are my choices to make, and I won't be rushed.

CHAPTER 4

DARIO

"BROKEN TRAFFIC LIGHT," I SAY, LOOKING OUT THE WINDOW.

Connor's on one side of me. Oliver's on the other. Tamara's behind us, decoding the dispatcher's messages into a coded shorthand, and Sarah's still behind a door.

Pedestrians make slow, steady progress below us as if everyone isn't separated from everything they love in the world, but the car traffic isn't doing as well. The light at the corner of Ninth and 47th blinks alternating flashes of red in both directions. The intersection is snarled with people who don't know how to manage a four-way stop.

"There was a broken light reported right before the last three greenhouse SWAT hits," Oliver says. "Could be coincidence."

"It ain't," Connor says.

"How long do we have?" I ask, knowing full well it won't be enough time to gently coax Sarah from hiding.

"Forty-five," Tamara confirms what I already know.

Forty-five minutes isn't enough to earn Sarah's forgiveness... but it's enough to escape and live to fight another day.

"Everybody out."

The chainsaw's tank has about a quarter cup of fuel in it. The way it stinks up the storage area in the garage, a guy could think that gas has been evaporating since it got those pine chips in the blade, years ago.

The red milk crate with the safety goggles and gloves sits on the floor under a sagging shelf of who even knows the fuck what. The single bulb hanging from a wire is so bright it hides details in hard shadows.

Behind me, the scrape of footsteps on the concrete is soft, but calculated not to frighten me into alertness. Careful and sure. Respectful but confident.

The gate is open, chain dangling with the open padlock at the end of it. Anyone could just walk in while my back is turned, but it's Willa, and she doesn't need an open lock to be dangerous.

"Dario." She uses her social worker voice. There was a time when it soothed me. Now the bite of saccharine opens to a bitter aftertaste.

"Go home." When I yank the chain, the motor spins and coughs. "Not to your apartment. Home, home."

"When Sarah Colonia agrees to come with me."

Never. My mind screams, but my lips stay shut as I yank the chain again. Any harder and it's going to snap, but the motor doesn't catch.

I pull the chain again. Same result. This ignored, unused

machine knows better than to start. This little cage isn't the place to run a chainsaw. What am I going to do? Bring it upstairs with a roaring motor? I might open a wall in the elevator. I might cut the building in two. New York City is too fragile for me right now.

"She stays here with me." I drop the chainsaw back into the crate and dig to the bottom of the one next to it, finding a little cardboard box.

"Why?"

"Because at some point, soon, I'm going to have to explain to her who the fuck you are." I read the printing on the box. Wrong. I toss it and hunt for another. "And I don't want you around, complicating the conversation."

"About me being your wife?"

"Yeah." Another box. Wrong again. "Sarah doesn't have a nuanced idea of marriage."

"None of them do. What I don't understand is why it matters to you."

The last box is labeled with the right size. I open it. Three spark plugs. I pluck one out and pocket it.

"I don't have time to explain it." Opening the motor cover, I find the old plug, and grunt as I remove it with my fingers. I have a wrench somewhere, but this is faster. "But having you around is going to hurt her, and I don't want her hurt. So, good-bye."

I grab the chainsaw and stand, facing her.

A light flashes from the parking lot behind her. Car headlamps. My team is doing what I told them and getting the fuck out of here.

"You don't get to decide what hurt she bears. Not after what you did." Willa steps forward, completely blocking the way out of the chain-link cage, touching nothing, hands folded in front of her, manicured thumbs tapping. The approach is utterly non-threatening and fully assured. Blessed are the peacemakers, for they shall give me a fucking headache.

"What I did was set us up to win a war you chose to fight with me." I approach the exit with a chainsaw in my hand and she still won't budge.

"While I was down there getting complacent, you were up here acting like a damn vicious monster."

"I did what had to be done."

"Bullshit. You changed. You're regressing."

"I want to protect her!"

"If you want to protect her, you'll send her with me."

Willa's right.

I have fucking changed.

The man who kidnapped Sarah would use her as bait. He'd throw her back to the pack of wolves he stole her from. She'd return home a broken woman with horror stories bad enough to force them to pause, and in that pause, I'd attack.

None of that is going to happen.

Willa's always right, and fuck her for it, but she's only seen a slice of the truth.

Everything's changed.

"Lock up on the way out." I brush by her as I leave.

She's perfectly capable of locking the cage, since she helped build it.

Breathless from running up the stairs, I burst into my apartment with the chainsaw.

We don't have much time.

Crossing through the living room, I slide open a hidden door.

On my wedding night, Sarah heard Nico and Oria in his old apartment, which can only be accessed through mine. I'd walled it off from the hallway until he comes home. Matter of security. Didn't stop them from walking through my residence to get to it.

I enter Nico's bedroom like a hurricane and yank the bed away from the wall.

I put my ear against the cool plaster and hear a scratching sound from the other side, as if she's clawing her way out, but gently.

Crouching, I open the chainsaw's motor door and snap in a new spark plug. As I do this, I realize the gentle scritch-scritch is her drawing on the opposite side of the wall.

"Sarah."

"Dario." Her voice sounds far away.

"We're leaving." I close the motor cover.

"I'll leave when I'm ready," she says.

"Step away."

"Why?"

I yank the chainsaw cord and it roars like a bear poked with a stick.

I bend and put the chain against the wall, squinting against flying plaster as I push the saw up and over, then back down to the floor, pulling it across the top of the molding. Then it sputters, kicks, and dies. Out of gas.

"Back up," I call, then shove my shoulder into the wall. It

25

cracks, and on the third hit, bends. I smash my body against it over and over, grunting, "Mine. Mine. Mine," with every impact.

The wall drops with a *pop* and a spray of dust.

Sarah stands in the center of the room, sweet brown eyes wide as chocolate coins. A dozen walls could not keep me away from this woman.

Mine.

Neither of us move over the line separating us.

I have to tell her to get her toothbrush and underwear before her family comes to take her away, but she's so beautiful, there's nowhere to run.

"You're ready." I step forward, onto the fallen wall.

"You lied to me," she says, stepping back.

"I told you our marriage wasn't legal." Forward again.

"You don't get a medal for that." She points at me while taking another step back. "You knew that if I knew you were already married—"

"You wouldn't have obeyed me. Damn fucking right. You would have screwed your ass tight to your Colonia bullshit... your loyalty. Your upbringing. That trash fire of a wedding I saved you from."

"You didn't care who I married."

"I *didn't!*"

What am I saying?

Why is my face hot? Why am I shaking?

How did it come to this?

"That was then." I put my hands on her shoulders. "This is now."

Why is she crying? God damnit, why is she crying?

No. Comfort is too much of a distraction. I need to get

her out of here before they take her away from me forever. Physically, she needs to be safe from the world. Her body is all I have control over. It's the only safety I can guarantee. I'll never be able to protect her heart and mind from me.

I bend, pick her up, and throw her over my shoulder.

CHAPTER 5

SARAH

Someone pulls Willa away, and her voice is lost behind a slamming door.

His own wife was trying to protect me, but I'm tired of being protected.

Dario throws me over his shoulder before I can tell him how sick to death of it I am.

"Stop!"

I just want this to stop. The taking. The forcing. The surprises and upheavals. But after Dario throws me over his shoulder, he doesn't even pause before taking me down the stairs. I'm whipped around corners, blurring the windows at each landing.

Twisting my body, I jab my elbow into the back of his head until he stops on a concrete landing and roughly puts me on my feet.

"You want to stay here?" His shout echoes off the walls. "They're coming for you."

"Who?"

"I have no time to explain it to you."

"Make time."

"Your family. They'll be here in under an hour, and you can either come with me or you can sit in that apartment and wait for them to come and take you back."

"They don't want me back."

He shakes his head, palms up, perplexed. Starts to say something. Finds it inadequate or maybe untrue, stopping himself.

"You staying with me... it makes them look weak."

"And if they get me back, *you'll* look weak."

"I'll be dead." He grabs my arms as if I'm about to run away. "I don't care how I look. I just want you to be safe."

"I'll be safe with them. As long as you have me, you're in danger."

He bows his head in a kind of overwhelmed resignation.

"I can't do this anymore. What if I just go back?" I ask.

"What if you do?" He stands straight, looks up the stairs as if considering that old life on the top floor, then back at me. His anger seems to melt into exhaustion.

"Right. What if I do?"

"Then I'll stay with you until your family comes."

"How long?" I ask.

"Half an hour."

"They'll kill you."

"I'm not leaving you here alone."

He's not talking about owning me or using me as leverage. There's only one other motivation for him to want to stay here when someone's coming to kill him.

"To protect me?"

"No." He presses his eyes and mouth shut for a moment,

as if looking inside himself to make sure he's speaking the truth. "To be with you. Before they find us. Before they take you back. I want that time. It's mine. I want every second of it, and if that means I stay here with you and wait for..." The sentence falls off the end of a cliff. He takes my hand. "Fine. It's fine. We've done it my way from the beginning. Now we can do it your way."

He starts to pull me up the stairs, but I resist.

"You'll stay here just to be with me, even though you think I'm staying to be rescued so I can get away from you?" I ask.

"I don't think you want to be rescued. I don't even think you want to get away from me."

"What do you think I want?"

He shrugs as if it's obvious. "You want to make your own decision."

He'd stay here and wait for his death just to be with me.

I squeeze his hand and lead him up the stairs. When we reach the top floor, the hallway is unnervingly quiet.

"I need to get back into my suite," I say.

He takes me through his apartment and the cut-out wall. The suite was only abandoned a few minutes ago, but there's a forlorn feeling in the air. The newly exposed interior of the fallen wall has released a stale, musty smell.

Dario closes the blinds.

"Give me a minute," I say, crouching in front of what's left of my mural to scoop up dropped pencils. "Let me get this together." I drop the pencils in the box. "I think some got stuck in the couch cushions if you want to check."

He doesn't move. At first, I think he's staring at the hole in the wall, but he's looking at the intact half of my mural.

Hands in his pockets, as if he's not interested in checking the crevices of the couch. Men are all the same. I rip off the cushions and throw them to the side.

"What does it mean?" he asks.

"I have no idea." I grab what pencils I can see and hunt around the seams for stragglers. "Just whatever I was thinking about." With the last rescued pencil in my grip, I toss them all into the box and shut it. "I'm going to have to carry this, I guess."

He takes the box and puts it aside.

"Let me move the couch away from the plaster." He brushes his lips along the length of my neck, and I'm rendered nonverbal. "Then I'll fuck you on it."

"We have time? I thought—?"

He silences me with a kiss I can't refuse, and I'm immediately made of softened butter, wrapping my legs around him so I can rub myself against his erection like an animal in heat.

"Fuck moving the furniture." He pulls my pants down and props me against the arm of the couch, grinding against my bare, wet pussy.

We must have time, if this is what he wants.

"First." He unbuckles, and I hold on to his neck. "I'm going to fuck this cunt like I own it. Then I'm going to fuck it slow, over and over." He releases his cock, fisting the thick shaft. "I'm going to die fucking you."

"Do we have time?"

He thrusts into me. "No." He pushes again, burying himself deep. "You're going to take my cock until you forget how it feels when I'm not inside you."

"But—"

"God, you feel so good."

He keeps his promise to fuck me like he owns me, grinding fast and deep while he pulls me against him like a doll. My legs are gelatin, and the rest of me is a simmering pot on the stove with the flame turned up to high.

He fucks me harder and groans with satisfaction, grabbing a breast and squeezing until I whimper because the pain delays the oncoming orgasm.

"I'm going to mark your soul," he says against my neck with the seriousness of a wedding vow. "You'll belong to me in darkness."

"Yes." I don't know what I'm agreeing to, but yes, yes, yes. "Make me yours."

"You won't know how to come without thinking of me."

"God, yes."

"You want to come."

"I do. Please."

Still inside me, he brings me to the center of the couch, his arms wrapped tightly around me, and fucks me until all the stars fall from the sky and fill my body.

As we come down, he kisses my face and neck, whispering sweetness I never thought I'd hear from any man.

"I don't want to get out from under you, but I have personal needs to attend to."

He laughs and gets off me. We're both still half-dressed, wrinkled and twisted. I hop to my bathroom, strip down to nothing, clean up, and dress in something clean and comfortable.

When I get to the living room, he's fully dressed with his back to me, facing my silly mural. The couch is even farther from the wall.

From behind, I slip my arms around his waist.

"I'm all over this thing," he says.

"I was just drawing whatever came into my mind." I stand next to him. He puts his arm around me. "You came into it a lot."

He kisses me and looks back at the wall as if he's on a rooftop looking over the East River.

"I'm ready," I say, sliding away. "I'll just take the suitcase Oria packed, then we can go."

"Agreed. I have better supplies at my place."

"You'll have to carry the art box downstairs. It won't fit." I snap up the suitcase handle.

He looks at me with his hands on his hips and his brow in a knot.

"What?" I ask.

"We're staying."

"I thought we were going."

"You said you wanted to make your own decisions," he says.

"And you said that if I decided to stay, you'd stay with me."

"Right."

"And we both know you have no one else here, so it's you against however many. So you have no chance. We talked about this. They'll kill you."

"I thought..." He stops himself, letting out a quick laugh.

"That I wanted you to die?"

"Not that you *wanted* it."

"That I didn't care? That I'd let you get yourself killed?" I put my palm against his chest. The pound of his heart is the

33

same. Not weaker or slower for the sacrifice he thought he had to make for me. "Dario. Really?"

He runs his fingers through his hair, looking away. He's as tall and powerful as he ever was, but his vulnerability is unbearable.

"We should go." He kisses the top of my head. "We're already behind."

CHAPTER 6

SARAH

THE WIDE, ROLLUP DOOR NEXT TO AN OPEN CHAIN-LINK STORAGE cage is marked DANGER—LIVE ELECTRICITY. Dario inputs a code that seems to go on forever.

"Aren't you going to get electrocuted?" I point at the yellow sign.

"That's fake." The light goes green, and he presses his finger to the pad. "This is our ride."

There's a loud clack and a beep, then the door rolls up, revealing a pristine black Audi parked in a tight space, another rollup door on the opposite side—in front of it.

"This is the ghost car." He reaches for a briefcase on a high shelf. "Registered to a fake name in a shell corporation. Untraceable. I have it maintained and taken out once a month."

"It's nice."

He pops the trunk and puts the briefcase, my art box, and my suitcase inside. "I've never even driven it."

Dario slaps the trunk closed, and in the echo, a word forms in the concrete cavern.

"Sarah?" The thick clap of a door closing follows.

I recognize the voice. The familiarity shakes my guard loose, and I turn to see one of my father's many security men crossing the lot from the stairway door.

"Sonny?"

He's big at the shoulders and bigger in the waist, with a full head of sandy hair and a mouth full of perfect teeth. Daddy called him Muscles, because he had them, and Rock, because he was as dumb as one.

"We found you." He seems happy to see me. His smile is relaxed and genuine.

I glance to the side, looking for Dario, but he's not there.

"What are you doing here?"

It's the only question I can think of besides, Where did Dario go?

"I knew you'd be down here!" He reaches for his pocket, and I flinch before I realize what he's pulled out is a phone. "I'll get you out before the swatters are done clearing upstairs."

"I don't want—"

Behind him, Dario appears, fast as lightning. A sleeve appears across Sonny's neck—an arm. Another arm locks the first in place.

"Sonny Graco." Dario swings the man to get him on his heels. "Nice to see you." Sonny claws at Dario's arm. "How many?"

Another minute of struggle and Sonny's legs flap like two flags in a storm.

"He can't breathe!" I shout, as if Dario doesn't know.

"How many with you?" He jerks Sonny's head to the side. "Show me!"

Sonny makes a gacking sound and holds up four fingers.

"Thank you." Dario lets him go.

I exhale, but it's too soon for relief.

Sonny's on his knees for half a second when Dario takes out a knife and slits his throat.

I've never seen a person die, so I don't know if it always happens in slow motion in the space of a blink. My senses are heightened. I hear the lights buzzing, smell the copper of fresh death. The air against my skin is warm and heavy.

By the time I gasp, Sonny is already on the ground.

"Wait," I whisper too late.

"We're going." Dario grabs my elbow.

"He has kids."

"They all have families. Come!"

I let him pull me away, into the car, wide-eyed and empty as he drives up the ramp, through the gate, and into the streets of Manhattan.

Along the East River, joggers slog through the gray foam air and the slabs of the Queens skyline are softened in the haze.

We're stuck in traffic, trapped between movement and stillness. We are bodies flung through the air on our heels, shoulders forward, chests back, waiting for the ground to hit us from behind.

Dario squeezes my cool, dry hands and says, "Welcome to New York," which is meant to console me about the traffic.

Timothy never had to take me far and always seemed to be able to avoid a jam.

I wonder if he's alive. And William. And how many more?

"Just so you know," he starts after a pause. "You don't have to worry about Willa."

"She doesn't have to worry about me either." I take my hand away and fold the left fist under my right palm. "You can tell her that."

"She's my wife by the law. You're my wife by scars."

I rub the sore lines on my fingers. The tissue is still sensitive. "I don't even know what you think that means."

"What do you want to know?"

"Why you feel comfortable saying your wife isn't really your wife."

"She's..." He stops himself with a quick wave and starts over. "It was a situation. I met runaways all the time. Hired them to do stuff. This one, Rosemarie... she was maybe thirteen. I knew before she even opened her mouth she was Colonia. Nico was the one to get the story out of her. She was sold into marriage to some old fucking pig. She got out."

"How?" I'm surprised. Once a girl is promised, she's in a transitory place, owned by everyone and no one. So she's protected and watched by both families.

"She's a smart, smart girl. Funny too. But once she told Nico shit, she never told another outsider, she got spooked. She ran off and got picked up by Protective Services. Willa was her social worker. So, I caught Willa on her way home."

"Ah."

"Ah, what?"

"You met her and saw how she was and you had to have

her." I shrug as if it's obvious. He shoots me a glance that says it's anything but. "Look at her. And she's so... I don't know... she knows her business. If I were a man, I'd want to marry her."

He looks away as if he can hide his chuckle. "It wasn't like that. I mean, maybe a little."

"Thought so."

"At first, she didn't believe me about the Colonia. But it got through when Rosemarie's foster parents reported a story the girl told about wedding scars. Everything clicked, and Willa... when she gets fired up, watch out. She was all in. Wanted to know all about them... you. The Colonia. First thing was to get Rosemarie a permanent home with people who knew what the Colonia was about and that was me, and now Willa. But the adoption was going through Catholic Charities, and they don't adopt to single parents."

"So you got married."

"We did." He faces me. "It was business."

"You cared about another person together." I turn away. "That's not business."

"Maybe. Everything after that, though. We were in the business of catching girls who escaped and getting them out. Willa's parents were on St. Maarten, so we settled on an island close by, where we could hide money and identities. There were bumps. We fight. She can be a fucking bitch, but we're close. Not husband and wife. We understand each other."

"You've both been living in the same world," I say. "Under the same laws. Where these scars don't mean anything. The only reason you learned what they'd mean to me is so you could hurt my family."

Maybe he's lying to me. Maybe he's lying to himself. Maybe he's expressing a disappointing truth. None of it matters. I want to be his as much as I want to be free, and I don't know how both can be true.

"You're crazy not to."

"Listen to me." He whispers so softly I have no choice but to listen. "I'm trying to tell you I don't love her. You have to believe me."

"No," I say in the same low whisper, then raise my voice just enough to speak firmly. "I don't have to believe you. You're not my husband. You lied to me. I don't want to want you, but I do. I accept that. I'm not who I was, and I'll never be again. I was innocent before you came, and I can't ever have that back. Those rules about obeying you and serving you... those are gone because you broke them. Whatever way I am now, you made me."

He digs my left hand from under my right and presses on the tender line at the base of my middle finger. "These scars, they're forever. They're not meaningless to me. Blood was drawn. Our names are cut into each other's bodies."

"Sweet words." I let him caress my hand, but not responding in kind. There's no lying left in me. I'm not obfuscating to protect myself from him anymore.

"I don't expect you to trust me, but you need to." He looks at me when he says it, and since we're at a dead stop, he can hold my gaze. "We're at war. We're being hunted. I can't let them find you, and when you run, you turn your back. Do you understand what I'm trying to tell you?"

I turn away to look out the front. "You want to face them."

Them.

Sonny was a *them* and now his throat is opened up into a bloody smile. I have very few memories of him. He was just there. He said hello and asked me if I was having a good day. He drove me places sometimes. I can't even remember where I went.

"I have to." He puts my hand in his lap. "But if you trust me, I can show you... teach you the things you need to know." In the stopped traffic, he faces me again. "I can fight knowing you can live without me."

"What do you mean, 'live without you'?"

"War is a risky business. People die. Husbands leave wives behind."

Arguing about whether or not we're married seems beside the point. He's talking about murdering and getting murdered.

"I don't want that."

"Let me worry about it then. You just get to learning."

"I don't want to learn how to kill someone the way you did."

The traffic opens up, and he speeds ahead. He's concentrating. Pensive. One hand rests on the bottom of the wheel, the other on my thigh.

The last time I rode in the front seat was the first time. Armistice Night. I didn't even appreciate it at the time, but now I like being able to know what's in front of me.

"I'm sorry you had to see that." He changes lanes.

"You didn't have to do it. We could have just run."

"They need to know I'll kill for you."

"I won't kill for you, Dario, so don't teach me how."

There's an island in the river, between us and Queens. It flicks by at a constantly shifting angle.

Am I a liar? Would I kill for him? Will I ever find out?

The sounds of the world are shut out. Even the engine and the tires under us are muffled. We pass two women jogging abreast in the fog, ponytails swinging. They're a flash in my sight, then they're gone.

"What do you want most in the world, Sarah? Not a *thing*. Any object you want, I'll get you. That's a given. Tell me what you want to *do*. Where you want to go. Who you want to be."

"No one's ever asked me that before."

"I'm asking, and I know you can't answer." He slides his hand over mine. "Not yet. But you will when I'm through with you. I'll teach you everything."

"But will you?"

"Why wouldn't I?"

"Because then I can leave you."

"I will." He slides his hand from mine and drapes it over the steering wheel. "And you won't. But if I ever leave you, you'll know how to decide what to do and who to be. You'll be strong enough to save yourself when I can't."

He's not threatening to leave me. He's not threatening anything. He's sharing his reality in all it's brevity and intensity.

I don't want him to die, or leave, or break himself off from my love, ever. I squeeze my eyes shut as if that will keep out the pain of the separations I imagine. He didn't have to touch me to brush away my anger. It wasn't his dominance or the contrast of his more soothing charms.

He's placated me with the promise of an education.

CHAPTER 7

SARAH

W E LEAVE THE WATERFRONT AND DRIVE INLAND. THE FEELING OF being stopped in time wears off with the needs of my body. I'm thirsty and I have to pee. He won't stop for food or a bathroom break or anything until we're "out of NYSD jurisdiction."

I don't know what that means, but it seems important. I can hold it.

Without being reminded of my increasingly urgent situation, Dario gets off the highway, makes a few turns into a neighborhood that's quieter and grassier than the one we left, and pulls into a strip mall.

"Stay close." He puts the car into park. "We're not safe yet."

He walks around to my side, eyes everywhere in a heightened state of alertness, waving to an old guy sitting at one of the little tables outside Tommy's Pizzeria, then he opens my door to help me out.

"You hungry?" Dario checks over his shoulder when a car creeps up behind us.

"I could eat."

"Good," he says before greeting the man at the table, who's stood up. "Tommy!"

They shake hands and fold each other into a back-slapping hug.

"Dario, it's been too long."

Tommy is in his fifties with a full head of salt-and-pepper hair, a ruddy, clean-shaven face, and thick, gray eyebrows.

"Been busy." Dario takes my hand, pauses with his eyes on our hands. Maybe it's the scars, or the snowflake ring, but he takes a moment before turning back to Tommy. "This is my wife, Sarah."

He and I can argue about the technical truth of that statement, but not about my immediate reaction. My heart doesn't resist it, nor does my mind shout out against it. Willa or no, for now, I am his wife or something close enough to it. I am comforted. I am accepted.

"*Signora Lucari.*" Tommy takes my hands and kisses my cheeks. "*Piacere mio!* Come in, come in." We follow him into the little restaurant. "Junior's making up his specialty. Sarah, you like *pizza bianco*?"

I don't know what he's saying, so I look at Dario. He speaks to Tommy in Italian, and Tommy says something back. They laugh, and we sit in a booth.

"What was that about?" I ask Dario when Tommy's gone.

"It's nothing." His eyes are on the windows and door. "You should have the *bianco*."

44

"Don't tell me it's nothing."

He turns back to me, head cocked. "I'll tell you what I like."

Direct confrontation is not even a consideration, but I offer the same tilted head and add a raised eyebrow. The same expression Grandma made when she was daring me to keep up whatever behavior would lead to a Correction.

Dario's concession is quick enough to surprise me. "He asked if you were the Sarah from second blood."

"I don't know what that means."

"Most people won't say the Colonia name in public. It's like speaking of the devil will summon him. So, they use second blood, for the church."

"Precious Blood?" I like the way questions feel in my mouth. The way they flick over the tongue. Even more, I love the way my mind opens in the expectation of an answer.

"It was built second. After the one Downtown. *Secondo sangue.*"

"And we're too scary to mention out loud."

"You are."

"Then why were you both laughing?"

"You ask a lot of fucking questions."

I shrug, and he fills in the blanks.

"You never had a *bianco* because you—your people—pretend you're American. You don't learn the language, the culture. Nothing. I can't speak great. But my dad spoke it in the house, and I learned enough to do business. You people? Nothing but red, white, and blue."

"We've been in New York since it was New Amsterdam."

Tommy comes over with water that I immediately gulp. "Junior's coming with the pie in a minute." He sits himself

45

at the end of the table. "Where you headed? Anything you need?"

"A bathroom?" I answer even though I wasn't the one he asked.

"Of course. It's right down—"

"I'll take her."

With his hand between my shoulder blades, Dario walks me to a narrow back passage and opens a door marked *Donne* in a carved plastic rectangle. He flicks on the light, checks behind the door, the corners, and inside the cabinet. He makes sure the window is locked and peers up at the vent.

Satisfied, he steps into the hall. "I'll wait here for you."

I check what every woman does when she enters a bathroom.

"Toilet paper." I open the cabinet under the sink and take out a fresh roll, holding it up for him.

He's already distracted by something in the parking lot. I close the door and do my business.

When I get out, our booth is empty, and a white circle of pizza sits in the center of the table.

I am actually very hungry.

Before I can slide off a slice, a man approaches.

"Let me get that." He's handsome, about my age, with forearms stretching the rolled cuffs of his chef's coat. "I'm Tommy Junior." He pulls the triangle-shaped spatula from under the crust. "Everybody calls me Junior."

"Nice to meet you. Do you know where Dario went?"

"Outside for a minute. The trick to this pie," he says without pause as he slips the spatula under a slice, "is you put a little pesto under the mozzarella."

46

Right around the word "pesto," I spot Dario on the far side of the parking lot, next to a black and white police car, talking to two cops. One smokes a cigarette. The other has his hand on his holster.

"Go ahead," Junior says, getting into the seat across from me and folding his hands on the table.

I take a bite, burning my mouth.

"It's hot," he says, handing me my water.

"Clearly." I polish off the water.

"Try again." He refills my glass and leans forward, observing me carefully.

I blow on the pizza's surface, then gingerly bite into it. No burn. Either the pie's cooler or I've killed the nerve endings in my mouth.

My taste buds work fine though.

"Oh, it's good."

"It bursts like a pop of brightness on your tongue and lets the ricotta blossom."

Still talking to the cops, Dario looks in my direction. I'm not sure if he can see through the window's reflection, but I wave to him and take another bite.

"Something is crunching," I say on my third bite.

"Ah, *pignoli*. I don't grind all of it into the paste. I take out maybe ten percent while there are still pieces, then put it back. Keeps it from being mush. Here, have another piece."

I start on the second slice like a starving animal.

"Did you know," he says, "Afghanistan is the third biggest exporter of *pignoli*?"

"Mm-mm." I tell him I don't while chewing.

"I was stationed there. Army. Made E-6."

I don't know what that means.

"Were you an army cook?" I say around my third bite.

He shows me a tattoo inside his forearm. Two snakes curling around a rifle, set over a red cross in the background. The word COMBAT above, and MEDIC below.

"Where did you learn to cook?"

"My mother. She always said, 'Junior, a woman might cook for you one day, but if you know how to cook for yourself, she'll be one less woman who's gonna have to.'"

I laugh around a bite. "Do you clean the bathroom too?"

"Nah, nah," he says, leaning over the table to get closer to me. "And my wife's not gonna either. When I marry a woman, she's gonna be a queen, because I'll be a king. Big house. Servants. A full staff. All she's gonna have to do is sit on the couch and watch TV."

"What if she wants to do something more?"

"Like what?"

"Be productive? I don't know actually."

"There's gonna be kids!"

Dario shakes hands with one of the cops and heads toward us in big strides, his gaze melting the window glass between us.

"Well, I'm going to make this for—" For a split second, I have to consider if I should call him my husband. I decide not to get used to it. "Dario, because he can't cook for himself."

"I got printouts of the recipe." Junior gets out of the booth with all the energy of a man who's found his purpose in life. "One second!"

The bell rings when Dario comes in.

"Hey, this is really good," I tell Dario. "You're lucky I saved you half."

"Finish it." He heads for Junior, who's coming around the counter with a piece of paper.

Dario snaps it away. Junior stands there with his mouth open and his hands out. He starts a reply, then claps his jaw shut. Dario stands too close to him, legs apart, knees bent, fists clenched. He's too tight. Too menacing.

Whatever this is, it's dangerous.

Dario isn't hurting another person today. None. Zero.

I swallow whatever I'd bitten off and run between them, taking the paper away from Dario.

"It's a recipe." I hold it up, but he can't see or hear me through his focus on Junior.

"You." Over my shoulder, Dario jabs a finger at the quaking younger man. "Don't talk to her."

"I'm sorry, I—"

"Hey, hey!" Tommy comes out from the back. "*Cosa c'è?*"

Dario seems to wake up with a subtle relaxing of his posture and an exhale.

"Nothing." He focuses on me, taking the paper. He reads it and looks past me at Junior. "Thank you. We'll pack it up to go."

I count this as a victory, but I don't know what I've won.

CHAPTER 8

SARAH

THE PIZZA BOX IS IN THE BACK. MY HANDS ARE IN MY LAP, THUMBS tapping. I wait for Dario to explain what just happened, but he doesn't make a sound. This is my silence to break.

"What did those cops say?"

He shoots me a look before turning back to the road. I give him a look right back. He might not be used to life after rule one, but I'm starting to like it.

"The sheriff's department let the Colonia in. They figured out they had the right place from something you left in the greenhouse. A garter."

"I didn't leave that. You did."

"Touché." He turns the corner, knowing exactly where he's going, which must be nice. "The sheriff's department left and let the Colonia file in like a bunch of fucking ghouls. They're probably trashing the place while the NYSD sits outside—hiding like cowards as if I can't see them—watching for us. Fuckers think we're going back."

"Aren't we?"

"No." His clipped denial hurts me more than it should. That building was the only home we ever had together.

"What about when the sheriff leaves?"

"We go back when I say it's safe."

Nothing will ever be safe to him, and I'll never be able to judge for myself.

Dario turns. The pizza box slides from one side of the back seat to the other. I check to make sure it's still upright. It's fine. I'm not.

"If you didn't want me to make you pizza," I say, "you could have just told me instead of threatening Junior."

"It's not about the pizza," he grumbles in profile.

"I know I'm sheltered and I don't know a lot of things, but I'm not stupid." I get more and more angry with every second that passes without his response. "You're an experienced person who knows me pretty well. So, whatever this is... you being angry... it obviously couldn't be about me talking to a man about pesto, so I'm going to assume it's about the garter."

"No." He holds his hand up like a crossing guard in an intersection. "Until you know how to live—how to work and pay a bill—you don't talk to anyone. *Anyone.* Especially not a man. What if he decided he wanted you? You couldn't even read a map to find your way home. You can't call me. You can't use a phone unless it's connected to a wall."

"That has nothing to do with you acting like that."

"It has everything to do with it."

We pass a red brick church with a sign that says FIND PEACE! He puts his blinker on and makes a left—functioning just fine when we're fighting, which makes me want to push his buttons just a little more.

"It was just a recipe."

He pulls into a gas station, slaps the car into park, and leans into me. "It's never just a recipe. Never."

I can't even look at him, but I can hear him, feel him near me, smell him every time I breathe. When he gets out, I'm thankful and disappointed at the same time. He'll pump his car with gas, pay with his money, and drive his marital property to another piece of his real estate.

But I'm not even marital property. The interior of the car clatters thickly when he puts the pump into the tank. The numbers on the pump flip.

How am I letting this happen?

I'm not. I get out of the car. We lock eyes over the roof.

"Get in the car, Sarah."

I slam the door closed and walk around to him, leaving the black gas line between us. He waits for me to speak, but he's bursting at the seams to answer.

"If you want me to be independent, I need to be able to talk to people."

"A man I do not know—who I haven't vetted—does not need to talk to my wife."

"I'm not your wife."

"I told you..." He holds up his hand so I can see his scars.

"You told me nothing." I growl for the first time in my life, and it feels good. Now I know why he does it. "You used me. And I knew you were using me because you told me what you were using me for... but after things changed, you could have told me you were married, and you didn't. So you're still using me. The only thing that changed is what you're using me for."

The gas pump clacks, and the rubber tube jolts.

"I can't fucking sleep at night worrying about you." He takes out the nozzle. "I think of what they'd do to you if they found you." He slaps it into the cradle and pulls his card from the slot. A receipt comes out like a paper tongue. "And I can't decide if I should hide you in the basement or cast you in steel. But you're obsessed with things I had to do before my life revolved around you. So if I'm using you, can you tell me... for what? I'm using you to worship? To take care of? To panic about? Did I need my entire world to drop from under me just so I could stop caring what was keeping my feet on the ground in the first place?" He snaps the receipt away and slips it and his card into his wallet. "All that happened with you. I've been ripped out of my life and thrown into space. All I care about is reaching one star—this single point of light—and that's you. Everything, *everything* has changed except my marriage to Willa, because it didn't exist. It was necessary in the moment, and that moment passed a long time ago. Now it's you. You. All you. I don't know where I'm going next, but every future I see either has you in it or has me dead."

"Stop," I say through my teeth. "Just stop. I want to be mad. I deserve to be mad."

"You deserve so much more than that." He holds out his hand. "Come."

The debate in my mind is between continuing this fight until one of us is beaten into submission or accepting the inevitable outcome.

I want to be mad, and I deserve to hold on to it, but I know I'll forgive him, so I take his hand.

He leads me into the gas station convenience store and paces the aisles while holding my hand as if it's the only connection that will keep me from drowning, then he stops in front of a bank of plastic-cased phones.

He puts me directly in front of him, hands on my shoulders. "Pick one."

"I don't know anything about these. What's the difference?"

"You just need to make calls in case of emergency. Or to talk to me."

"I guess?"

"What do you mean you 'guess'? You going to put your pesto pizza on Instagram?"

"Is that what people do?"

He leans his forehead against the back of my head.

"I don't know what to do with you." When I try to turn, he holds me still, facing the phones. "I should send you away for my own fucking sanity, but I'll go crazy without you."

"Send me." I grab a random phone and turn, pushing the package into his chest. "Just make sure I'm ready."

"I'm not sending you anywhere."

The promise is meant to reassure me. It's made in a world where he's the only one who can make my decisions. I don't intend to live there forever.

He takes the phone to the front. He takes cash out of his wallet to buy it, then plucks a spoon with a key on the end from the counter.

"Put up a sign," he says to the guy behind the plexiglass, dropping a hundred-dollar bill in the slot. "Bathroom's out of order."

"Yes, sir!" He snaps a Sharpie from a cup.

Dario pulls me outside and around to the back of the

building, where a door that's been painted in beige enamel dozens of times is cracked ajar. Broken brown floor tile and the edges of a white toilet with no seat are visible in the slit.

"I just went," I say. "Do you need to go?"

He pushes me inside, follows as he slams the door, and flips the latch. The light flickers on automatically. With quick, feral glances, he checks every corner of the tiny room for danger, then turns to me.

"We have to talk." He tosses the useless key on the sink.

"Here? It's filthy."

The sink drips. Halos of brown water damage radiate from the ceiling vent.

"The only time you listen is when my cock is inside you."

My insides melt and my attention narrows. "Is that so?"

I don't know what I did to earn his intensity, but I'll do it again and again to keep it.

"Just so we're clear." He takes me by the shoulders and turns me to the sink, putting my left hand against the rust-pocked mirror. He puts his right hand next to it and asks, "These scars say you're my wife. Period. Not Willa. You. *You* are my wife. That means I get to defend and protect you. I get to fuck you, and I get to punish you."

He's fought to bring me into the outside, and now he's fighting to keep me from it. He could maintain my captivity if he wanted. Keep me sheltered, chained, ignorant of the world. But he's not saying he won't teach me how to live in it. The struggle is with himself now. My body gets the benefit of being the battlefield.

"Do it all while you can." I lower my hand.

"Oh, my prima." His face is obscured in the rusted

mirror, but his movements as he yanks his belt open are unmistakable. "You're playing a game you can't win."

"Maybe we both win."

"You're going to be sorry."

"Make me sorry."

He sticks four fingers in my mouth and pulls me close, his erection against my lower back. "You're asking to be punished."

I nod because he's right. I need to be punished for wanting to win. For wanting the choice to stay or go.

"You're asking," he says low, lips moving against my throat, "to get fucked."

When I nod this time, bubbles of drool drop from my chin.

"I can't let you scream." He takes out his hand and snaps his belt from the loops. "You're going to shake your head if you want me to stop. Understand? Say it."

"Yes."

"Open your mouth. Wide."

He straps the belt between my teeth, loops it tightly around my head and pulls back.

"Look at my wife." He jerks my head back. "On a leash with spit running down her chin like an animal. Do you want me to fuck you like this? Gagged?"

I nod, tasting the leather.

"Of course you do. You know who owns you. Pull down your pants. Let's see if you're telling the truth."

The position he has me in makes it hard to obey. That's by design. What's obedience worth if it's easy? Would it send shocks of desire through my bones if I didn't have to struggle to get the waistband past my hips? Even humiliation has to be earned.

"Gorgeous." He caresses my bottom, and I sigh at the compliment, then suck a breath past the belt when he puts three fingers in my pussy. He takes them out to slap it. The gasp turns into an exhale of surprise and pain. "Show me how you tell me to stop."

I look over my shoulder and shake my head.

"You want more."

I nod.

"You want to show me why you can't leave me." He jerks my head forward and slaps my pussy again. I squeak in pain but stick my bottom out for more. He pushes my face against the dirty mirror. "My sweet little slut." Again. And another slap. "Spread your cheeks apart so I can punish my property."

I'm open now, and he slaps my ass, my wet lips, my thighs until I'm a sodden, whimpering mess with a chin slick with slippery drool. In the mirror, past the grime, I see him use his free hand to release his dick.

"You want me to fuck this sore little cunt?"

Yes. Yes, I do.

I'm so wet he slides right into me. He's angled me up against the sink, so his shaft rubs against my clitoris as it enters blissfully slowly, stretching inch by inch.

"Here's how it's going to go, little princess." He fucks me from behind at a leisurely pace, pulling on the belt. "When I teach you how to use a cell phone, it's to call me. When I teach you to get around, it's so you can get back to me. Everything you learn is so you can stay with me. Do you understand?"

I nod, in a state of total submission, stretched between degradation and ecstasy.

When he's buried deep, he swats my hands away and pulls my ass cheeks apart, pressing his thumb against the hole. "What if I fucked your ass right now? Made you scream and cry?" He takes a slop of spit from my chin and rubs it against the tight ring. "I'm getting so hard thinking about my cock coming in your ass."

Two fingers inside. I squeak and groan with the hurt, while the pleasure from his cock grows more intense.

He takes them out. "Not today then." He yanks my head back by the belt. "But I'll have it, my wife. I'm going to fuck your ass. My ass. I own it. I fuck what I own, and I own what I fuck."

Nodding into the mirror, my mouth is cut by a leather line and my chin is slick with spit.

"Good." He takes my hand and puts it between my legs. "Now, be a good little wife. Show me how you help yourself come."

I hesitate. I've touched myself a few times. But I was alone, my shame hidden behind a closed door, furtively exploring what my husband would get to know.

He's asking me to do something more debasing than anything he's done to me.

"Do it, Sarah." He takes me by the hips and drives deep. "Give it to me."

There's no threat. No *or else.* He fucks me as if I've already obeyed him.

My fingertips touch his cock where it's sliding against me, then up to the hard, sensitive nub. My touch sends shockwaves through me.

"Do it like you mean it."

I touch myself with more urgency, gasping with how good it feels.

"That's right."

His words get lost in a groan. I feel his orgasm in my fingers as mine builds. When he drives deep, his thick, warm liquid seeps out. My fingers catch some and slide it against the demanding nub. The lubrication changes everything. Everything.

When I come, my toes flex and my knees bend as if I'm trying to launch myself through the mirror. My lungs empty, flatten, and my throat emits a muffled cry.

CHAPTER 9

DARIO

To protect her, she needs to be armed with knowledge, so she knows how to live. I always knew she'd have to be trained in the ways of the world, but she was supposed to be far away—a dot on the landscape of my mind. But she's in the foreground of my heart, and to protect her is to give her the power to leave me.

The fear in my blood isn't funny. It's hot and angry. It takes losing this woman very seriously. The fear isn't loneliness or even death. It's a deeper separation that I can't even get my thoughts around until I know she'll be all right without me.

She won't stay leashed. There's mischief in her. It's dangerous. She could slip out of line. Reveal herself. Step outside the carefully placed boundaries she needs to stay safe.

When she touched herself, for just an instant, I caught a glimpse of her private self. The girl discovering something she should have known already. The connections she missed.

I want more of her eyes lighting up. Her face opening like a window. A chain of breakthroughs. A life invented moment by moment.

I make sure she's the cleanest thing in that filthy little bathroom, kissing her where she's exposed herself to me, vowing to safekeep her vulnerabilities. The world outside this dank, cinderblock nightmare pushes against the door with a constant mental pressure. Once we're out, the consequences of my vengeance will chase us down.

Crouched in front of her, I kiss her belly while drawing up her underpants.

"Are you all right?" she asks. I look up at her while she strokes my cheeks.

"I'm supposed to be asking you that."

"I'm just a little tired."

I am too. I'm so tired of being tired. Sick to death of demanding death.

"You need to relax." I pull up her pants. "Let's get you comfortable."

After picking her up, I carry her across the parking lot to the ghost car. I buckle her in, give her water, lower the back of the passenger seat, and put on the sound of ocean waves. She seems to like that, and she falls asleep before we're on the highway.

Something has to change. I can't train her to live in the world and run away from it at the same time.

Maybe I got lazy. I'm not—in a million years—supposed to feel desperate for Sarah Colonia, but I feel a creeping softness that leaves me inside-out. She's the center of it—the cause and purpose of it. Without her, I'm helpless to make myself right.

The two-story Tudor is fifteen minutes from the last edges of the Bronx but behind a gate and surrounded by acres of forest, so the property feels like the country.

She's still sleeping when I pull up to the front. Lips parted, lashes dark on her cheeks, the car's dome light glowing on her skin. Safe.

Her flip phone sits at her feet, harmless in its plastic case.

Mentally, I list the things she has to learn to do.

Read a map.

Use her phone.

Make doctor's appointments.

Benny, the caretaker, rushes to the car. I roll down my window and put a finger to my lips. He sees Sarah and nods.

"Sir," Benny says quietly, head bowed slightly. I haven't seen him in a while, and the diameter of his bald spot has grown. "It's ready."

Benny's servility is not to be taken as weakness. He needed a reason to get out of the business of killing people. Keeping my safehouses ready means he can retire in comfort, while I have them maintained by a man who can commit murder if he needs to.

Open a bank account.

Pay a bill.

"Thank you. Give me a minute."

Read labels.

Drive.

For God's sake, driving involves built-up social knowledge she's been denied.

"Should I stay?" Benny asks. "Heywood and Glen are ready, but I haven't greeted them yet."

He's talking about two massive houses on streets marked Heywood and Glen. They'll be full of my people by now.

"Go. Make sure everyone has what they need."

"Of course."

He runs off. I'm ready to settle in until Sarah's awake, but when I close the window and look over, her brown eyes are staring back at me.

"How are you feeling?" I ask.

She closes her eyes and opens them again. I expect her to claim she's fine, or sleepy, or satisfied. I shouldn't be surprised she opens with a question, but she'll never stop surprising me.

"What else did you lie about?" There's no accusation in her tone. She's not rigid or guarded. She wants facts. My words, placed next to some kind of objective reality.

"Besides Willa?"

"I lied about a lot. Little things. Sometimes to protect you. Sometimes to hurt you."

"Like when?"

I don't have a list of bent truths or outright falsehoods. Since rerouting a limo on her wedding day, I've been trying to do the impossible. I told her whatever I had to tell her. Searching my mind for something... anything, to admit to, I can only come up with a series of statements I thought were lies when I uttered them but that now hold a deeper truth.

"When I said I adored you."

"That was a lie?" Her lips twitch.

"And treasured you?" I put my hand over hers. "Remember?"

"Yes."

"And honored you?" When I brush my finger over her jaw, I feel it quivering.

"Enough, Dario." My name cracks in her throat. She sits up. "I get it."

Taking her at the back of the neck, I pull her toward me, so we're face to face. "It was all a lie of omission. I was saying enough to keep you from the truth."

She swallows, looking down, eyelashes casting shadows on her cheeks.

"I want to be a man you honor, and adore, and treasure, and I'm not."

"What makes you think that?"

"I haven't earned it."

"Shouldn't I honor, treasure, and adore you no matter what?"

Of course she should. A wife's unquestioning devotion is not just the rule of the Colonia. It's what I expect. What I demand.

"No-matter-what isn't good enough anymore."

Her shrug says she doesn't know what's good enough, and that's wrong. Of everything she needs to learn, she needs to learn how to demand more of everyone, including me. Especially me.

I get out, walk around the car, and open her door.

"Come on, wife." I wedge my hands under her and pick her up the way I did to get her into the car, and at Armistice

Night, and the way I'll carry her whenever she needs it.
"Let's go home."

She puts her arms around my neck. I kick the car door closed and carry her to the house, over the threshold, and into the new life I will create for her.

CHAPTER 10

SARAH

DARIO ISN'T NEXT TO ME, BUT I SLEEP DEEPLY WITHOUT HIM UNTIL the sun shines on my face as if its only job is to wake me.

The bathroom connected to the bedroom is done in white stone with blue glass tiles at the edges. Everything I need to take care of my business has been laid on the marble sink. I find a robe on a hook behind the door and put it on over my underwear. When he laid me down last night, I thought he'd make love to me again, but I fell into such a deep sleep, I didn't even feel him undress me.

The bedroom's back window opens onto acres of spindly trees on a bed of dried leaves. I can't see the edge of the property from here. There's no wall or break in the forest. The next house over has a peaked roof of gray shingles. The next house out the side window is closer, but still a bit of a walk through the woods. I close my eyes to hear the birds and bugs. The breeze. And far away, the whoosh of cars on a highway. Downstairs, pots and pans clack together.

Maybe Dario's the one making a racket, but those are

kitchen noises, and that man does not know his way around a kitchen.

The short hallway leads to a three-step stair with a door at the end. I try to open it, but it's locked, and an alarm squeals so loudly and so suddenly, my heart stops, afraid to take another beat.

I've heard this exact pitch before, and that's why I'm frozen in place.

Precious Blood's alarms make the same sound, and for a moment, I was pulled out of this house and into my past.

"Hold on!" Dario's voice could be right here or across the ocean. I can't tell with that blaring siren.

Then it's gone, and all that's left of it is a ringing in my ear. I go up the three steps to find him coming down the hall toward me. The shock of the alarm has reset my mind, and it's as if I've never seen him before. He seems taller, more purposeful. He is a god of terrible beauty descending from heaven on a beam of light.

He's frightening, but I'm not scared of him, because he's stretching down from the sky for me, only me. His hand opens, reaching down, and he's not taller. I am two steps down. The beam of light comes from the window behind him, and his terrible beauty is just Dario Lucari in jeans and a sweater.

"Come on," he says when I take his hand. "The eggs are going to burn."

He takes me around a corner to a wide set of stairs that reach the first floor. With the sun up, I can see the shiny dark wood floors and pale leather couch. The white walls and matte black molding around the windows. He pulls me through so fast I have no time to gather another detail before we're in what I can only assume is the kitchen. The walls are flat slate with hair-thin seams creating different-sized outlines.

"I hope you like eggs." Dario pushes yellow liquid around a pan with a wooden spoon.

"I do." I reach for the spoon. "I can do it."

"So can I." He takes my hand and kisses it. "Coffee's in the pot."

"I don't drink coffee."

"Right." There's no apology in his words, but his face has a thin, barely perceptible veil of shame over it.

"I didn't expect you to know that, necessarily," I say.

"I should." He touches the corner where two seams meet and a drawer of potholders pops open. "You're my wife."

"Am I?" I guess where the plates are and push the corner where two seams in the wall meet. A door pops open, revealing a cabinet full of dishes. Got it on the first try.

"As far as I'm concerned, you are. Which makes me your husband, and it's a husband's job to know what his wife likes."

The way he looks at me sends blood to my cheeks. He's talking about more than breakfast.

"My friend Denise has been married since she was seventeen." I put two plates on the counter—next to a stick of butter—and stand close to him. "It wasn't until last year —her fourth baby, when she was laid up in the hospital— that her husband found out her slippers didn't match."

"Did he buy her a new pair?"

"It wouldn't have helped." The toast pops. I grab it with bare fingers. "It was the sizes that were different. One of her feet is bigger than the other. She has to buy two pairs of shoes, which she doesn't do often because it's expensive, and she has to hide the boxes with the odd ones."

Dario pushes the eggs around, mouth tight enough to hold back a tirade. I find the butter knives before he has a chance to tell me where they are. This kitchen may want to hide its function, but it was set up sensibly.

"He should have noticed the first time he kissed her feet." He taps the spoon on the edge of the pan and clicks off the heat.

"Marco isn't much of a foot-kisser." I scratch the soft butter onto the toast and drop my voice as if sharing a secret. "He's more of an ass-kisser."

"You don't have to whisper here."

"Everyone says yes to Daddy." I shrug, turning my volume up by half a notch. "But Massimo said Marco was a super-brown-nose, so if Denise needed anything, I'd tell my brother and he'd tell Daddy to make him do it. If it came that way, it was... safer. For Denise. But it had to be done carefully."

He scrapes eggs on one plate, then holds the pan over the other. "On top of the toast or on the side?"

"Side."

"So, Denise couldn't ask Marco for anything."

"Well..." I drift off, staring into the middle distance. We weren't supposed to ask for help from our husbands unless we were at our wit's end. Men had their own problems. "Grandma always said it was our job to make a man's home as stable and uncomplicated as possible. Asking for something outside the necessities of the house means we're falling short."

"Sit," Dario says, pulling out a chair for me. While I was

thinking about the rules I'd grown up with, he'd set the plates down with forks and glasses of water. My job.

I obey with a sigh, sitting while he pushes in the chair.

"You are first," he says with a light touch on my neck. I turn to look up at him. He holds up a finger. "*Prima*. First. You can ask me for anything. Do you understand?"

He towers over me, offering to put himself at my service.

"Yes."

"Good." He gets in his seat and picks up his fork. That's when I can start eating.

"How long are we staying here?"

"Until it's safe to leave or dangerous to stay." He brushes crumbs from his fingertips. "Today, first thing. You need to unpack whatever you have in that suitcase. Make a list of anything you're missing... no. Anything you *want*. Anything. Got it?"

"Mm-hm." I agree around eggs that are smoother and richer than any I've ever made myself.

"Then I'll show you the house. Get you coded and printed. But until then, don't open any doors."

"What about food? Do we have enough Quick Lick?"

He smiles as he chews. "The pantry is stocked."

"I'll be the judge of that."

"I guess you will be. Eat up. We have a lot to do."

I do as he says, eating the breakfast he cooked for me while I slept the morning away. It's more delicious than I thought eggs could ever be. Does he want to stay home and cook while I go out in the world and do his job?

This plate of eggs and toast isn't just good. It's a challenge to my domain.

"These are good," I say, then shrug. "For a man."

"The trick is butter. Lots of butter."

"I appreciate you making breakfast." I push away my empty plate. "But I'm cooking dinner."

"Good."

"I need fresh basil."

"Put it on the list. Benny can pick it up."

I clear the plates and bring them to the sink.

"I want to make the pizza," I say while my back is turned. "Junior's pizza."

"Fine." He's behind me, kissing my neck. When he saw Junior talking to me through the window, he burst like a ball of pent-up violence. Now he's kissing me without a whiff of anger about me using Junior's recipe.

"Dario?"

"Mm-hm?"

I turn to face him. He tenderly brushes hair off my cheek.

"Would you have hurt Junior?"

"Yes."

"Why?" I ask.

"I know how men are."

"He just wanted to talk about pizza."

"No, he didn't." He touches my nose. "And if he did 'just want to talk about pizza,' it's because he hadn't gotten around to trying to fuck you."

"Dario."

"Trust me on this."

I trust he knows what he's talking about, but I also believe Junior wasn't excited about anything more than pignoli nuts. The consequences of that excitement could have been so dire for Junior, the way they were for Denise— just because she was in a basement alone with Marco. I saw

71

CD REISS

it happen to different girls in different ways over and over, and I just accepted it. That was my world.

It's not anymore. I'm outside now. How can everything still be the same?

"What are you going to do when I go out by myself?" I ask. "Half the adults in the world are men. How many do you think I want to take to bed?"

"One." He pulls me close, and I fall into him.

"Good."

"But they'd take you in a minute."

"All of them?"

"Don't worry, they'll never get past me."

He acts as if he'll always be there to protect me from the evils of men.

Husbands leave wives behind.

Running his lips over my face, Dario doesn't seem dangerous. His arms feel like security, but they are violent and unpredictable. The body that electrifies mine lives in service of vengeance. He is a killer, but he could be killed, and all the competence in the world won't fill his place in my heart.

I push his chest, looking him in the face.

His expression turns to suspicious concern, as if he can tell where I'm heading.

I almost lose my nerve. Dario and I aren't really married. He already has a wife.

Maybe there's power in that. A *wife* can't ask for anything.

Maybe I can.

"You said I could ask for anything."

"I did."

He doesn't seem to regret the offer.

"You said we're staying here as long as it's safe."

"I did, prima. What is it?"

I run a nail over the knitting of his sweater. "Why not make it safe right now?"

"There's a security system." His voice is flat, suspicious, as if he knows I'm not talking about alarms and locks.

"I want it to be even safer. So. What if you made peace with my father and brother?"

"Peace?" He loosens his hold on me, and desperation fills the place where security lived. "With the Colonia? After everything I told you?"

"Maybe you can work on all that without getting killed? Then we can live," I say quickly. "Just *live*. Be together. Happy."

His face cycles through anger, impatience, hesitance, and with a blink, acceptance.

If only happiness stuck to a soul for as long as anger does.

"That's not going to happen." He steps back. "Not just because you ask. Not even if I wanted it."

"It's what I want."

"Ask me for something else. Anything else. Not that. It's impossible." Before I can press him further, he turns his back to me. "Follow me."

CHAPTER 11

SARAH

Dario leads me through the house. He names every space we pass, opening doors to show me that I can enter the second bathroom, the second and third bedroom, the sunroom, and the mud room without tripping an ear-splitting alarm. The garage, the front door, and his office all have biometric locks that open with a fingerprint.

So does a door under the stairs, where he stops and uses his thumbprint to open it.

"We have those kinds of locks." I'm delighted to already know a thing.

"Where?"

"Whenever they update a door in Precious Blood, they put one in."

"I prefer when they're backward." He indicates I should go through. "Go on."

The overhead light goes on, revealing a short-ceilinged hall. It leads to a small, dark room with TV monitors showing empty halls, alleyways, the house we're in right now, the gate at the end of the drive. Flickering shots of the surrounding forest from every angle.

"You had something like this in Manhattan."

"I have them all over."

Reaching behind and above me, he makes something beep and sigh. I look up at an open flap of wall. He removes a flat device from the hidden compartment and places it on the counter.

As he sets it up, I look at the screens. I recognize some of the places from the other security room. This one has a path around the house we're in, a service road out the back, some forest, and a gate that's more utilitarian than the cast-iron one in the front. Garbage pails are lined up next to it.

"Where's this?" I ask.

"The service entrance." He keeps his attention on his setup. "Out back."

"Huh." I get closer to the screen. There's a tiny gap between the hedge and the gate. "Is it open?"

He checks it immediately. "Fuck. Good eye."

"What is it?"

"Garbage day." He looks down again. "That shit's gonna stop right now."

The light from the device's screen shines on his face, and I see what I hadn't seen before. He hasn't been sleeping. I lay my palm on the back of his neck. I don't know how to fix this for him.

On the screen, a rectangle appears. I recognize it.

"I put my thumb there." I hold out my thumb and he takes it gently.

"You did this for Precious Blood."

"Yes. To get to the food stores. The big kitchen in the basement. Here and there."

He presses my thumb inside the rectangle, rolling it back and forth. Red swirls appear in the shape of a thumbprint, getting more and more defined until the device beeps and a blue checkmark appears.

"So I can open which door?"

"The pantry's in the garage." He taps buttons, swipes away screens, types on a screen-bound keyboard. "And all the interior doors should work for the lady of the house."

"Oh, I have a title now."

A little smile teases the corner of his mouth. "I have to restrict your access to the front gate. It's not because you're a prisoner. You should be here with me because you want to be, but if you don't want to be here, I still can't let you leave."

"How's that different from being a prisoner?"

"You have to trust me."

"I don't want to run away. I want to go to the store."

"I'm not worried about you." A lock of hair drops over his forehead. "Come, I'll show you."

He leads me out of the little room to a door near the kitchen and gestures at the keypad. "Go on. Let's test it out."

I press my thumb to it, the way I do for some of the important places in the church and rectory. A little light turns from red to green. Dario shoulders the door open.

"It sticks." With a flick of the light switch, he ushers me into a large, concrete-floored room with a covered car next to the Audi we drove from Manhattan. A tool bench sits against a side. The wall against the house is lined with cabinets. Dario opens one side of a double door, revealing shelving filled with cereal and cracker boxes. Flour. Sugar. Pasta. Cans stacked on cans.

"Well, it looks pretty stocked," I say. "We should have enough for dinner."

He opens the cabinet next to it. This one has keys in the door and half a dozen rifles hung vertically against the back.

"Oh," I say, reaching out. "What—"

"No touching." He slaps my hand away. "They're loaded."

"Are you supposed to have loaded guns lying around?"

"No one's supposed to be in this house but people who know better. And now you do. Because I trust you, and you're not my prisoner." He scans the rows of keys dangling from the interior door. "If I need to use a gun here, in this house, then every second counts."

"That's your reason for not making peace?"

"It's reason enough." He snaps a set of keys off the interior door. The keychain says MET 5th AVE. "Everything is now a risk. Our life is land mines and armor with weaknesses we won't know about until it's too late. We'll never be some nice, happy couple living on a ranch. But soon you'll know how to use these rifles. You'll know how to drive this car." He holds up the keys and reaches across me to the car cover, pulling it off partway to reveal shiny black paint. "You'll know what to do, no matter what."

His phone chimes. He looks at the screen and puts it away.

"You have to go?" I ask.

"Yes."

"Past one of the screaming doors?"

He looks at my hands and I realize I've been wringing them so hard the skin is red. He takes them.

"My palms are all sweaty." I try to pull away, he won't let me.

"I made you scared."

"I'm being silly." I squeeze his dry hands with my wet ones. "We're in a fortress and I'm as safe as you can make me."

"Listen to me. Every day you're here, you're going to learn how to be as safe as you can make yourself."

"I don't even know what I'm nervous about." I fold our hands together so our scars match. "Will you be home for dinner?"

It's such a wife question that the tightness of his mouth breaks into a looser smirk. "Wouldn't miss it."

The kitchen is infuriating. Every cabinet looks like a wall. There's a drawer that's actually a refrigerator. A faucet behind what I think might be the stove, except there are no burners or coils. A piece of counter slides over to reveal a bank of buttons with little pictures as if I'm a toddler who can't read, not a grown woman who was reading grownup books before anyone else in my cohort.

Out here, in the world, that's not enough. I don't know what I don't know.

Some buttons work the lights. Others open window blinds. The vents blow warm air. Then cool. A television pops up out of the counter. There's a news show on. I've seen boring television news before, but infrequently. A woman in a red jacket looks at the audience—me, everyone —and talks about a murder, a robbery, a panda.

Why is this so surprising?

Either this television is different, or I'm different.

I comb through the cabinets, making a list. I need to check the garage pantry for something I'm sure I saw. Pressing my thumb against the pad like Dario did makes a red light turn green, but the door is stuck.

"I have that," a man says as he enters. He's in a black suit without a tie. His hair is slicked back and his face is cleanly shaven, but he has a five o'clock shadow at noon. He presses his thumb on the pad and the door unlocks like a sigh. "I'm Benny. This blue button is me." He shows me a little blue circle on a panel of buttons. "Whatever you want... just press it and my phone rings. All right?"

"Thank you."

"I'm sorry about this."

"I'm used to sticky doors." I hope he doesn't feel as if he has to explain that to me.

He shoulders the door open the way Dario did. The cool, musty air of the garage streams into the house.

Will Benny follow? Is it okay to even talk to him? What if he follows me into the garage? And we're alone? And Dario sees us? Will he hurt Benny?

"Thank you." I try to put on airs, hoping he hears the dismissal in my tone.

He nods and steps back. "When should I come for your list?"

"Half an hour?"

"I'll be back then." With a short bow of deference, he's gone.

No harm done. I've dodged a hundred bullets in five minutes. Or none. I can't figure out anything anymore.

I get to the pantry inventory and stuff the expired and stale into a plastic bag I find under the tool bench. Then I reorder the shelves, taking down the things I want for the inside kitchen.

Being alone with Benny wasn't a big deal. Dario wouldn't have hired him if he didn't trust him.

I don't remember being this nervous when I was alone with Vito and Gennaro in the suite. Thinking back, I'm sure I wasn't. Ripped away from my life and stuck into a world that felt completely alien, I was too afraid of death or rape to concern myself with what made Dario angry. My mind was too paralyzed with what was different to realize all the things that were the same.

We were taught that outsider women were as unrestricted as men—having dangerous jobs and loud voices but walking around in a constant state of terror. Grandma said outsider men do not protect their women.

But when I press a button near the television, the images change, the stories change, and I see how much I have to learn about being a woman.

CHAPTER 12

DARIO

I FIND WILLA TAKING UP RESIDENCE IN ONE OF TWELVE STUDIO apartments I own on the other side of the highway.

"Well." She looks me up and down, wearing a green silk bonnet. "I knew you'd show up at some point."

She steps away to let me pass, then snaps the deadbolt.

"Thanks, nothing for me." I respond to an offer that wasn't made.

"What brings you?" She mutes the TV and takes a sip from a travel cup of Diet Coke. I peer into every corner of the studio.

"You already unpacked." My people have been with me forever. They know where their safe house is, and Benny keeps them clean and furnished. Willa's bed is made, of course. The pillowcases will be silk, and the television is on the most innocuous thing available.

"There wasn't a speck of dust." Willa runs her finger along the windowsill and shows me the result.

"I have staff to take care of it."

"You included my space in their rounds?" She tosses a coaster on the table and puts her Diet Coke on it. "How sweet."

"You need to go home."

"Why?"

"Your presence... your existence is causing me trouble. Yesterday, I got an earful about what a liar I am. And manipulative. A user... all because you decided to show up here."

"No, Dario. Because you're a manipulative liar, but I have to say... the way you were rendered completely speechless when you were caught? She raises her eyebrows to mimic the surprise she felt. "Shocking. It was like you cared."

"I do care."

"Oria told me, and I didn't believe it. I thought she was just projecting. But there it was, in front of my own eyes. My God, Dario. You love her. What an utterly misguided, unfortunate, stupid choice to make."

"I don't *love* her."

"You weren't even supposed to actually fuck her."

"One has fuck-all to do with the other."

She opens the fridge. "You think?"

"I didn't marry you because I fucked you twice."

A can of ginger ale goes flying through the air. I catch it.

"I know what we were and what we are." Willa closes the refrigerator. "Don't flatter yourself. We both have needs, and neither one of us has done without because of a stupid piece of paper. I'm talking about *her*." She jabs her finger at me. "Every girl who came through us was treated with care. They came to me untouched by any more trauma than they'd already gotten from the Colonia."

"She's not the same." I open the can. It fizzes, and Willa waits until I drink off the foam. "She's royalty. You knew that. She was a weapon from day one."

"You never preyed on the weak ones."

Violence almost leaps out of my skin to strangle her. The insult cuts where I didn't know I was exposed. Not that she called me an animal. I may dress in clothes and use a knife and fork, but I've never played at being anything besides rage and desire held together by a sack of skin.

I'm bristling at the idea that I'm preying on Sarah, even though that was the plan from the beginning.

"She's not weak," I say, defending her strength so I don't have to think of what I've done.

"I'll be the judge of that once she's away from you, with the girls on St. Easy."

The nickname for the island we set up to rehabilitate Colonia women used to be a private joke. It's not funny anymore.

"She's not going."

"Then I'm staying." She pours herself fresh soda.

"You don't belong here."

"Oh, I know that. I have a whole life and none of it's in this hellhole. I have a man who loves me and who I love. I have purpose and I have peace."

"Because you don't have the stomach to do what I do here."

Leaning her hands on the counter, she takes a deep breath like a woman gathering strength from the air. "You forget what I used to do for a living."

"The job you left because you couldn't watch people get hurt anymore? What do you think you're going to see if you stay? When I get my hands on Peter Colonia, you're going to wish you were back on a tropical island with that man who loves you."

No snappy response. She knows the truth.

"This is my fault," she says. "I was down there getting complacent while you were up here acting like a vicious monster."

I'm not going to stand here and argue about who she thinks I am or what she thinks I've morphed into.

"I have this. I'll take care of her. I'll teach her what she needs to know until she can stand on her own two feet. Without me," I say.

"What have you done to help her so far? Instructions on how to suck your dick the way you like?"

"I'm the only one who can help her."

"You won't teach her a damn thing because once you do, she can leave you."

"Just go."

"I'm not staying here." She swallows hard, then makes the next statement as if it's the most difficult thing she's ever uttered. "But I'm not leaving without Sarah."

Out of respect, I hold back laughter. "You really think you get to decide this?"

"Don't test me."

She's getting tested. We all are. And I'm not the one deciding who passes or fails. It'll be Sarah.

CHAPTER 13

SARAH

BENNY FULFILLED MY LIST PERFECTLY, REMINDED ME ABOUT THE button I had to press if I needed anything else, and disappeared. I eat lunch and figure out the stove—more or less. When Dario cooked eggs on it, I was so entranced with the hidden cabinetry that I failed to notice the glass on the range didn't get hot—like an electric stove would—but the water boiled anyway.

I make dinner with my eyes on the television. I see a show about a family with a disobedient wife and messy children where invisible people laugh at the way she treats her husband. When she hugs him at the end, the invisible laughers say *aww.* I figure out how to change the channels with a detachable black box. I see women cops. Women who use guns. Rifles. Pistols. Laser guns that shoot light. Lawyers. Doctors. Bosses. Women with children and without husbands. Women alone with men. Women doing things, feeling things, saying things that shock me.

Mostly, I see women who are not afraid.

When it gets dark outside, the kitchen lights brighten automatically, and when Dario gets home, I shine brighter because darkness has entered.

When we're done eating and I've cleaned up, he sits me down at the kitchen island and crosses to the other side of it.

"The only way to keep you safe is to make sure you're competent in a crisis." Dario props himself on the kitchen island counter by two fists, sleeves rolled up.

He places the phone I chose at the gas station between us, closed like a mouth, freed from the plastic, charged, and set up. On a barstool opposite him, I tuck my hands between my knees, palms outward so my pants can absorb the sweat.

"Have you considered not having a war?"

He looks at me flatly, mouth closed. I'm only a little sorry I brought it up.

"Open it." He pushes the phone to me. The time is displayed on the top in green over black.

I open it the way I saw him do it. Another little screen lights up. The time again, but in white on a blue field. An envelope. A folder. A tiny map.

"What do I do with all these things on the screen?"

Dario comes behind my barstool and cups his hands under mine. "Nothing. The only things you need are these buttons. With the numbers."

His chest presses against my back. I feel him breathing. His heartbeat is a faint rhythm between my shoulder blades. No phone will ever make me feel as safe as he does.

"I want you to memorize my number."

"Okay."

"Are you ready?"

He recites it, and with each digit, he kisses my neck, sucking away my brain's energy so it can flow between my legs. I touch the numbers on the phone without pressing them, engraving the shape of the motion in my fingers, the way I did on the landlines at home.

"I can't think when you're doing that."

"What's the number?"

I imagine the shape and recite the numbers.

"How did you do that?"

"I remember which corners and sides, and they make lines between, in my head. It's a pattern."

"Do it again."

Again. And again.

"Without looking," he says.

He kisses me. I make the shape in my head and repeat the ten digits until the swirl of need in my core could heat the city. I open my legs and throw my head back against him, reciting the numbers correctly.

"Dario."

"Again."

"Take me first."

He stops kissing my neck. I turn and wrap my legs around him, pulling him into me. He's hard. Very hard.

"No." Even as he refuses, he puts the contour of his erection between my legs.

"No?"

"No." His hips grind, pushing his hardness against me. "First, we wait and make sure you know it."

"I know it. I swear."

Hands under my knees, he pulls them wider to get better access. "How do you call me?"

"I put in the number, then I don't know."

"Press the green button. Do it."

"I can't call you while you're doing this to me."

"Try me." With a smile, he switches to a side-to-side motion that's guaranteed to distract me.

I hit the wrong button and have to start over. "I think you're enjoying this."

"You have no idea."

"There!"

"Green button."

My screen says *Calling...* then *Connecting...*

His pocket buzzes.

"I told you I knew it."

"I feel something against my balls," he says. "I wonder what."

"Pick it up. I want to talk to you."

He takes the vibrating phone out of his pocket and looks at the screen. "Who's this?"

"It's me! Answer."

"I'm not home." He slides the phone between our bodies where it buzzes against the nerve center under my pants. "Hang up, if you want."

"Oh my G—" The vibrations are lightning. The opposite of his teasing mouth. If I cut the call, I'll cut the stimulation.

The sensation escalates. I lean into the short back of the stool.

Then it stops like a car at a red light.

He's smirking and can go right to hell.

"Do you know how to leave a voice mail?" he asks.

"I know how to use a *phone*." I hold it up so he can hear the disembodied woman describing how to talk after the beep. Even I know that. Massimo and Daddy's phones had the same message. After the beep, I say, "Hi, Dario. Please take my pants off."

I press the red button, make the shape of his number, then press the green. The vibrations resume. He lifts my shirt to expose my breasts, pushing the phone hard against me while thumbing my nipples. He exhales with his own arousal, then it stops again.

"Again. Call me until you come."

It takes three more calls before I'm jerking with climax.

"Do you believe me now?" I ask, putting the phone on the counter. He keeps himself pushed against me.

"My plan was to send you out without a jacket." He pulls away and lowers my shirt. "Make sure you can dial when your hands are shaking."

"That's a little extreme." My legs drop.

"Smarter men than me have died underestimating the Colonia."

"Have they had me at their side?" I stand and pocket the phone. "No, they have not."

"You're not 'at my side.' You're my wife."

"Yes, I am, and no, I am not."

He raises an eyebrow and tightens his mouth. I can't tell if he's angry. All I can see is the massive bulge in his pants. He catches me looking and yanks his belt open.

"Get on your knees."

I lower myself without thinking, kneeling like a supplicant at the altar.

"That mouth's getting insubordinate, and it's going to

89

get you killed." He exposes himself, hard and thick, throbbing from the vibrating phone. "Hands behind your back."

He puts the head against my lips, leaving a trail of precum along my lower lip.

"I still know your number."

"Open that smart mouth for my cock."

I do it slowly, just to claim a little bit of control. He takes me by the back of the head and pushes in so fast my tongue doesn't have time to get out of the way.

"Now open your throat so I can fuck the defiance out of you." He gets out of the way long enough for me to breathe and press my tongue down, then he's in my throat. "You need to do what I tell you." He should pull out now, but he shoves himself deeper. "You suck when I tell you. You fuck when I tell you." He pulls out a little, but not enough. "You breathe when I tell you. Now. Breathe." He pulls out completely. I suck in air. He fists my hair and makes me look up at him in the distance, past his spit-coated dick. "I can't teach you anything if you don't do what I tell you. Breathe and open."

I do what he tells me, and he feeds me his dick.

"When I'm out, breathe, then keep it open wide. Don't close your lips around it. Don't breathe again until I tell you."

I nod around his shaft, and he pulls out. I breathe. Open.

"You mean everything to me," he says. "And I'm in over my head. If I lose you..."

He doesn't finish, deciding to fuck my open mouth instead. I don't close my lips around him. I let him use my throat, holding my breath as he pumps against my face, holding my head still.

He stops. "Breathe."

I do it, and he starts again, telling me to breathe one more time before holding me still, nose pressed against him, balls pulsing against my lower lip.

"Sweet girl," he groans, unloading down my throat. "I knew you could breathe on your own."

CHAPTER 14

DARIO

BEFORE I AGED OUT OF THE SYSTEM, NICO AND I WERE WITH A couple who left us on our own in the apartment for weeks at a time. We lived on nearly expired eggs the convenience store owner around the block sold to us at a discount. Sometimes he threw in a loaf of not-quite-stale bread. In the summer and fall, I made the potatoes we grew in the strip of soil between the apartment building's fence and the next property over. We ate. We lived to plan revenge.

I don't need much. I can survive on what I find in the dirt.

When I've felt powerless, that always calmed me. Nico and I could cut it all off and start over with nothing.

There's more than Nico in my life now, and I am not comforted.

It's not enough that I feel safe in the world. Because of me—my actions and my lies—Sarah does not.

What if I made the peace she wants?

Could we live on potatoes and weary eggs in anonymous peace, without the enriching soil of revenge?

No. It's impossible.

I decide this in the time it takes me to go through the door under the stairs and pass through to the security room. I'm in front of the flickering bank of closed-circuit monitors when I realize what happened.

She got to me.

I've traded my comfort for hers.

My password and thumbprint turn on a monitor behind a sliding panel, revealing a secret monitor.

She got to me, and I didn't even see it coming.

The secret monitor flickers on. There's a moment where I hold my breath. Nico's supposed to be the only person on this screen, but this time, after his missed meeting with Oria, I fear it could be Peter, or Massimo, or some curious Colonia trying to climb into a higher position.

But it's Nico—outside, in a park, walking along a trail. The video is vertical and shaking with his stride. Behind him, joggers come up fast, passing with either annoyed looks in his direction or laser-tight focus on their zone.

Relief floods my veins with the threat of complacency.

I open the conversation with a bark to shake myself out of it.

"Your woman's been in a state of panic for days."

"They were using my equipment to find you." He throws himself onto a bench set against a wall. He looks behind him anyway. "Tell her I'm fine."

There's no honey-bear-boo-boo in his manner when he relays the message. No flourishes or sweetness. He and I are very much alike without a woman present.

"You're calling off schedule," I say. "That's not fine."

"I couldn't risk it. There was a wall broken down in my old apartment."

He's describing the wall I chainsawed to get to Sarah.

"You didn't leave anything behind. Unless they can read the DNA in the sheets."

"I left a passport in the wall... just in case."

My fingertips wake into a numb tingle. "Did it have your name?"

"Nah. Fake name. It was the picture. I was thinner and younger. Coulda been me with more hair and a goatee. Coulda been some Maltese asshole. Took some questions. They started out as jokes, but it got pretty uncomfortable."

"Do you need to get out?"

Oria would be thrilled if Nico extracted himself, and frankly, I wouldn't be too upset about it either.

"Yes, but no." The shadow of a jogger with a swinging ponytail passes over him. "We have... they have Dafne."

"Where?" I lean forward enough to jump into the screen.

"I don't know. There's video. Supposedly too nasty to see more than the metadata from the security logs. Your security logs. It was the greenhouse security cam."

"I saw them trash it." I flip open the keyboard and pull up the greenhouse footage to look for the nastiness he's talking about. "Saw NYSD sniffing around."

He looks away, checks behind him, but it's still a wall. "Next night."

"Do you have the timecode, or do I have to scroll through every fucking hot minute?"

He rattles it off from memory.

I fast forward, expecting the feed was cut at some point,

but though the camera wasn't hidden, when the Colonia and NYSD took over, they didn't shut it.

When three men and a woman appear in the abandoned greenhouse, I freeze the frame.

This is why they left the camera alone.

"Shit." I leave the video frozen and lean back. I don't want to see what happens just yet. "They do not like traitors."

"They do not."

"Is she alive, or do I have to watch to the end?"

"No clue. The plotline's not in the metadata."

My finger hovers over the spacebar. All I have to do is tap it, and it'll play again. Once I see this video—no matter how it ends—I'll be pissed off. My decisions will be painted red.

"Let's say she's dead." I move away my finger. "What then?"

"Business as usual. We chip away. We have them where we want them."

"They just found our center of operations and destroyed it."

"Wrong. They took forever to take advantage of your mistake and lost you, lost Sarah, lost everything. They have a building they can't use. They look like they're in control, but ever since Sarah's been with you, nothing's gone right for them."

"You're closest to losing when your opponent's cornered," I say.

"Also? Something about a man with nothing left to lose, and yada yada, danger."

"What if she's alive?"

"She'll be hollowed. She won't be allowed to speak. So

she can't say what happened or who did it." His jaw is tight, and his words come out in hard, muffled barks that won't alert anyone but me to how angry he is. This is not the man who calls Oria *boo* or—for her sake—underplays the danger he's in.

"Calm down."

"I hate them so much. And being here, talking to these men. The righteous. The pious. The way they think they're fucking superior. I'm getting more and more pissed off every day I can't strangle someone."

"Do you need out?"

He hesitates. Averts his gaze. Exhales slowly.

"Today, please," I say.

"Fine. Let's make a deal. If you get to the end of that video, and Dafne's dead, I'm out in forty-eight hours. If she's alive, I'll stay to get her location. I'll stay to help the rescue. *Then* I'm out."

"And if they kill her before we get there?"

"Set me up a flight out of Teterboro airport the next day. Tell Oria I'll meet her there."

"Agreed."

"Good."

"I like it," I reply instead of looking at the video.

"Today, please," he says.

I look at the frozen frame of the greenhouse. I recognize two of the men from Peter's inner circle. The third has a blurred face. A tap of the key to the next frame will clear it up and their identities will be known.

"If she's alive," I say, stalling further. "They hollowed her. Like you said."

"Like I said." He looks past the camera into some

unknown future on his side of the city. He pinches the skin on his chin. Thinking.

"I want to watch Peter Colonia die."

"Even with me here at the servers... you'll never get to him again, and even if you got in, you wouldn't get out."

"That's a big prediction, Nostra-fucking-damus."

"Watch the video before you decide what you're getting in and out of, Houdini."

There's nothing left to say. I take a deep breath and exhale slowly. When my chest is empty, I hit the spacebar.

CHAPTER 15

SARAH

DARIO WAS GONE ALL DAY. BEFORE HE LEFT, HE TOLD ME TO CALL him with my phone at two o'clock. I did it, and over the headset, he directed me to give myself an orgasm, which I did. He came home after dark, ate dinner, and after his phone buzzed, he disappeared into the depths of the house.

When everything's in its place, I wonder where he is. Unable to find him in the usual places, I start for the bedroom, but notice the door under the stairs isn't fully closed. I go to close it, but I check first. The monitor lights flicker.

Well, I figure he knows I'm a snoop, and maybe I'll find him on one of the screens, doing whatever he does.

But Dario is right in the room, sitting in profile, eyes glued to a screen that lights his face. I've never sneaked up on him before, and I'm not sure how to tell him I'm here without him reacting with either fear or aggression.

Whatever's on the screen, it's taking up so much attention his guard is down. Barely breathing, I lean over to see what he's looking at.

I see people moving, then recognize the greenhouse I came to loathe. The rest comes in a flash. A woman. Naked. A ball of fire in the corner. A cigarette lighter. Someone's smoking. The woman is pulled down to her knees.

It's not me.

I am not the naked woman on her knees in the greenhouse.

Maybe I gasp. Or maybe my body made the room's temperature that much warmer.

Dario spins around to face me.

"Fuck!" He slides a cover over the monitor. "Sarah. What are you doing here?"

"What's that? What's happening?"

"It happened already. You need to go."

"Who is that woman?"

"Go upstairs and wait for me."

"Show me."

"No."

He tries to hustle me out the door, but I push him off. He grabs for my arms, but I flail, kicking his legs, screaming, "Show me!"

"No! Sarah, No!"

I jut my arms forward and push him away. He falls back a step, and I reach for the screen. I'm too slow, or he's too fast, but I'm not giving up just because he has my wrists. I have legs and I have feet. I have a head with a hard skull I can swing against his face.

"Ow! Jesus!" He lets go of me to cup his nose.

"Oh! I'm sorry."

And I am sorry. But I need to know what happened. In the split second I have, I slide the cover away to expose the screen. The frame is filled with darkened shapes frozen into blobs. There are no buttons or switches to flip.

"How do I make it go?" I demand.

"How do I make you go?" He uncovers his face. It's as beautiful as it ever was. "How do I make sure you don't see the abomination that happened under my roof? You won't get over it. It'll fuck with your head. Is that what you want? To see something so fucked up, you never get your feet under you?"

"I'm not scared."

"You're not scared enough."

"You sound like my grandmother with all her bogeyman stories. They never worked."

He shakes his head then looks at the screen with a sadness that may make him look powerless right now, but it's red meat for anger.

"There are bogeymen, Sarah." With the keys and a final tap of the spacebar, he speeds up the video until black and white figures rush around the greenhouse under patches of digital static. "They raised you."

He taps, and the video goes at normal speed. The static disappears. Two more men pace around. The one in front of the naked woman is Raymond. My cousin. And the men are Gino and... I think...

"Marco?"

The woman can't be me because the man isn't Dario. The woman punches Raymond's thighs. He pulls her nest of hair, revealing a long braid that's coming undone.

"So, it is Dafne."

In the fight, they're both pivoted to profile. She's not pantomiming fellatio. There's no tricky angle or playacting.

"That's her," Dario says. "In my house. With them."

My cousin, who liked my Christmas cookies, shoves his dick in my teacher's mouth like a piston, then stops deep. She's choking and he's coming.

"Dafne left the Colonia because she loved a man her father didn't want her to marry," Dario says. "She vowed another man would never touch her."

Marco pulls Dafne up by the hair. His dick is already out. When Dafne won't open her mouth, he slaps her. Somehow, that's more horrifying than what Raymond just did to her.

Gino kneels behind her while Marco wedges her mouth open.

I tap the spacebar. The image freezes, but that's an illusion I created to save myself.

"Did they kill her?" I can't believe what I'm asking.

"She leaves the room alive."

I want to cry, but I can't. I'm dry as a bone.

"That's my cousin." I tap Raymond's face. "He liked picture books with trucks."

"Remember that kid. He's gone." Dario takes my face in his hands and looks at me so deeply, I'm sure he can see how badly I want to forget what I just saw. "Are you going to insist on seeing the rest?"

"I get the idea."

"I'm sorry I showed you." The light from that image shines blue on his face, shadowing the hollow places under his cheekbones. The video is poison. It's a contamination.

"You had to. How else would I know what they are? What *we* are?"

"Shush. You are not like them."

But we choose not to be, and choices are weak. They can be unmade and remade. Sequestered behind walls of poor reasoning, I can reject what they did, but I'm one choice away from being one of them.

"This won't ever be over, will it?" I ask.

When we've been silent too long, he says, "I have humiliated my enemies. They wanted me to think they've moved on. But that's over. They don't take their licks and forget. They're relentless. They'll hunt us down. They'll keep me alive and make me watch them hurt you before they kill me. And if I die before they catch me, they'll hunt my family. They'll kill my friends. They'll burn down everything I ever touched and destroy everyone I care about. Starting with you."

Dafne. Dafne. Dafne.

No. I won't think about what I just saw. It hurts too much. I want the hope back. The menu of possibilities.

"I know you wanted peace," he says. "Now, do you understand why that's not possible?"

"I'm not afraid of them," I say.

"You should be."

"I can't be your prisoner forever."

He holds me and makes promises in my ear. "Not forever."

In this little room behind locked doors, it seems impossible that anything bad could happen to us. I feel safe here with him. Even knowing this feeling is a reckless luxury, I can't help but own it.

The images from the greenhouse smash into the barriers I erect to protect this coin of peace. They crack. I

MAKE ME

cringe, holding back those thoughts. I can't let them through.

"Dario," I say breathlessly, picking up my head from his shoulder, "you were right. I feel scrambled. Everything is wrong. I need to feel something is right."

"How can I make it all right for you?"

"Do what you do." I pull up my skirt and lower my underpants. "Remind me it isn't like that with you." I sit on the counter and spread my knees. "Please. Make me feel it."

Lifting my knees, I beg for it by showing him the source of my need. The intensity of his gaze is as physical as a touch. With a hand on each knee, he spreads me wider, drawing his hands down, inside my thighs, then he spreads my lips apart.

"You're wet."

"Thinking about you. Please take me. Help me block it out."

I'm convinced he'll do what I ask, but he pulls over the chair. Is he serious? Does he want to have a conversation? I close my legs and start to get up, but he pulls them apart and pushes me back, then sits.

"Relax." He runs his lips inside my thigh. "Try to relax. Think about how good it feels when I fuck you." He spreads my lips again and kisses where I'm wet. "Relax and let me take care of you."

There are no threats of punishment. No rough penetration. No pain at the margins of pleasure. Just the soft strokes of his tongue and the caress of his lips. His mouth savors the taste of my pleasure.

Without pain, it's almost overwhelming—and yet, I can't come.

"Faster, please," I gasp.

"You're too beautiful like this." He sucks me quickly. I buck. "You're too hot to finish. With your legs open for me, begging for it, my dirty little girl." He sucks my clit tenderly, and when I'm sure he's going to let me come, he stops to kiss the perimeters of my pleasure. "My dirty, beautiful wife wants to come."

"Please."

"But you're so pretty when you beg." Another suck, then a series of tongue flicks that forever halve the distance between me and my orgasm.

"Please, Dario. I'll give you everything."

"You already have. You just don't know it."

"I do! I do know it!" Is he listening? Or just licking me into madness? "My body is yours. My mind."

My heart?

"Only think about me. You think about nothing I don't allow in your head. Do you understand?"

Without waiting for an answer, he takes such a hard suck on my clit that I gasp from the bottom of my lungs.

"Yes!" I cry.

I expect him to revert to form. Hurt me with his teeth. Use his fingers to bruise and grab. I expect roughness and pain, but his portions of pleasure are so indulgent, so controlled, so sadistic that tears fall from my eyes. I can't beg. I can't speak. All I can do is weep from the whispers of attention from his mouth as he draws me along, going more slowly as I get closer.

"You want me to make you come?" He's watching me over the length of my body.

"With you." I pull his head away. "With you, please."

In moments, he's inside me, meeting the last of my needs by filling me with him and connecting our bodies.

"Look at me." He holds my face to his. "Keep your eyes open and look at me."

He's the only thing in my vision. He's everything. Dario is up, down, every point on the compass. Sobbing with every breath, I lose sense of space.

I am grief, and joy, and desire.

I've wept for all of it before and I will again.

"Dario," I say the only word in my vocabulary, and it's the only one that matters.

That acceptance is the last thought I have before Dario leads me home, and I'm lost in rapture with him.

When I find myself, the world is a clearer place.

There will be no peace. There will be war, and blood, and uncertainty.

But there will be love.

CHAPTER 16

SARAH

With the morning sun on his white shirt, Dario stands at the foot of the bed, fully dressed while I'm still wrapped in sheets.

"I know you want peace." He straps on his holster.

"And I know that's impossible now."

"Not while they have Dafne." From below, his face is even more angular when it's clean-shaven. My eyes see him, but all my mind sees is Dafne in the greenhouse.

"You won't attack while Dafne's in there because you care about her." I get up on my knees. The sheet falls away, exposing my naked body. "After seeing that video—I'm angry. I want to set fire to something too. But there are so many people *I* care about who'll be in the way. They didn't do anything."

"How do you think I can spare them?" There's no sarcasm in the question. He's really asking, so I really answer.

"I don't know."

Gently, he leans down, pausing before our lips touch.

"Neither do I."

He kisses me with careful tenderness and then leaves the house to make war with my past.

Making a ragu means standing over a pot for hours, stirring and thinking with the television on. I watch. Stir. Think. I find myself staring at the center of the red whirlpool, listening to the news. Faraway countries go to war. Someone lies. Everyone hears it. The truth is drowned out by grief.

I decide what I want, then change the channel from reality into fantasy.

"What smells so good?" Dario asks as he enters.

"Dinner."

"Sunday gravy in the middle of the week." He grabs the lid on the pot and snaps his hand away.

"It's hot." I snap his shoulder with a towel, then use it to lift the lid, releasing a cloud of steam and the smell of Grandma's sauce. He leans over it. I rip a piece of bread off the loaf, dunk it, and hold it up for him. "It's for tomorrow. Tonight is Junior's pesto pie."

"You sound like an American ordering cheese pizza with pineapple." He bends over the bread, looking at me, and blows. The way his lips narrow and tighten makes me want to fall into a puddle, but then I'd drop the bread before he bites into it.

"That sounds delicious."

He scoffs and takes a bite. When he kisses me, his lips are still warm. He looks over my shoulder at the little TV. "The *Avengers*?"

"This woman?" I point out the copper-haired warrior in the oily black outfit. "She beats up men—big guys with scars and armor—coming right at her. She knocks them out all the time."

He shuts off the show. "It's a comic book movie. It's not real."

"I know that. I'm not an idiot. But no one around her thinks it's a big deal. It's not shocking, so it must be *possible*."

His laugh is pure delight, and his next kiss is unguarded appreciation. "After everything you've been through, you want to be Black Widow?"

"Is that an option?"

"Everything is an option," he says between more kisses, lifting my shirt so his fingertips can brush the expanse of skin, leaving trails of sensation like lines in desert sand. "Anything you want."

"Anything?" I'm caught between his body and the counter.

"Anything possible." He finds the hook of my bra and frees more open desert.

He thinks I'm talking about learning how to kick high enough to hit a man's face.

"This morning, you asked if I could find a way to spare the people I cared about."

The oven beeps. I slide away to shut it off, then turn my back on him to get the potholders.

"I've thought about that more than you." He holds me still against the island counter by the base of my neck. "And you think you solved it?"

"I did. I know the Colonia better than you."

"Do you?"

In two words, he reminds me that I came to him ignorant of anything he finds important. He's wrong.

"My friend Denise. She's a good person. If I met her and told her what Marco did to Dafne, she might—"

"No."

"Why not?"

"Too dangerous." He whispers wetly in my ear. "What if her shitbag husband sees you?"

"He won't. I know exactly where to meet her. I can do it. I want to. Alone. You can't even go with me."

"There's no place you are that I can't be."

His warning is thick with meaning, slick and suggestive. My core hears the message loud and clear.

"I'll do it whether you let me or not."

He can't possibly like that answer, but his dick hardens against me. "Pull your skirt up."

I do it, shaking with anticipation as he opens a drawer next to me and makes sure I see him remove a metal spatula. I can't help but gasp at his intentions.

Without being told, I bend over the counter.

"Look at you," he says, stepping back to stroke my bottom. "My stubborn little wife."

When he removes his hand, every nerve below my waist jangles with the expectation of pain and pleasure. He taps my underwear with the flat of the spatula.

"Just do it," I whisper.

He grunts a *hmph* and taps a few more times.

"When I tell you to stay here..." With a *whoosh* so fast it practically whistles, the metal lands on my ass. The thin fabric barely dulls the sting. "It's to protect you." He smacks the other side. "Until you can protect yourself."

"I know."

"You know." He hits each cheek one time. My bottom is already on fire. "But here you are."

"I don't want Denise to suffer any more than she has already."

He pulls down my underwear with one finger, then with a hand between my shoulder blades, presses me against the counter. "Do you want me to make your ass red?"

Resistance drains out of me, leaving a hole as big as an ocean. Only he can fill it, and when he's done, I'm still doing what I need to do.

The unbuffered spatula is built for pain. My body jerks against him and tears spring from my eyes. I let out a high-pitched squeal when he slaps it against my bare skin again.

"You'll stay here." And again. "Until I say..." And again. "... it's safe to leave." Again, and I see every color in the rainbow. "I don't want to beat you into obedience." Gently, barely touching the skin, he strokes my behind. It burns like hell, but with an electricity that tingles. "I want you to obey because you understand."

"I do. But I can't."

"Why not?"

"You can't see the danger to her. You don't know."

"Don't I?" His fingers brush between my legs, then my folds, and he sighs. "You're so wet." He inserts two fingers without resistance and I groan. "Open your legs a little. Show me how much you want to do what I tell you."

I set my feet wider, and he goes deeper while his pinkie flicks my clit.

"I'm going to save her. I mean it."

"Do you?" He rubs inside me, finding a hard little spot I didn't know existed.

"Oh God, Dario."

"I'm not done." He hooks his finger, torturing the interior nub with pleasure.

"This won't work."

"I'll be the judge of what works and what doesn't. When will you understand that?"

He quickens the stimulation, rubbing that hidden, hardened spot.

"What are you doing?"

There's a box of explosives inside me, and he's picking the lock.

"I know, Sarah. I know your deepest places."

"Oh, God." My whole body is flushed warm as the pressure builds past where I'd usually find release.

"All the secrets they keep from you. I know them."

My entire body shakes with release, but not completely. Not enough before another wave crashes, and his fingers speed up. He says I'm a good girl. He says I'm sexy and hot. He keeps talking and I keep coming in flood after whole-body flood. The orgasm is not rigid. I don't arch, but loosen. It belongs to my hips, my breasts, my arms and legs. I feel as if I'm being squeezed from the inside out for the last little bit of tension.

He pulls his hand from me and catches me when I try to stand.

"I think the pizza's cold," I say.

He laughs and helps me pull up my underwear, then leads me to the table and sits me down before he stands at the sink.

"You can't contact Denise." He washes his hands thoughtfully. "I don't want to have to tell you what'll happen if they find out."

"You think I don't know?" I put my fists on my hips. "We all know about hollowing."

"If you knew." He twists the faucet off as if he wants to break it. "You wouldn't stand there and talk about putting your friend, or yourself, at risk of it."

"Grandma told us stories about traitors. The men are killed. The women... she whispered it so Massimo couldn't hear... between their legs, their parts are removed. The parts that make us feel. The parts you like best. All gone. I was young. I thought they were just stories when I got older. But I'm wiser now. I believe them, and I know what the outside folds are for, I understand what that means."

"Thanks to me." He snaps the towel off the rack to dry his hands.

His shirt conforms to the bulk of his arms. It teases the contours of his chest. Even domestic chores take on power when he does them. Opening the drawer with quiet menace. Plucking out a potholder with assurance. Checking the oven like a cop with a search warrant. Sticking his bare hand where he can get burned.

"Pizza's still warm." He uses the potholder to grab the

tray and closes the door with his foot. "Come on. Let's eat. Forget about all this."

He kisses me as if that'll make me forget, and it does, for a minute. I can't tell him this isn't the last he'll hear of Denise.

CHAPTER 17

DARIO

SCRUBBED CLEAN, I STAND ON THE BEDROOM BALCONY.

The penthouse on top of the world had become a kind of home. I could see everything from my bedroom, and if the view was blocked, I could go up to the greenhouse and see more. See everything. Of course, I couldn't really see the outlines of whatever problem I was trying to solve. But the illusion was enough to clear out the cobwebs and false connections.

But now I'm on the flattest part of the flattest part of the east side of the continent, at the same level as anyone else, and I can't see shit from the second-floor balcony. The trees hide us, but they also obscure my enemies.

I'm not sure if this house is a secure location where we can plan our attack, or a trap.

I've never doubted myself this much.

Sarah joins me, opening and closing the sliding door as gently as she can. From behind, she puts her arms around my waist and rests her head against the base of my neck.

"You all right?" she whispers.

"Yeah."

She doesn't pick apart my answer. For a few minutes longer than anyone else would wait, she's just there with me.

"Thank you," she says, letting go to come to my side. "For bringing me here with you."

"You think I wouldn't?"

She shrugs, looks at her hands on the railing. Her snowflake ring glints in the moonlight. "It would have been easier to send me with Willa."

"You would have gone?"

"I would have."

"But you would have hated me."

"No. Not hate. Maybe not trusted you ever again. Maybe —once I got on my feet—I would have come back and found you."

"When I hide, I'm not an easy man to find."

"You'd never hide from me."

She's right. I'd never be able to stop watching her, and to leave those lines open is to be exposed to danger. I'm the one who wouldn't be safe if we were separated.

"What's that light?" She points over the tree line. "Every ten seconds."

"You've been counting."

"Yes."

"What do you think it is?"

"If it was irregular, I'd say probably cars coming over a slope or something. And if was fast like flash-flash-flash, then I'd say it's the lights on a fire truck or police car. But they would be red and blue. See? There it is again. Ten seconds. It's weird."

Sarah has never owned a cell phone. She'd probably never touched a laptop in her life.

Yet she figured out the induction stove. She watches television like a mermaid just up from the deep, trying to learn a new world from a box. Do I have to tell her what's real and what's fake? Will she try to wave a magic wand or kick a six-foot bruiser in the face?

Not as long as she notices flashing lights on the horizon and counts the seconds to make sense of them. She's fast without speed. Smart without an education. She's practical about dangerous things.

"It's not weird," I say.

"So, what is it?"

"A lighthouse."

Even by the light of half a moon, it's obvious how exciting and surprising the answer is to her. I've just made her night.

"I've never seen a lighthouse," she says.

"You still haven't."

She elbows me. I put my arm over her shoulder, and we watch the sky flash every ten seconds.

"It's on Executioner's Island. In the Sound—it's just a rock with a lighthouse on it."

"Why do they call it that?"

"I don't know." I squeeze her, but not hard enough. I'll never be as close to her as I need to be. "Before your wedding day—"

"The one you interrupted? Or the one you forced?"

"The first one. I was in a little landlocked town called

116

Secondo Vasto. Over the river from a college town. Nowhere."

"Why?"

"Remember Santino and Violetta? From Armistice Night?"

"How could I forget?"

"It's his territory. *Their* territory now. I went for a handful of men no one here would recognize."

"Vito and Gennaro?"

"Yes. And another, who decided to stay. But while I was there, a war broke out. Santino disappeared and I took over because there was no one else. Or so I thought. We're upslope in this fucking fortress, looking over the town, and his wife is driving me crazy. She spits and fights and thinks she knows more than I do about how to run a fucking war."

"You didn't try to spank some sense into her?"

"She's another man's wife. At the time, that was the reason. Also, not my type."

"Not submissive enough."

I laugh because she's gotten it exactly right. "I kept telling her to go cook something. Sit with the women. Get out of my way before she got herself killed and I had to answer to Santino DiLustro."

"He seemed pretty scary."

"I'm not scared of him, Sarah."

"I wasn't saying you were. You were in his territory, surrounded by his men. It's bad odds."

She sees everything so clearly and I kept her locked up. I stole a block of marble and brought home a work of art, carved by a genius.

"I did everything I could to take away her power." I look

away, ashamed of the memory of what I tried to steal. "She had her men lock me in the basement."

Sarah startles. "What? You?"

"I underestimated a woman and she made me her prisoner. Then I came back home and did it again, with you. I took you for a pretty little doll and then you're out here counting the seconds between flashes of light so you can deduce what it's coming from." I let my arm slip from her shoulders and fold my hands on the railing.

This feeling of helplessness is as pleasant as a cattle prod up the ass. There's too much. It's all too much. I can't get my arms around it.

"I forgot Dafne for a minute," she says. "Already."

"I haven't forgotten. We're going to get her back."

"How? Are you going to kill everyone?"

"No." I want her to believe me.

She closes her eyes and bows her head a little as if praying.

The moment seems so private I back away and sit in one of the chairs.

Finally, she turns and says, "I really didn't know what my people were doing."

"I know."

"I should have." She comes forward, standing over me. Is she bowing her head in shame or looking down at me? It's the same thing.

Taking her hand, I pull her between my knees. "No, Sarah."

"It was right under my nose."

"That's why you couldn't see it." Hands under her skirt, I stroke her legs, her hips, her ass. "You did nothing wrong.

118

You can feel shitty about the situation but blaming yourself isn't allowed. It keeps you from doing something."

My fingers explore her folds. I can't see her expression in the dark, but she breathes sharply and bends into me a little.

"Does it?"

"Yes." I hook a finger in the fabric to draw down her underwear. "Step out of these so I can fuck you."

My dick is out by the time she's done. I pull up her skirt and draw her close, a leg on each side of the chair.

"I want to make it right," she says. "I want to help."

"You will." I push her down enough for my head to rub her clit.

"Tell me how."

"Show me how you fuck." I line up to her entrance. "Show me how it feels good."

"That's not what I meant."

"I know." Pushing her down, I bury myself in her in one stroke. She gasps. "Show me what you like anyway."

She starts off timid, moving in all the ways I like. I shift her a little, and she groans.

"Go ahead," I say. "Use me."

She moves against me one way, then another, until I help her find a groove. Her mouth opens while her eyes close.

"Dario, wait."

"Why?"

"Are you ready? Because..."

"Don't worry about me."

"God, oh..."

"Come, sweet girl." I take her face in my hands and put it close to mine so I can feel the orgasm on her breath. Catch the vibrations in her throat before she cries out. Hold her in my grasp while she takes what belongs to her. "Take what's yours."

She takes it, and when she's done, I give her what's mine.

The thought that started as a cloud I couldn't hold takes form.

It's not an idea. It's a decision.

"Sarah, will you marry me?" I hold her to me, my nose buried in her hair.

I know the answer before she says it.

"I don't know," she replies with her head on my shoulder. "I can't be your partner while I'm a burden. I can't live... function without you." She puts her nose to mine. "I don't know if you should."

"I should." I hold her face where it is, where I can see the moon's glint in the whites of her eyes. "And I will. When you realize how much you give to me, I'm going to marry you."

"Maybe you will," she says. "Maybe."

I'm left wondering, does she doubt my commitment? Or her own?

The bolt is stuck. All I want to do is change a hose, and I'm stuck with my arm in an engine, trying to unscrew something designed to be unscrewed. It's a stupid part to get held up on and I'm this close to sawing it off. Connor's arms are crossed, feet apart—a silhouette against the frame of the open garage door.

"We need Dafne's exact location," he says. "We go

snooping around and she's not where we think, or maybe she is? We're gonna be caught with our dicks out and wind up dead as a fistful of doornails."

"Look, Connor." I stop to turn the wrench with everything I have. Fail. "Nico's got nothing, and the only place he can't access is the clinic on Eighteenth Street."

The black 1970 Skylark's been on blocks for years. The hoses are dried out and the lube's broken down. Oversight on my part. A car like this deserves care.

"And you want to carefully search all five floors for what? The Colonia Memorial Hollowing Center?"

"We don't have her location." I pull my arm out of the Buick's engine. "That's not going to change. Can you get me the orange can?"

"We need to go in like a fucking storm." He crosses out of the light to grab the spray lubricant from the tool bench. "We can't leave Dafne to rot while we peek around corners." The can turns into a streak of orange when he tosses it. I catch it.

"Until we can guarantee her rescue." I take the can and adjust the light so I can see the bolt. A little grunt escapes my throat as I try to loosen it. "We're not storming shit."

Even with my eyes and hands on a 350 V8, I sense his suspicion.

The bolt finally jiggles loose.

"I mean no disrespect." He warns me he's about to drop a garbage bag of disrespect. "But this is *her*. She's making you play a game of cricket when we can just hit them with the bat. Why not turn every last one of them into pink mist?"

"Because it makes a mess, Connor." One last twist and

the bolt comes free. "We're not in some DiLustro backwater where we can bury bodies in the front yard. We're packed tight in a fucking city. We can't even blow up that church without greasing a city block. This isn't a fight between butchers. It's a war between surgeons."

I pull out of the engine and lean on the chassis. A streak of grease blots out the StyTown tattoo on my forearm.

He runs his fingers through his hair and averts his gaze.

"Now." I toss the old bolt and wipe the grease off my hands. "You can either be ready to extract Dafne like a pro, or you can get on a plane and go the fuck home. Because Connor..." I put my hand on his shoulder. "If we lose, my wife's a sitting duck in this house. Look at me."

After a moment, he meets my gaze.

"Am I fucking around?" I ask.

"Are you?" His eyes won't lie with deferential bullshit.

"I am not. So unless you see something, or have an idea that's better than pink mist and cricket bats, I need you to do your job like it's the only thing between you and a bullet."

He looks away, mumbling, "We shoulda done to her what they did to Lissey—day one."

The thought of it is a spark on dry kindling. That'll never happen to my Sarah.

"Shut up, Connor."

He commits to the image. "Done her up like a pig."

"We are not animals!" Before I can think better of it, I become the animal I deny, putting my greasy hands on his white shirt and forcing him against the tool bench. "Do you understand? If you came here to act like a savage, you wasted your time."

"You woulda." He pushes back on his heels, knocking me against the bench.

I would have. In the first days, if I'd needed to, I would have done worse to Sarah than what was done to Dafne. Was I stronger then? Or weaker?

I'm fighting to a draw. Connor and I have each other by the throat, red-faced, in a race to choke the life out of one another before we get choked ourselves.

Connor is ex-military... a Digger who served in East Timor.

I grew up on the streets, fighting for scraps.

We were evenly matched before I had something to lose. Now I'm on my back and my ears are ringing so loudly I can barely hear her voice as she comes in.

"Please!"

Downward pressure bends my elbows. The grip on my throat loosens. My fingers lose their leverage. We separate, breathing like drowning men. Sarah crouches between us, her arms spread as if she has the strength to keep us apart.

"They took her from me." Connor's voice is rough. "They put her in a shipping container. In a cage. They stole her and used her like a piece of meat." He points at Sarah. "They sold her life. Her people did it."

Sarah's hand is at her chest. She bears no culpability for what the Colonia did, but I can't take care of her now. When Connor gets like this, nothing moves forward until he calms the fuck down.

"I know."

"I came to you for justice. *Justice.*"

"You'll get justice." I get my feet under me and offer Connor my hand. "I swear it."

"Fuck you yanks." He takes my hand and gets his feet under him, looking at Sarah while talking to me. "This cunt's been in bed with traffickers her whole life. She was raised on their teat."

The way he's looking at her—with distrust he's kept hidden this whole time. Now he doesn't care if we both know how he feels about her.

"I was," she says softly.

"Sarah." I try to shut her up before she pisses him off, but it doesn't work.

"I didn't know."

"Sure," he says sarcastically.

I put my hands on his shoulders. "She's helping get you your justice."

"*Our* justice, mate." He steps back. "Everyone. And fuck you for forgetting that."

"Thursday," Sarah says, shutting Connor's mouth. "Ten in the morning, give or take. I'll get you Dafne's location or get to someone who can get it."

"No, Sarah," I croak as if Connor's hand is still on my throat. She's started making a promise he'll want her to keep, and if I undo it now, I'll seem careless with my own team.

"How?" Connor asks.

"A friend. Her aunt's a nurse in the clinic. I can find out if she's there. Maybe what floor she's on. Will that information help?"

He nods slowly, then shifts his gaze to me. I have his trust now, because he thinks I always intended to send Sarah to her friend for intel. Fuck this. I hate it. I hate being outmaneuvered and I hate that I have to go along with it.

"If we do this," I say to Connor, "I want guys on every street corner on Thursday. I want them on roofs. I want the NYPD walking the street. If anything happens to her—"

"Yes, boss," Connor says then turns to her, as if he knows I'm not the one who can tell him. "Where?"

She points her chin up a little. "McKinley Park. On 4th Street, between First Avenue and—"

"I know it," Connor says, a little soothed. "'Ta, for that. Busy corner. Fully in the open."

"No, it's not." She looks at me, and I'm sure she can read my mind. "Not in the ladies' bathroom."

"Right." He nods.

"Expect two to four mothers," Sarah adds. "Six to nine kids. An aunt named Clara watching them. No men. No one's going to be armed."

"We will be," I cut in, drawing a line in the sand and highlighting the danger of the situation.

"It's good enough," Connor says. "I have it from here."

He turns and walks out. It's just Sarah and me. I take her by the chin and look for lies or misdirection in her brown eyes. There's none.

She inspects my throat as if she knows I'll never burden her with minor injuries.

Thursday. She'll never be ready to face the outside world without me by Thursday.

"You got what you wanted, Sarah. You get to see Denise. I hope it's worth it."

"Who was Lissey?" Still inspecting, she runs her fingers over my shoulders. Grease-streaked arms and stained hands. Caring for me as if she values me.

"You have to stop snooping." I pull her hands off me. "She was his sister. One of them."

"And the Colonia... what?"

"Trafficked her." I squeeze her wrists. "Do you know what you just did? With Connor?"

"The right thing."

"You put me in an impossible situation."

"I've been in an impossible situation since we met." She tries to wrench her arms away, but I have her. "I'm doing everything I can to be useful."

"Do less."

"You need to let go."

She's not talking about my grip on her arms, but I let them go anyway.

"I'm going into the ladies' room with you," I say. "You and all the women in Manhattan need to deal with it."

"Denise isn't going to talk to me if you're there."

"Get it into your head, Sarah. I am not letting you off this property without me. Ever. Get a credit card. Use a phone. Learn to drive. None of it matters. As long as I'm alive, I'm staying with you. You're either here, behind these gates, or I'm in arm's reach."

"It's going to be fine!"

"No, it's not. You have no idea how not fine it's going to be." I hold out my hands in frustration as her eyes go bigger with the realization that she's bitten off more than I can chew. "Look, I can't teach you anything now. There's no time, and I just end up fucking you all day anyway."

"So you quit?"

"I have a different solution to the problem... and I hope you like it."

CHAPTER 18

SARAH

I CAME DOWNSTAIRS TO FIND DARIO AND WILLA FACING OFF ON opposite sides of the kitchen island, not saying a word to each other across air as thick as cold bacon fat.

"Dario," I say in a voice barely louder than a whisper. "This was your solution to the problem?"

"Yes." He doesn't look at me.

Blood pounds in my ears. My vision gets dark in the corners. If I don't say what I need to say right now, I'm going to faint or worse... lose my nerve.

"I don't want to go."

Suddenly, four eyes are looking straight at me.

"What?" Dario asks.

In the background of the noise in my ears, Willa laughs.

"I want to stay with you."

"Oh, honey, this man isn't letting you out of his sight. It would be cute if it wasn't so vaguely threatening."

My eyes meet Dario's for confirmation.

"You're not going anywhere," he says.

The thrumming in my ears stops and my vision clears. A little nervous laugh is released from my throat.

"Good, okay," I say, clapping my hands. "Nice to see you, Willa." I fill the teapot. "Did you want coffee?"

"I'm all set."

"Dario? How about you?"

"I'm fine."

"Good." I turn on the magic burner, because I want tea, and what I want is enough. "Willa, have you seen this? It heats the water but doesn't get hot."

"That's called an induction burner, honey. It uses magnetic—"

"Oh!" I interrupt with excitement. "Dafne started..."

...teaching me about magnetic fields, but now she's...

"I'm just going to make some tea." I finish with a dumb narration to fill the hole that the video of my teacher opened. "If you change your mind, just say."

"Willa's here to get you started," Dario says. "She's not taking you to St. Easy or anywhere."

"Good," I say, reaching for the teabags. "I was going to try to figure out the second oven."

"It's a warming drawer." She slides open a hidden panel under the lip of the countertop and I bend with her to look at it. "Keeps dinner warm if your husband's going to be late."

"Oh." I stand straight—tea canister in one hand and the lid in the other—look at Dario, then Willa. "Was this house for you guys? Together?"

Willa laughs. Dario is not amused.

"This was a bad idea." He jabs his finger at Willa. "You're going to confuse her."

Willa and I answer at the same time.

"No, I'm not."

"No, she's not."

We smile at each other. I lay down the canister and get myself a cup.

"You're right," she says. "This house was supposed to be for Dario, Rosemarie, and me, but I took her with me to set up St. Easy, and well... she never came back."

The teapot whistles.

"It's fine," I try to reassure them both.

Willa and Dario get into a staring contest again. If eyes could shoot daggers, I'd be scrubbing blood off the white kitchen tiles. And yet, Dario still trusts her. That much is clear.

"I'm glad you're here, Willa." I say her name to get her attention back on me. "After you show me around the kitchen, I'd like to learn how to drive a car, please."

"Untapped ambition." Willa shakes her head as if I amuse her. "Every one of you Colonia women is a stark-raving-go-getter."

"You won't have to coddle her," Dario says. "She catches on quick."

My cheeks may be hot from the boiling water I'm pouring, or from the way Dario's dancing with complimenting me to Willa.

"Do you catch on quick, Sarah?" she asks.

"Depends."

"Willa," Dario says, trying to sound nonchalant and failing. "Go to my lawyer's office and get some divorce papers drawn up, would you? Take Sarah. Show her the ropes."

"Of getting a divorce?" Willa smirks.

"Never." His fake coldness turns real hot, but her amusement does not melt.

"After she has her tea." Willa leans toward Dario on her elbows. "I'll show her the ropes. You can go."

With a flick of her wrist, Dario is dismissed.

It takes Willa hours to show me all the buttons in the house, because she doesn't just show me what happens when I press them. They all connect to the internet, and though I know what that is, I have little experience using it, and I certainly had no idea appliances could talk to it.

The Colonia only buy things with cash, so she shows me a checking account and credit card bill with a single transaction, so I don't get confused.

Then she tells me we're going to the lawyers, where she'll divorce my husband.

Benny brings her little brown sports car around. It says Jaguar on the side and in the front, a silver jaguar leaping off the end of the front hood. I wait for someone to open the passenger side, but Benny is nowhere to be seen and Willa crosses to her side, spinning her keyring around her thumb.

"It's unlocked." She opens her own door. "Go on."

I've seen car door handles before, but not one with a button. I slip my fingers behind the handle and pull. Nothing happens. I look at Willa. She's not giving any hints.

When I push the button with my thumb, it opens. We

get into the two-seater. I click my seatbelt and smile. The things I know already are as much of a victory as the things I learn.

"All right," she says, pulling out of the gate. "This is how it's going to go. You aren't married to him."

"I'm not, actually."

"Good girl." Her hands rest comfortably on the wheel, and she manages the pedals as if she's walking—unaware of how special she is. "Let me do the talking. We got married for bullshit reasons, and we'll get divorced for the same."

"When do I learn to drive?"

"Let's see." She pulls into a parking spot. "Switch."

"Wait, what?"

"I get out and sit there and you get behind the wheel."

She puts her hand on the door handle as if she's ready to get out, and I'm supposed to do the same. We'll leave the car, then get back in on opposite sides. It's obvious and it's not a big deal because everyone drives.

But I'm frozen in place, eyes so wide they ache, heart racing so fast it feels as still and heavy as stone. I don't want to disappoint her, but I cannot move.

"Right," she says with the conviction of a woman whose worst suspicions have been confirmed. "When you don't have that particular look on your face, you'll learn to drive."

She pulls out of the spot, and I look forward with my jaw tight.

"Don't get your panties in a twist," she says. "Watch what I do, and it won't be so scary."

I watch the dance of her feet and hands. Where she looks and what she does.

"Getting a divorce," I say. "Is it hard?"

"Shouldn't be. There's a waiting period, then we're done."

"Then he's mine?"

"All yours, if you still want him."

I do. I am sure I do. Even after I can drive a car and go wherever I want, I will still want him.

Willa doesn't seem as sure.

CHAPTER 19

DARIO

EVERY DIAMOND UNDER THE GLASS SPARKLES MORE THAN I'VE EVER seen any gem sparkle on a woman's hand.

"You look like shit." This observation is the second thing Oria says when she walks into Tiffany, right after "what do you want?" We came in separate cars even though she's taken up residence half a mile away from our safe house.

"Just tell me what you women like."

"'You women' meaning 'women' or 'Colonia women'?"

"The second."

She sighs and peers into the case. "We don't get an engagement ring. There's no tradition around it."

"You think I want to get her a Colonia ring?" The implication disgusts me.

She shrugs.

I point at a yellow gold ring with a big center stone surrounded by sapphires and smaller-karat diamonds. "What about this one?"

"Keep it simple."

The woman behind the counter has been attentively inattentive—hands folded in front of her, a thin, neutral smile of brown lipstick—until Oria points at a single stone in platinum.

"Would you like to see it?" Her lips disappear when her smile turns to teeth.

"Yes," I say.

She unlocks the case and takes out the ring with a reverence usually reserved for statues of the Virgin Mary. Oria scrolls through her phone as the woman shows her. Ignored, the clerk hands the box to me.

"Do you want to try it on her?"

"Oh." Oria finally looks up. "It's not for me."

"Same size finger," I say. "Close enough. See if it fits."

She lays down her phone and puts on the ring.

"This is a one-and-three-quarter carat solitaire set in platinum," the saleslady says, finally knowing what to do with us. "The round cut is excellent and the clarity rating of VS1 is—"

"What does that mean?"

"It's nearly perfect."

"I don't want it if it's not perfect."

"Jeez, Dario. You'd think you weren't already married to someone else."

The saleslady clears her throat but remains neutral.

"Will she like it or not?" I ask.

"Yeah." Oria holds her hand out flat, considering it. "She'll like it."

"We can place a new diamond in this setting," the saleslady says. "I'll show you our collection of perfect stones. Is this size what you were looking for?"

"I want bigger."

"No, he doesn't." Oria takes off the ring and picks up her phone. "You're going to freak her out and she won't wear it."

The lady leads us to an area in the back meant for people looking at the expensive shit. Exits locked and the archway in is narrower. Easier to secure. Two security guys. Alarm system cleverly hidden, but not invisible. There's probably another layer of security I can't see.

Doesn't matter. I'm a paying customer.

Attention on her phone, Oria wanders off to a couch upholstered in robin's egg blue leather.

"Did you see the video?" I'm not in a sitting mood, so I stand over her.

"No fucking way I'm watching that."

"I don't blame you."

I'm suddenly nervous about the entrances and exits. The foot traffic outside. How did I wind up in Manhattan? Jewelry stores aren't hard to find. I could have gone to one upstate, but I had to have the best for Sarah, and the best is here.

"What are we going to do about it?" Oria won't look at me.

"We're pulling our stock from Newark."

"Is this the 'stock' you've been working on for six years?"

Guns. She means guns and so do I.

"Six and a half, but yes."

"Why are you telling me this?" She puts the phone aside. "You never tell me this shit."

"I can stop telling you this shit." I sit next to her. "Your choice."

She squints as if a tighter lens will bring my motivations into focus. "So it's stock or... what's the other option?"

"It's all stock."

The ceiling lighting is hidden behind beige panels. Only the glow is visible because it's the only thing that's needed. The ugliness of wires and plugs is hidden.

"I've been thinking..." I can't finish. Once I tell her, it has to happen. If it doesn't, I'll have to deal with the blowback. "About you and Nico."

"Yes?" She tilts her head. I have one hundred percent of her attention. She can tell something's off.

"I get it."

"Get what?"

"Why you want him back. Why it's hard to be apart. Why you want peace."

"I'm sorry? I don't want peace with them. I just don't want him inside with them... and what the actual...? You want a truce?"

This is the blowback.

"Not anymore."

"You were even thinking it?" She scans my face and decides I was. "You were thinking of accepting what they do? Just letting it slide because you got bored?"

"I'm not *bored.*"

"Then what is it?"

"Can't you figure it out?"

"Jesus." She plops her bag onto her lap but doesn't open it. "You love her."

"I don't know."

"No." She shakes her head. "You're confused. When it

comes to 'love,' you're incompetent. It's the one thing you've always admitted you didn't know how to do."

I've lived a hundred years inside my short life, but I've never said the words she's looking for. Even in my mind. Even about my own brother. Or my dead mother.

"I care about her. Deeply."

She scoffs. "You cared deeply about every woman who came through."

"This is different." I keep my voice low, but I'm failing to keep my cool.

"I mean, you're fucking her so, yeah."

Reducing my feelings for Sarah to fucking should piss me off, but we're in public, and the comment isn't meant to insult. Oria is holding up a fact to indirect light.

"What does fucking have to do with caring?"

She puts her head against the back of the couch and looks at the ceiling, whispering curses. "All I want to do right now is wait for Nico to come home. And all you have to do is let that happen."

"Done."

"What?"

I shrug and look away as if it's nothing, but it's one of the reasons I had her meet me here.

"He's coming back."

"When?"

"Once we get Dafne out." I look at my watch while she sits on the edge of the couch like a kid waiting for her birthday present. "Or we confirm she's dead. Then he's meeting you at Teterboro. He'll probably talk to you himself, but I wanted you to know. He's coming out."

She throws her arms around me with such force I'm almost pushed off the couch.

"Thank you." She squeezes the breath out of me.

"Okay."

"Thank you so much, you fucking asshole. Thank you."

"You're..." I push her off and she finally lets go. Her eyes are glassy with tears of joy. "You're welcome. It was his idea. He's ready."

"I can't believe it." She digs in her bag and comes out with a used tissue to dab her eyes.

She'll believe it when it happens, and it will. It has to, for the same reason I have to keep Sarah with me. The world is not real without her. Oria must feel the same about Nico.

I haven't felt this good about someone else's happiness in my life.

The saleslady comes out with a tray of diamonds, followed by an armed security guard who looks no more threatening than any big guy in a suit. I meet them at the counter. Oria stays behind.

She starts her pitch. "These three stones are—"

"Which is the best?" I'm losing patience with this whole process.

"It depends on what you're looking for."

She's not getting it. She's used to people coming in here either knowing what she's talking about or eager to learn.

"I'm looking for a ring that won't look insignificant next to the size of her heart, with a diamond as perfect as she is. It has to be a color that's bright, but not overpowering. It has to be like her. Humble and priceless at the same time. Do you understand?"

The saleslady nods slowly, blinking once.

"This one." With tweezers, she pulls out a stone and holds it under a light. "Two carat. Perfect cut and clarity. We have more colorless stones, but I think you might appreciate something on the warmer side."

I can't see the color difference she's talking about, but she's right.

"That one."

"Have you thought about a wedding ring?" she asks. "We have sets for bride and groom."

Another thing to do? Of course. My eyes settle inside the case—on a ring with large diamonds around the entire circumference. It's not simple, but neither is Sarah. It's a ring for a woman who deserves the most beautiful things in the world.

I choose her.

There never lived a woman in the world who could tease this kind of feeling out of me. But here I am. Sarah Colonia. I've never loved a woman in my life, and now I'm so inexperienced I think love is my choice to make.

"This one."

"It's lovely," the woman says. "Also platinum with seventeen round cut—"

"Wrap them up. I need them both today. Now."

She drops her gaze, and her lips get even thinner. "Our diamond setter is gone for the day."

"It's important," I add. "I've kept her waiting long enough. We can get some engravings later. The dates and..." I rummage through my brain for things people carve inside wedding rings. "A nice quote or something. Another time."

"Even with that, sir, we simply can't get it done before Thursday."

I could be dead on the floor of a park bathroom in two days.

I look at my watch as if new hours are going to appear. They don't.

I'll have to wait to propose until after Sarah and I meet with Denise.

"I'll be here Thursday afternoon," I say, signing on the dotted line. "Or not."

CHAPTER 20

SARAH

The dim ceiling light flickers in a steel cage above the bathroom stall. The toilet is lidless and seatless—just a wet, open mouth ringed in stained porcelain lips.

Of course, Dario is in the McKinley Park women's bathroom with me. He stayed at my side from the car, past the swing set, and through the door of the little brick building that clearly says "WOMEN" beneath the silhouette of the figure in a dress. There was no one around to tell him the men's room was on the other side of the building, so here we are.

Forty-five minutes later, in the second-farthest stall from the door. I don't know why I thought he'd let me sit in here alone for an hour, waiting where he can't see me.

If I'm being honest with myself, I'm glad that last bit of my plan failed. I'd rather have him near me than anyone, as long as he stays quiet and lets me do the talking.

We haven't said a word or made a sound in all this time. I'm jumping out of my skin. Dario's patience is awe-inspiring. The beauty of his posture—heels against the side of the toilet, arms crossed, back against the wall—is enthralling. He doesn't move from his tensed position to relieve the pressure on his knees. He crosses his ankles once, soundlessly, never touching the floor or exposing his presence.

The only active thing he does in that time is stare at me, head to toe, as if doing some kind of math. Not a word though. Not a sound.

It's midday of midweek, so the park is populated with kids too young for school, their nannies, and their parents. Mostly women, mostly mothers. They gather in small groups, clutching paper coffee cups and metal water bottles. Except one group of young women who come together. They meet on the corner of First and 10th with their children every third Thursday.

I don't have children, so I don't go, but Denise told me she sometimes leaves the kids with the other mothers, gets in the last stall, and just sits there for as long as she wants.

When anyone comes into the bathroom, Dario looks for my reaction. Kids. Women. Girls. I shake my head. There's a water fight when a group comes in to fill up balloons. No. A woman shoos them back outside. No. Another woman comes in muttering. Rattles the door. Dario puts his finger over his lips. I shake my head. Teenagers skipping school, giggling. No. A toddler looking for his mother. No.

In this series of snapshots, we hear slices of life in Manhattan, but not Denise.

I look at Dario and tap my wrist. He finds a way to shrug without moving his shoulders as if to say, "I'll stand here in this bathroom, wedged between a toilet and a wall, with you as long as I need to."

I mouth the words, "What if I'm wrong?" without adding all the things I could be wrong about. The time. The date. I'm counting on my friend's life to be the same, and what if it's not?

Dario shakes his head. He won't be moved. I know that much. His trust in me is nice, but what if it's misplaced?

I wipe my palms on my pants.

"Matty! You have to wait for me and Auntie Clara!"

A babble of little-boy sounds follow. Then a hearty adult snort, right from the sinuses.

Allergies.

Dario's gaze goes from my knees to my eyes—from seduction to question.

Yes.

That's Denise and her little son, Matty. Aunt Clara is there to make sure the mothers aren't left alone too long. Public parks are dangerous, after all.

"Pee-pee!" Matty rushes into the farthest stall, next to where Dario and I are, and slaps the door shut. "Me-self! Me-self!"

"All right," Denise says, giving her son what she can't have for herself. "Just put the pee into the bowl, okay, sweetheart?"

"Kaykay!"

"Lock the door like I showed you."

Metal clicks. Through the crack, I see her. She looks as tired as she sounds. When she leans against the stall door, our stall shakes. Fabric rustles. Water hits water.

"Good boy." Denise faces the floor, arms crossed, arms closed.

I wish I could hug her, but all I can do is silently beg her to take ten minutes for herself.

"Ball now!" Matty cries.

His mother recites all the things he has to do before he can play ball, and it seems like he does them, until it's time to wash his hands.

"Matty! You have to..."

And her voice is gone in the chase. I look at Dario, eyes wide.

Did we lose her? Will she come back to wash his hands or give up and let him play ball?

Again, Dario puts his finger to his lips.

Men are the most patient predators in the animal kingdom, and Dario Lucari is at the apex.

But me? I've been patient enough. She was right there, and instead of whispering her name or showing my face, I let her go.

I put my hand on the little silver lock, ready to get out, when Dario leaps from his perch and pushes me against the door, his hand over my mouth.

"Not yet." The words are spoken as loud as a breeze, with a body tensed against mine and eyes that remain in a state of peace.

He moved so quickly and pinned me so accurately, I don't have a choice but to heed him. The confidence in his eyes and arms. The unbroken line between his intentions and his actions.

"Like, a minute!" Denise calls from outside. "He's fine as long as he has the ball."

There's a pause. Dario lets me go and gets back on his perch.

"There's no other way out," she says, closer. "Like always."

"On Monday, I thought you fell into the toilet and we were going to have to pull you out of the sewer in the middle of 14th Street," an older woman says. That'd be her Aunt Clara. "By the time you came out, all the bread was set out to rise and you hadn't done a bit of kneading."

She shuffles in front of the stall next to us. Empty. I scoot to put my back to the toilet. Her shadow shows her bending to look for my feet. She'll see them, but not Dario's. I look up at him, a hawk on the roof's edge. He smirks at me.

The third door swings and clicks against the wall.

"Take your monthly constitutional," Aunt Clara says with the hint of jokey commiseration. "But don't take your time. I'll be outside to make sure there are no unwanted visitors." She makes the banal description sound vile and frightening.

Denise chirps gratitude and locks the door. Her aunt Clara goes outside with the kids.

Dario's nod is more than a sign to begin. He's telling me I can do this. He's with me the whole way.

I take a damp, folded note from my pocket. Its corners are darkened from half an hour in my hand. I'm supposed to hand her the tiny square under the stall, but in this last minute, I realize that's not the best way to do this.

I unfold it while Denise pulls down her pants. On one side is a phone number Dario set up to forward to him. On the other is a greeting.

HI, STINKPANTS. IT'S SARAH.

. . .

When her second baby was so big she got a fistula, I helped her with her chores and called her stinkpants. I was a casually unkind, nasty bitch. I don't like using the name now, but it's a way for her to know it's me before she sees me.

Dario watches as I read it. Does he approve of the cruelty? Does he even see it?

While Denise pees, he folds one hand over the other and knots his brow. A question or confirmation about unfolding the note. I nod. It's fine. It's better. I've decided. And in response, he nods and folds his arms, accepting my decision without further inquiry.

Good. I don't want to be told what to do right now.

The pee noises stop. Denise snorts. There's no rustle of clothing. No rattle of toilet paper. She's staying in the quiet to think. I look to Dario for strength, and with a simple, confident nod, he gives it to me.

Reaching down, I pass the note under the stall, insult up.

Nothing happens.

Time passes. Too much time. Maybe three seconds with Mississippis in between. Then I feel the paper slip from my fingertips. I don't expect silence, but that's what I get. My attention on the space under the stall, I reach for Dario and catch the hardness of his forearm. He puts his hand over mine, and I finally breathe enough to use half my voice.

"Denise?"

"You're dead."

Is that what they're telling everyone? Jesus. Was there a funeral? What did Daddy and Massimo say over the closed casket?

Or maybe she means I'm dead to her.

"I'm here." I rub my palms on my pants again. I'm going to need a stain remover to get the sweat out of them. "Remember when Marco Junior was a baby? And you gave him rice cereal for the first time? And he went crazy? Grabbing for the bowl with these little arms he didn't know how to use?"

Her response is to pull up her pants and flush. I expect her to say something, ask a question, express excitement. I don't expect the stall's wall to rattle, then hear her gasp from above me. She looks over the top, pressing the note in a triangle halfway over the edge.

"Hi," I say. Even wide-eyed, staring at the man wedged between the toilet and the opposite wall, her face is like a letter from home. "He's okay."

She tears her attention from Dario and puts it on me. "Is this him? The one who did it?"

"Yes." I put my fingers on the wall, ready to climb to her. She looks back at Dario, grinding her jaw. I realize too late what she's about to do. "He's okay. He didn't harm me. I promise he won't hurt you."

With a sharp *kkst* from her throat, a glob of spit flies across the space and lands on Dario's chin and chest. I suck in a breath, but in those first moments, he doesn't move.

"Good thing we checked for toilet paper." He gets down with fluid, catlike grace and reaches for the paper.

"You animal."

He wipes his face and shirt. She can insult him all day long and he won't react. This next part is mine.

"Denise." I get up on the toilet to talk to her face to face over the stall's rickety wall. "Listen to me."

"Why should I?"

"Please." Something about my plea breaks her, and her rage turns to despair.

"Oh, Sarah, I miss you so much."

"I miss you too."

"Come home. Please. Kick him in the balls and come home."

I'm not coming home. Not today. Not ever.

"Denise. You haven't screamed for your aunt. You haven't run away. Why not?"

"Maybe I will."

"A part of you trusts me... and that part of you, it's the part that always knew Marco was bad for you."

Her eyes narrow. Years of defending him for her own peace of mind won't let the slight meet the truth. I've overplayed my hand.

"We'll leave you alone," I say. "But we want to know... has Aunt Clara mentioned seeing Dafne Tamberi? Our teacher from the lower grades?"

"Why are you asking?"

This is as good as a yes, and I'm formulating my next question when Dario cuts in.

"Where? What floor?"

She shoots him a look. "What's it to you?" Her attention turns back to me. "And you should be ashamed, standing here with him while she's barely alive from what he *did*."

She spits out the last syllable. Of course, her aunt told her Dario was the one who hurt Dafne, because that's what she would have been told. The important thing is that Clara was told *something*, which confirms the clinic has her.

An instant of amplified sound forces us both to turn

toward Dario standing beneath us, phone in hand. The noise is gone too quickly to identify, but I can still see—and I'll never forget the video he just muted.

"Dario," I say. "Don't."

He's not going to listen to me. She accused him of what the Colonia did, and he's not going to leave this bathroom without countering it.

"Denise." I shift close enough to her to block out Dario. "What floor does Aunt Clara work on? Just tell us that."

Her eyes scan mine, left to right. She snorts, then her gaze moves over my shoulder.

Dario's holding up his phone, and Denise can't take her eyes off the screen.

"Denise." I put my hand on her arm.

She lets go of the sweat-stained note, letting it drift to the floor.

"This is who did it," Dario hisses. "Now where is she?"

Denise's lips go slack, as if watching this monstrosity is taking up the energy her body needs to breathe, to swallow, to answer his question.

"Dario," I whisper. "Turn it off."

He doesn't move it away or stop it.

"You need to tell us or find out."

She'll need the number on the note. I get down to retrieve it, but as I stand back up, Denise reaches for the phone's glass. It seems like she's going to touch it. Maybe play the video again. That's how she gets close enough to grab it right out of his hand.

"No!" Dario shouts.

Denise jumps down and unlatches the door. Then Dario. He's going to catch her.

But Aunt Clara's voice echoes in the small chamber. "Denise?"

"I'm right here."

Dario puts his back to the door, looking up, mouthing the word *fuck* over and over.

Through the crack, I see my friend putting the phone in her back pocket. She and her aunt Clara walk out, and Dario finally finds his voice.

"Fuck!"

Dario curses all the way to the car. Once we're both safe inside, he holds out his hand to me. "Your phone."

I give it to him, and he makes a call.

"Thank fucking God that fucking house is locked down or we'd have to fucki—Tam."

As he talks to Tamara, he seems so cut off from me it's unbearable. After what just happened, seeing Denise, showing her the video, knowing how painful it was for me to see, watching her face fall—it must have been ten times more painful for her.

I hear Dario tell Tamara what to do about his phone and I see his rage at himself, but it's all through a filter of the memory of that bathroom stall.

"...erase everything. And the lock screen..."

"Don't," I say.

Denise resisted helping us, but for how long? She can't unsee what her people—*our* people—did. Her own husband.

"...shouldn't even have a keyboard..."

"Unlock it. Dario."

"What?" He stops himself mid-sentence to look at me as if I've lost my sense.

"If unlock it means she can see it... she needs to look at that video as many times as she has to. She might put it away and never look at it again. Or she might show people inside. Think of what that would do? A mass waking. Then she'll help us get Dafne out." I pause to check his reaction. All he does is blink, and it's all I need. "Leave the video. Can the forwarding number be somewhere?"

"In the contacts," Tamara is barely audible from his phone. "It's not a bad idea."

"Can you make it so when she calls it, it comes to my phone?" I say it loudly to make sure she hears me.

"Fuck, Sarah," Dario mumbles.

"Yes." Tamara's voice is definite. "Dario?"

"She's going to hang up if it's you. If it's me, she'll talk." I put both hands on his thigh and lean closer to him, pleading. "She has liberation in her back pocket."

He thinks. From a thousand miles away, Tamara asks if he's still there.

And though he doesn't answer, I can tell he's still here. The invisible wall that seemed to separate us is gone. He is one hundred percent in this car with me.

"If she's caught with it," he says, "and they punish her, that'll be on us."

Us.

I've dreamed of sharing a home with a man. Children. Old age. Sharing responsibility isn't a dream come true, because I never dared imagine it was possible, or that it would be this fulfilling.

"She's smart." I put my hand on his. We are connected. I am here with him, anchored in the storm. "She'll be fine. And if she's not, she'll call me, and I can ask about Dafne."

He shakes his head, but I know it's not about Denise. He's denying something deeper and more personal.

"Tamara," he barks toward the phone. "Do it." When he hangs up, his head drops back.

"I know."

He squeezes my hand but looks out the windshield to a place far away, rubbing his chin with his thumb. "I just want to be with you, and I'm so tired of the rest of it."

"I'm with you."

He puts the car into drive. "I'm getting you home, then I have to pick something up."

CHAPTER 21

SARAH

I N THE M ANHATTAN PRISON I LEFT A WEEK AGO, IF D ARIO WASN'T around, I knew he was in the office behind the double doors at the end of the hall. I didn't think about that until he left the grounds of the safe house and disappeared to some nameless place my mind couldn't picture.

There's an empty room on the other side of the house. If he can decide how he's coming and going without telling me, I can decide this is my space. I bring in paper and my art box. A table. I go through a few chairs before finding one I can sit in for hours. I eat lunch, then I draw what's in my head.

His hands. The place his arm cap meets his shoulder. The delicate map of lines on his brow.

Outside. The tangle of bare tree limbs. The shape of roofs on the horizon. My memory of the tree line's clear silhouette every ten seconds.

Benny checks on me, asking if I'm okay.

I miss my people. My family. Safety. I miss the sense that

I wasn't on my own and every choice was lovingly made for me. That I was surrounded by a community that cared for me.

Like Denise.

I wish I knew what was happening with her, but there's been no news. All I can hope is that she hid the phone and never took it out again.

"Is there a clipboard anywhere?" I ask Benny.

"I think so. Hang on."

He brings me one. I clip as much paper to it as I can and go outside where I can get a closer look at the trees.

I go around the back and find the service road I saw on the security monitor. The sun makes a hatched web of shadows on the soft bed of leaves that crackles under my shoes. I've never been in a real forest. I've only seen trees in parks, where they're tamed and bound. Their spacing seems random, but when my pencil records it, there's an order bigger than the paper can contain. But I try.

Up ahead, a twig cracks. It's not me. I step ahead. Cautious. Curious. Safe enough to be open to any possibility. The next broken twig is close enough to stop me.

The deer is already staring at me, a piece of leaf hanging from the bottom of its chin. Pale brown. White spots. Big ears radiating from the head like antennae. Its eyes are black and still, filled with a terror that anchors it to me.

I look away but keep it in my sight. I don't expect it will let me any closer, but I don't want it to run. I don't want it to be afraid. I hug my clipboard, shifting my shoulders forward as if I carry a weight, the way I did at home and school when I wanted to escape notice.

You hunch like that every time Grandma's around.

Massimo didn't understand. He never had to make himself small.

The deer's ear wiggles. It bends to eat something on the ground. Out of the corner of my eye, I watch, standing as still as a tree, postured to look as unthreatening as a woman. The deer picks up its head, turns to me, checking to see if I've moved, and finding me still, turns its back on me. I dare to look up. It's checking the ground, but finds nothing, and casually trots away.

My smile is spontaneous, but it gets so wide my face hurts.

I could have scared it. I could have brought a moment of fear into the world, but didn't, and I won't.

From now on, I'm going to be the counter to the suffering I've seen and felt. The exact opposite. The world will be better because of me.

My legs churn under me as I look at the crossed branches above in their sensible, chaotic beauty. I don't realize how far I've gone until I hit a chain-link fence. It's ten feet high with a coil of barbed wire strung across the top. The other side is more forest and brush. Over it, I can see the roof of another house. Not the one I have to get back to. I can't see that one anymore.

How big did Dario say the property is? Too big for me to find my way back home.

Following the line of fencing, I look for a better angle, hoping to see the driveway or the house itself. But all I see is a camera mounted on the top of a fence pole.

When he realizes I'm gone, he'll go to the little room under the stairs and check his screens for me, but who knows when that will be?

I tuck my clipboard into my elbow and take out my phone. Open it. Brush the keys with my thumb. I know the shape of Dario's number. I know the shape of Daddy's office from calling it every day to let him know what was for dinner. I know Massimo's cell phone shape from calling him to check on Daddy's every need or drive me someplace if Timothy wasn't able to.

Do I remember it?

One-two-three-four-five-six-seven-eight-nine-ten points on the shape. Right. And then I automatically press the green button.

Calling... appears with its ellipses running.

Calling... quickly becomes *Connecting...* then becomes a timer counting up from zero.

"Wait."

What did I do? This isn't what I want.

When I hit the red button, the timer is replaced with the clock.

I feel like I dodged a bullet.

But why?

Is calling Massimo to say hello the worst thing in the world? Just to talk?

Dario's right. I don't know enough about the world to function in it, but I do know how to call him.

I'm about to do it when the phone buzzes in my hand. I press the green button, because only one person has this number.

"Dario?"

"Where are you?" he asks.

"I don't know." I look around. "I saw a deer."

"Am I supposed to use that as a landmark?" I hear

stomping feet on his side. A door opening and snapping shut.

"I'm waving at a camera."

"Stay there."

"You're coming?" I ask.

"I'll always come for you."

"Okay."

"Hang up."

I hang up. Do I need to tell Dario that I dialed Massimo's number if we didn't say anything? Will he go back to thinking I'm ignorant and incapable over such a silly mistake?

Four minutes later—according to the clock on my phone —his dark figure appears between the trees, breath huffing in cold clouds, scarf under his chin, jacket waving in the wind his speed creates. His kiss arrives in time to keep his promise.

"You're not supposed to walk this far." His hands cup my face, and he has to bend to level his eyes to mine.

"Are you worried I'm going to climb over the fence?"

"I'm worried you're going to get lost for too long." He puts his arm around me and guides me back. "It's cold. You'll call me a snort and I won't hear it."

"If someone calls you a snort in the forest and you're not there to hear it, are you still a snort?"

"I am your snort." He kisses the top of my head. "I'll always pick you up and bring you home."

"Have you heard anything about Denise?" I try to ask casually.

"Not yet."

"I bet she threw your phone in the trash."

157

"Maybe she did."

It's not long before I can see the house—far away, in the spaces between the trees.

"Can we stay here?" I ask. "In this house? Can it be ours?"

He seems to think about it for a few steps, then stops, facing me, then looks down at our clasped hands. "If you like it that much."

"Do you not like it?"

He hesitates, looking at the house, then the path we just walked down. "I bought it for another woman, for a specific purpose. You deserve a house of your own. Made for you, not a castoff I bought for someone else."

"That's not the way I think of it at all."

"But it's how I think of it."

That's the last word for him. He takes my hand and leads us on a stroll to the house again, twigs and leaves crackling underfoot. The scarf around his neck unwinds and blows behind him. The ground feels soft and unsure. Mud sucks at the soles of my shoes, and wet leaves slide against each other if I don't pick up my feet.

"A week ago, you were trying to send me away," I say, taking the last word from him like a thief. "You made up a passport and bought me a ticket on a plane. Now you want to build a house around me. And this house in your head, I can't even picture it. But this house? However or whyever it's yours now, I can see it. It's got rooms and furniture. It exists. I can grow from here. Branch out. Figure out who I am—that's all I want."

"You will. You'll have it all."

"When?" I don't want to sound like a demanding child, but I don't know how a demanding, powerless adult sounds.

"As soon as this is over." He swings his arm to indicate *this*, and I know what he means. This violence. This war. This plan.

"It's not going to be over." I stop him at the door of the house that was never, and never will be, mine. "Dario, this thing you're doing, it's not going to end for us, or for my family, or anyone."

"It will."

"Do you think you're the first person who's come for us?"

He flinches ever so slightly. I wouldn't even recognize the expression if I didn't know him. He knows he's not the first, but he's never considered that he may not be the last.

"What if we ended this?" He looks at me, a little brighter, a little more hopeful. "What if I had a secret place on a tropical island?"

My heart drops into despair. "I don't want you to send me away."

"What if I went with you?"

"With me?" I'm not playacting at confusion.

"Do you want me to be there with you?"

I hadn't even considered the possibility, and now that it's been offered, I can't tie it onto my assumptions.

"How am I supposed to know?" The spool of insecurity unwinds in a single sentence. "I'm not sure what you mean when you tell me what you want, and I can't be sure what I want until I know what you mean when you tell me what you want."

"I get it." He holds up his hand, closes his eyes, and

collects his thoughts. "I've known what I want since the day my mother died. Destroy the Colonia. Wipe them from the earth. I still want it. But now I want more. I want you."

"You have me."

"Do I? As long as I'm at war with your family, do I ever have you?"

My hands are warm compared to what happens to my heart.

"So stop the war."

His laugh is short and hard. He takes me by the shoulders. "When we get Dafne, I'll stop it."

"Of course." I'm ashamed I forgot already.

"Then we'll be in St. Easy together."

"St. Easy?"

"That's what we call it. You're going to learn everything and be with people who know what you need. Including me."

The terms of the offer are now clear. It fits in a slot between my desire to stay with him and his desire to send me away.

"So I stay here until then?" I ask. The steam of our breath mingles. "With you?"

My head is like a pot of overcooked rice. I can identify individual grains of thought, but everything is stuck together.

"For now, I don't want you thinking about any of this. All I want you to do is get up to speed. Once we get Dafne, I'll have them on the back foot. I'll broker peace, then we go."

"Together?"

"Together."

CHAPTER 22

SARAH

TOGETHER, WE GO INTO THE HOUSE DESIGNED FOR SOMEONE ELSE, that exists, and that I feel safe inside. He closes the door.

"Do you trust me?" He unbuttons my jacket and slides it off my shoulders.

"Yes." I shouldn't answer so quickly, but the heart doesn't hesitate.

"How much?"

"Why?"

"Because what I'm going to do to you, it's going to hurt at first."

When I inhale, the air is fire in my lungs, igniting a kindling in my belly. "I trust you."

Pensively, he runs his fingers down my shirt, circling the nipples. "Go up to our bedroom. Take your clothes off and wait for me."

I do as I'm told, and when I get to the bedroom, my breath isn't short from the run up the stairs. My hands aren't shaking as I undress because I'm scared. The flush in my cheeks isn't from heat, and the tightness of my nipples isn't from a chill.

It's the promise of hurt. His hurt.

He's still fully dressed when he comes in. He takes off his scarf. "Turn around."

I turn my back to him, and he covers my eyes with the scarf.

"Now." He spanks my bottom. "Walk to the bathroom."

"But I can't see."

He spanks me again. "Go anyway, or I'll tie your hands behind your back and send you on your knees."

I want to make him proud. Prove myself. I know where the bathroom is, so I reach out for the wall, taking unsure steps. I'm in control of my thoughts and movements. Right or left? The choices are mine to make. But I'm hobbled without my sight, and I run into the corner of the bed.

"Right direction." His voice echoes as if he's already in the bathroom. "This way."

Am I in control? Do I want to be, as long as Dario can wield power over me?

"Can I take this off?" My arms wave in front of me like a kid playing pin the tail on the donkey. I take another step.

"No." The tub faucet goes on at full blast, sounding as though it's coming from every direction and making his voice hard to follow. "A couple more steps."

"Can you talk again?"

"I love seeing you find your own way to me."

My foot touches cold tile. I smile.

"I made it!" I put my arms out for him, but he's not in range. I step forward. No Dario. When I reach for the scarf's knot, he grabs my hand from behind and places it on top of my head.

"You made it." He puts the other hand over the first. "I knew you would."

He touches me from neck, to breasts, to belly. I can't decide if he's behind me or in front, because it feels as though he's everywhere. His hands push my feet apart, and it feels like he's kneeling in front of me. His lips brush against my shoulders, and it feels as if he's ten feet above me. No part of me is beneath his attention. My ankles, inside my elbow, the expanse of my back—they all turn incandescent at his touch.

When I'm glittering with sensation, he takes my hands off my head.

"I'm going to make this good for you."

"I trust you." My arms droop to my sides, completely relaxed.

"I know you can take it, but if it's too much, you say so. Do you understand?"

"Yes."

He pushes me forward, and though I'm convinced my legs are too loose to walk, I take a step.

"Lift your right leg."

I'm not sure I can command my knees to bend, but they obey what my brain cannot. He guides me into the tub, on my knees, and bends me forward like a doll, putting my palms on the tile of the wall. He shuts off the faucet. The steam is wet on my face.

The hot water flows from a pitcher, warming the parts of me that are exposed to the air. From behind, his warm hands take my breasts before one drifts between my legs and pulls me back into him.

"Do you want to see?" he whispers. "I can take the scarf off."

"Can we leave it? I know it's getting wet."

"Leave it." He circles my clit, holding me tightly. "Open your legs."

When I do, the hot water laps against me.

"This is mine." He slides two fingers inside me.

"Yes."

"Lean back." He puts his hand back between my legs, but this time, he settles on my tighter opening and circling it. "Is this all right?"

"I can't believe how good it feels."

"Believe it." Slowly, he pushes in his finger. "Do what I tell you, and you'll feel so good. Next time, you'll beg me to take your ass."

Deeper. I feel as if he's discovered a part of me I didn't know existed. With a second finger, I'm dissolving into his arms and the embrace of the hot water. With his other hand, he circles my clit. I gasp with the intensity of the feeling.

"When I put my cock in your ass, it may hurt. But it's better if I get you close to coming and keep you close."

I feel the cock he's talking about against my lower back. It's a battering ram. It's going to tear me apart.

"Okay."

He speeds up the stimulation of my clit. "You're so tight back here." He buries two fingers in my ass. "So hot. It's going to feel so good to fuck this little virgin hole. Show me how much you want it. Spread your ass apart."

I reach down and spread my cheeks apart, and he gets his fingers in even deeper. "Do you want to come?"

"Yes."

"Will you?"

"No."

"Good girl."

He removes the two fingers and the hand that was on my nub. I gasp with the loss of them. Behind me, a cap snaps open, and he shifts me away from him.

"What are you doing?" I ask.

"Getting ready."

I take off the blindfold and look behind me. A tube of lotion floats in the hot water. He's leaning back, wet from the chest down, fisting his dick. At this point, it looks bigger than it felt against my back.

"Hands and knees, beautiful. Show me your ass."

"Now?"

He pushes me forward and I land with my hands on the tub wall. Then he pulls up my hips and squirts warmed lotion on my tailbone before smearing it down to my waiting ass with his two glorious fingers. It's not long before I forget the thought of that monster in my bottom.

He takes away his hands. "Ready for my cock?"

"I don't know."

"What don't you know?" He flicks my clit, and I groan.

"It's so big."

"Yes, it is. And you can put it in as slow as you want." He leans back, pulling me with him, and wedges his cock between my cheeks. "Just relax. Breathe."

I feel it hard against my anus, demanding and predatory. Waiting until the right moment to break down the door.

CD REISS

"You're not breathing."

"Right."

"Let me see it. Breathe."

I inhale slowly and deeply. He pushes. Gets nowhere.

"Good," he says as if we were successful. "Again. You this time."

I breathe again and push myself down. My ass opens a little, and I squeal. He pulls back.

"Again."

"I'm scared."

"Are you telling me to stop?"

"Would you, if I was?"

"Yes. Without hesitation, I'd stop."

I'm curious enough to want to keep going. I trust him when he says he'll stop, when he says he'll make it good for me, and when he says it will hurt. I trust all of it.

"Then do it. Take it. Make me love it when you fuck me there."

"God, you're so fucking hot."

He puts four flattened fingers between my legs, circling gently, using the promise of pleasure to encourage me. I lower myself little by little, until his head is in. I cringe, biting back a scream of pain because his groan of pleasure makes it all okay. He likes it. I'm giving him myself.

"Slow, now."

"Okay." The shape of the pain has a dozen points, like a stamp on a certificate or a volatile star. The pleasure is rounded, yielding, curved, and sloped like an approaching tidal wave.

Another inch. Stretching me, unlocking a door to fill a place I didn't know was empty. The pain dulls, becoming a

166

constant ache as his cock slides in, inch by inch. Then something changes and the points turn to petals.

"Oh, God. That's..." My body buckles when he pulls out and slides back in.

Am I crying because of the pain, or because I've been reduced to shapes with edges that roll and vibrate?

"That's what? Does it hurt?"

"Yes. No. Please. Let me finish."

"Good girl."

We take it so slowly that when I try to go faster, he redirects my every move with gentle sureness, as if it's all about me.

Then he groans, sucks in a breath. "I need to feel..."

He doesn't define it. He just increases his movements on my clit and the tidal wave becomes a circle, bigger and bigger, even after I'm sure nothing inside me is that big, and I'll never be able to contain it. Like a balloon filling with heat way past just enough. Past what it should reasonably hold. The rubber holds together, thinner and thinner.

"I can't!" I sob.

"You can." He grunts, shoving deep.

And I do. The balloon gives up and finally breaks. Splatters in a wordless scream. He puts both hands on my hips and moves me up and down on him.

He pulls me into him as his crescendo comes in a rumbling breath. We lie like that in the cooling water, my back to his front as if I'm a skin's-width ahead.

I am broken, and filthy, and at peace.

That night, I'm alone. Dario is somewhere being a man no one's ever learned to control. To counter the emptiness of the house, I turn on a game show.

"I'll take *Friends of Alice* for 400."

"This substance, often used in haberdashery, is said to be responsible for making many a hatter mad."

My phone makes a noise.

"What is mercury?"

When I look at it, I expect to see a call from Dario, but it's a message from Massimo's number. Holding my breath, I open it.

—*I know your voice,*
even with one word—

Did I say one word?
Wait.

—*Tell me where you are*
and I'll come get you—

No.

Never come get me.

If I leave a message, he'll send something back. I shut it off. If I ignore him, maybe he'll go away and leave me alone.

"According to Shakespeare, nature teaches even beasts to recognize these."

Before I admit to myself that I don't know, one of the contestants beeps in and says, "What are friends?"

"That is correct."

They move on to the next box, but the question lingers.

What are friends?

Friends laugh. They joke. Share secrets.

Friends embroider diaper covers and clean the apartment when your husband gets mad and lays you up in bed.

Friends tell you he's not that bad. That you can redeem him. One day, he'll stop.

Has Marco found the video? Or just the phone?

I take out my phone, turn it back on, and let muscle memory dial the shape of Denise's home number. Four in the corner. Diagonal. Up twice. Middle. Corner again. Middle. Zero.

It rings. What will I say to her?

She'll ask about me first. I'll say I'm fine. She won't offer to come and get me, that's for sure.

Ring.

I'll ask her how she is.

She'll say she's fine.

Ring. Ring. Ring.

I'll listen to what she says and what she doesn't.

Ring. Ring. Ring.

"Come on."

I don't hear Marco's voice telling me to talk after the beep.

I know they have a machine, but it doesn't pick up. It just rings and rings.

This is worse than her swearing she's all right.

CHAPTER 23

DARIO

I FIND SARAH STANDING AT THE COUNTER, WATCHING THE television, tapping her eraser against a new sketch pad.

My life can be order. It can be whole.

I kiss the back of her neck.

"Dinner's in the oven." She says it as I've always imagined my wife would—as if she knows damn well she's the still center of a universe in chaos.

"What are you watching?"

"It's called *Jeopardy*. It's a backward contest about... things. Facts I don't know."

"What did Willa show you today?" I kiss the back of her neck again and move her shirt to expose more skin.

"The library." She drops her pencil and slides a little booklet out of her sketchbook pages. "I got a card. Then we got a study guide from the DMV."

"And then?" Barely looking at it, I take the booklet and lay it on the counter.

"She left. Benny too. Something about a water heater

breaking." She faces me. My lips cannot resist her throat. "How many safe houses do you have?"

"Not enough." I take in her scent of milk and honey and rose petals.

"Any news from Denise?"

"No." I put her on the counter with her legs wrapped around me.

"Can you tell if she watched the video again?"

"No."

"Can you check on her?"

These aren't things she should be concerned with, so I change the subject. "Did you pick up the papers from the lawyer?"

"Yes. You're divorced. Officially. Legally."

"It means nothing. I feel exactly the same as I did yesterday."

"Really? I was so relieved I think I lost ten pounds. Then Willa took me out to lunch to celebrate and I gained it all back."

Her happiness is contagious, but I don't want to get distracted from the reason she was out with my now-ex-wife in the first place.

"What else did you learn today, my prima?"

"Willa told the lawyer you're an asshole."

"You knew that. What did you *learn*?"

She smirks, and I let her run her fingers through my hair.

"When someone stops short in front of you, you say, 'You want a Honda up your ass?' provided you're driving a Honda, which we weren't."

I lean back. Fucking Willa.

"If someone cuts you off and you see them at the light,"

she continues, "you roll down your window and say—very nicely—'Today you fucked around and next time you're gonna find out.' When the car in front doesn't go for a green light, you gently tap the horn and say, 'That's the only shade of green it comes in.' Asshole can be tacked onto the end of any of those. Or fucknut."

"Anything else?"

"If you want to cuss at a woman, you call her a sweaty dickbag, and if it's a man, you call him a dirty whore. This confuses them long enough to run away. Tomorrow, we're going to try them out."

"No, you are not."

She bursts out laughing.

"You should have seen your face," she says between breaths. "It was..." She tries to make an angry, kill-to-the-death expression, but it's impossible when she's laughing. "Very Dario face."

"I do not look like that."

"All the time. You're a serious man who makes a serious face."

I lift her shirt. "You should see what it looks like when I'm licking your pussy."

"Is it serious like this?"

She's probably trying to make a face, but I can't see it while I'm kissing her breasts and belly.

"Maybe." I lift her skirt, then look at her. "Or maybe I'm smiling."

I kiss the insides of her thighs and lick her pussy until she comes so hard, all I can do is grin.

When the sun is up, I'm already awake to meet it. I can't remember a time when I slept more than a couple of hours. I work out until I ache. I think. I focus. I plan.

But ever since Sarah gave the last part of her body to me, I've been distracted.

I own her fully, but I haven't given her all of myself.

Offering to go to St. Easy with her isn't enough. Asking her to marry me isn't enough. Buying the ring isn't enough. Nothing I ever do might ever be enough, but I'm holding back, and I know it.

I just don't know how to close that gap.

So, I'll try this morning, and tomorrow, and the next day. I'll find where I can do better for her and do it.

Today, with the engagement ring in my pocket, I make her breakfast. Pancakes, the way my mother used to make them for us. Huge and fat and soaked in syrup. I set the table with the fork on the left. I remember which chair she sits in when she's not told where to sit, then I move it because she's learning to do different things.

I stand over the table, wondering if she wants to sit in my seat, facing the back garden. It's the best view.

Yes. That's the way to go. I'll ask her to marry me right here. I'll ask like I mean it this time—with a ring. Maybe on one knee.

When she comes downstairs, I'm in the middle of moving her fork.

"What are you doing?" Her hair is nested in morning knots and her white silk robe is cinched crooked at the waist, allowing one side of the neck to droop and expose the shadow of a breast. Her bare feet flatten against the kitchen floor, one long toe set at a hard bend. She's gorgeous and perfect.

"Making you breakfast." I set down the fork.

"Why?"

I could let that robe slip off her shoulders, or I could rip it away and tie her legs open with the belt. Bite that little curve of tit or kiss it. Scream or moan. Cry or weep.

"Because people need to eat. Are you not people?"

Her brow screws tight. "If you need me to get up earlier, I can make it for you."

Taking her face in my hands, I kiss the beautiful line of dry, chapped skin on her lips.

I'll give her this ring and beg for her hand after I make her beg for my cock.

"Since I'm up early, I can make it for you."

Her stomach grumbles in agreement. I guide her to her seat and hold out the chair at my place for her. She hesitates, but when I nod, she sits where I tell her.

I get the pancakes from the warming oven. As I pour the syrup, I check on her. She's looking out the window, sun on her face. She likes the view of the garden. Good. That's her seat now.

When breakfast is out, I sit diagonally from her so I don't block her view.

Her hands stay in her lap. She's not going to pick up her fork until I pick up mine.

Fine.

I pick up her fork and cut her a piece of pancake.

"Open your mouth," I say, holding up the fork. "Just pancakes. I'm not going to sneak my dick in there."

She smiles before she opens up.

"Good girl."

"Oh, this is delicious." She chews around the words.

"I'm glad you like it." I hand her the fork, handle-first. "Eat."

"You don't have to do all this, you know." She takes the fork and uses it.

She's right in that no one's forcing me to do anything, but she's wrong in that I don't have to do it. I do.

"What are you doing with Willa today?" I ask.

"The subway."

"What time is she coming?"

"Um..." She turns my wrist to look at my watch. "About an hour. I better hurry."

"Finish. She can wait."

"Mm-hm." She agrees with a full mouth, ready to finish by hurrying. Obey me and be punctual for Willa at the same time. Always out to please everyone. She catches me staring. "What?"

My heart makes a decision on the answer before asking my defenses. "I haven't been the kind of man you deserve."

"Shush." She puts her fingers over my lips. "Before you say something I have to agree with."

I kiss her fingertips and return them to her so she can eat. "I'll make it up to you."

"You've been terrible, Dario." She barely pauses her meal as she speaks. "You took me and locked me away. You've humiliated me, hurt me, and treated me like a slave. But the worst thing you've done to me is made me believe you're not a monster."

How have I not noticed how quickly and efficiently she

eats? Her meals had to be wolfed down between chores. Of course, she never got to take her time and enjoy her food.

"What if I am?"

"No. You're not. You tell yourself that so you can do things like kidnap me. But—" She swallows. "After Denise, I feel like I'm involved. Anything that happens to anyone is my fault."

"No, Sarah."

"Yes." She puts down her fork. "Everything that *you do,* I've made happen."

"That's not how this works."

"Make a promise. I know there will be consequences, but... no more hurting anyone. No more killing. End this war without blood."

"That may not be possible."

"It has to be. You have to make it possible. Every part of me wants to be with you. Here..." She picks my right hand off the table and presses my fingers flat. "Swear it. Say, 'I, Dario Lucari, being of sound mind and body...'"

"My body's just 'sound' to you?" I can't help but laugh. Maybe I'll make her beg for my cock before I beg for her hand.

"Say it!" She's serious, but also trying not to smile.

"I, Dario Lucari," I repeat, pushing my plate away so I can lean over the table. "Being of sound mind and pretty fucking effective body..."

"... do solemnly swear..."

"... do solemnly swear..." I draw my free hand down her throat, teasing the skin I'll taste after this little performance.

"... that from this day forth..."

"... that from this day forth..." I push the neck of her robe aside so I can mark with touch the places my tongue will go.

"... to not intentionally hurt or damage anyone."

"Interesting you say both hurt and damage."

"I'm making it up as I go. So say it. '... to not intentionally...'"

The diamond solitaire is a rock in my pocket.

I will get it on her finger, then fuck her on the floor.

"... to not intentionally hurt or damage anyone unless they're a threat to you, in which case I will gut them and not even feel bad about it."

"Dario!" She lets go of my right hand.

"Now I want you..." As I push her robe off one shoulder, my phone buzzes on the counter. I ignore it. "To pledge something to me."

The buzz is followed by two more. Not the usual pattern. Not Nico's buzz, but one I set to demand my attention.

I take my hands off her body and lean forward to kiss her lips. They taste like maple syrup.

My first order of business is protecting her, so I pull away. The ring will have to wait.

"You'd better get in the shower before Willa gets here."

She's halfway up the stairs when I pick up the phone, and I'm forced to forget about the ring.

CHAPTER 24

DARIO

HORROR EXISTS. YOU CAN READ ABOUT IT EVERY DAY, OR YOU CAN see it up close. A shaking Colonia woman you pick up on the corner of 65th and Second, with her worldly possessions in her husband's duffel bag, can tell you about horror in the front seat of the car, sobbing while you say "there, there," and biting back rage so you can rush her to someone who can actually help her.

Horror is a story you tell yourself when you feel safe. You pretend you've experienced it, and maybe you have—in some form—but the potential for worse is always fulfilled.

Even the horror-stricken can experience horror. It's always new. Always fresh. It can find an unwounded place on the soul—a place where only a story might have existed —and pierce it with experience.

Horror starts out looking like a normal street on a normal day. It looks like going around the block a few times, looking for a parking spot when you're actually double-checking for spies and traps.

"And the sheriff's department left just like that."
Connor's question is a statement wrapped up in suspicion.
He drives.

I crane my neck to see around every corner. "NYPD says
they're gone. Colonia too. Can't guarantee there aren't
stragglers or booby traps. But the street looks clear.
Agreed?"

"Aye."

"Pull into the parking lot." I look out the rear window
and wave to the car behind me.

"The cops do their job and check for said booby
traps?"

"I talked them out of it." I turn back to the front. "Whatever the Colonia left behind is my problem."

The site being abandoned is an invitation to return, and
we've RSVP'd yes. There's a trap here, or a message, or just
four floors trashed for a week and a half.

"Us first," I say to Connor when he parks. "I want to
make sure we're clear."

Four cars have pulled in behind us. My guys get out after
Connor and I do. Each one's been touched by Colonia
violence. All of them want to be here and are fiercely loyal to
the cause against that organization. That's the benefit of
operating with a motive greater than profit.

"The blokes will follow on our signal." The elevator
doors slide open. Conner checks it and holds open the door
so I can join him. When the doors close, he says, "The other
day, in your fucking suburban garage..."

"Forget about it."

"I wasn't trying to have a go at you."

He's not going to just accept forgiveness for definitely

and unequivocally having a fucking go at me. Damn tenacious, this guy.

With an eyebrow raised in disbelief, I throw his lingo back at him with the full weight of my New York accent. "You were mad as a cut snake."

"That I was, mate. That I was."

"Feeling better?"

"Sure am."

"Keep it that way."

There's no need to speak of the time he tried to strangle me ever again.

"It's going to be a disaster area," I say when the elevator slows.

"I expect arse piss on the walls."

"What is that?" I turn to him.

"What comes out when you eat a dodgy fish."

"Right." I face front as the doors open. "You have higher expectations than I do."

I'm joking because they're as low as possible.

But that's a failure of imagination. There's always a new nightmare waiting.

We clear the three floors of apartments first, and the guys start coming up.

The rooms look better than we anticipated. We track a stink of dead things to a ninth-floor apartment and find an open fridge too warm for the ground beef left inside.

"They got hungry." Connor shuts the door.

"Must have been some good leftovers."

"You want to bring a couple of guys with us up to the penthouse?"

My floor won't be this clean. I know it from the fact that they found Nico's spare ID packet.

And there's the greenhouse.

"Pick two with strong stomachs."

Conner doesn't go right away. All he does is raise an eyebrow.

"For the ass piss, or whatever. Guarantee you at least one of them shit on my pillow."

He leaves, and I go right up the stairs without them. Whatever's up there, I'll handle. Tripwires. Ambushes. Booby traps. Maybe I'll clear the greenhouse too, before they head up.

The hallway is empty. The double doors to my office are open.

So much has happened in this hallway. I begged Sarah to open a blocked door. Kissed her. Invited her into my apartment.

The office has been ransacked. Papers everywhere. Cords ripped out of the walls. Phones thrown.

At my feet, a lone postcard from St. Easy. I pick it up and flip it over.

Dearest Dario—
You should see the beautiful girls here... and they'd love to see you.
All my love
—Willa.

Stupid. All of us. Willa was stupid to send this thing. I was stupid to not burn it as soon as it came. The fucking

Colonia are stupid for not seeing it's the key to my entire operation. I tear it up and put the pieces in my pocket.

The entry to my apartment is open. There, too, I find no traps, but the furniture's been shifted. Cabinets opened. A few dishes broken. Someone made a sandwich and left half of it behind.

No one shit on my pillow, but the sheets are half off the bed.

When I reach the wall I chainsawed open, I pause. There are tracks in the plaster dust. Some are shoes. Some are bare feet. They're irregular. All directions. Sliding and half-stepping.

Sarah's suite is on the opposite side of the open wall.

More tracks. They're dark in the sprinkling of plaster in front of the wall, and white as they tracked the dust away.

There's nothing unexpected here, but I have a profound sense of unease.

I observe every cranny and crack without moving. I listen for any sound out of the ordinary. There's something. Not the traffic outside. Not the heating unit. Not water whistling through the pipes. Not the door to the stairway, way out in the hall, swinging open. Not the footsteps of Connor and two men with strong stomachs.

"Stop!" I bark, palm up to them.

Through the doorway, they're frozen at the apartment's entry. I put a finger to my lips, close my eyes, and listen.

Not the traffic outside. Not the heating unit. Not water whistling through the pipes. Not the men breathing. Not my heart beating.

But a scratching.

I know this scuttling scrape-tapping.

From a warehouse in Newark. And the tunnels under the subway. I know it from the storage room where I kept Don DeLillo's body to prove I was the one who did him—and thus the one who should fill the power vacuum left behind.

Crossing over the broken wall in a heightened state of awareness, I see the winding plaster trails are from bare feet, and I smell the blood. The white powder rat tracks fade and disappear like ghosts.

When I get to the bedroom, the scratch-scrape-tapping is as loud as crumpling paper, and on the bed, a sea of gray fur undulates like shaking sewage.

"Connor!"

When I shout, the rats scurry away toward me, over my shoes, down the hall behind me.

"Fuck, what?" One of the guys, surprised by the flow of rodents.

"Damn." Connor. Right behind me, looking over my shoulder.

There's a body on Sarah's bed, arms and legs tied to all four corners, face eaten away.

Dafne.

Her skirt's over her waist, and the space between her legs is covered in a blood-soaked bandage. I grab a balled-up pillowcase from the floor and approach her with it. Her mouth is open. Four front teeth missing. Bruises on her neck that are so fresh they're barely visible. The rats have started shitting on her. I cover her face.

"They did this?" Connor asks.

"It wasn't Santa Claus."

One of the guys excuses himself to throw up. So much for strong stomachs.

"They hollowed her." Conner indicates the bandage between her legs.

It's funny to me how easy it is to forget that no matter what you've seen or experienced, there's always a new horror.

I've spent years hearing about the details of "hollowing." It's why so few women run from the oppressive life inside the Colonia. The carrot that keeps them there—besides brainwashing from birth—is a stable life, the promise of a good family, a stipend when it's needed, free fucking healthcare with their nutbag doctors.

Hollowing is the stick, and it's a horror reserved for traitors like Dafne.

"Probably did it in their clinic," Connor says. "Then brought her back here."

"Why?" Gingerly, I pull the bandage away. "Why do it if they were going to kill her?"

The blood stopped clotting, so the bandage comes away easily, revealing a flat area, shorn of labia and clitoris.

Hollowed.

"And why bring her back here?" I put the bandage back and notice the dress isn't blood-soaked.

It's red.

"Because she's a message," Connor mutters. "We have to kill them. All of them."

We will. Every last one of them. But the path between my brain and my mouth is broken as I trace the lines of the gown. Its plunging neckline. The mass of red fabric gathered above the knees.

It's Sarah's dress from Armistice Night.

"Those fuckers," I whisper.

Connor's right. This is a message, and we have to kill all of them.

"Bury her proper first." Connor. Sensible. Practical.

What they did to Dafne is reason enough to slaughter them.

The message they're sending about Sarah...

"Those. Fucking. Mother. *Fuckers!*"

... is the blinding fire that's going to burn this city.

"Dario?" Connor. Curious. Scared.

"Get me one of them."

This is what they do to traitors.

"Who?"

Connor is red. This room is red. This building is red. The earth it's built on is a smoldering pile of red so black, it's white.

"Bring me a Colonia. A driver. A soldier. A fucking janitor. Get me a living body with a dick I can rip off. *Do it!*"

My voice is thunder. I draw it from the depths of the earth, where my need to protect Sarah sits uncomfortably with my horror.

CHAPTER 25

SARAH

THE SUBWAY LOOKS EXACTLY LIKE I THOUGHT IT WOULD. THE STARK lighting that's somehow bright and dim at the same time. Posters advertising things in bright colors or plain black and white that catches the eye. But the track-rattling, horn-hooting, brake-squeaking is louder than I expected. Some people have voices that carry across the length of the entire car, but most voices fade into the forest of sounds.

"I didn't think I could ever miss this," Willa says as we're jerked back by a sudden acceleration. Everyone in the car sways.

I tighten my grip on the pole to keep from falling. I feel a tap on my shoulder. A skinny man with brown skin and a goatee gets up from his seat and points toward it. I look at Willa.

"He's giving you his seat." She smiles at the man. "Thank you, sir."

"Thank you," I add, sitting between two passengers.

He nods and leans against the door, reading a magazine. Willa stands in front of me.

"Is that normal?" I ask.

"Sometimes."

"Because I'm a woman?"

"Because you almost fell on your ass." She chuckles. "And maybe being a woman has something to do with it. You never know."

I can't tell if he cares about me or not, but he's not some outside demon Grandma was convinced would rape and murder me as soon as look at me.

"Can I ask him?"

"Oh, Lord, girl. Leave the man alone."

She's not afraid of him. That much I can tell.

The conductor rattles off something I can't understand, and commuters gather their things and stand. Placements shuffle. Willa gets a seat next to me and tells me how to read a horizontal poster with a red line across it. It's a map apparently, and like everything else I've learned today, it's brutally simple once you know how it works.

The conductor mumbles again, and the train stops in a station. Most everyone gets off, including the man who gave me his seat, who doesn't even spare me a glance on the way out.

The doors beep and close. The conductor mumbles. The train whines before it moves. There's an uneven but repeating pattern to it.

"They're changing trains." I point toward the poster with a red line across the middle. She shakes her head. "No?"

"Yes. You're right." She pats my hand. "If you keep this up, I may get home soon."

St. Easy. Home for her. And maybe home for Dario and me. Or we'll stay where we are. I'm in an in-between place where I can hope for everything.

"Do they miss you? Down there in St. Easy?"

"The women? Some do. Some, I'm sure, are glad I'm not there to boss them around." She chuckles to herself. "You know Nella Faria?"

"Kind of? I saw her in church, but we weren't in the same... I guess you'd call it a social circle."

"Same cohort." She confirms the word I assume she won't use. "Well, Nella came to us about a year ago. Caught dancing numerous times apparently." She *tsks*. "Now, she dances all the time, which you'd think, 'good for her,' but she tries to do things, jumps and such, that she shouldn't be doing. We have no coach down there to teach her to do it right. So she winds up concussed, and without me? Neil's got his hands full already."

"Who's Neil?" I figure, at this point, I should learn about St. Easy before Dario and I join her there.

Her expression warms and her head tilts, as if my question triggered happy thoughts.

"Neil is a doctor. Educated in London, born and raised in paradise." She can barely speak, she's smiling so hard. "Heart as big as his... well. He's a good man."

"How did you meet him?"

"That island... we have three vets and two pharmacists. But he's the only doctor, and I had to call him once a week for Joanne Mongeluzzo. She was in bad shape. Anyway, every time, he was like, 'Where did this girl come from?

What did you do to her?' And I couldn't tell him because who would believe it? Let's just say he did not appreciate that. We were like this." She bumps her fists together. "Then one day I brought Rosemarie in for a fever, and he grilled her like a criminal, thinking he'd get to me. Now, most of you fall apart when a man's the least bit stern, but Roe? She shut him *down*. 'Don't you talk to me like that.' And 'Who do you think you are? You're gonna cure my fever. Willa saved my life.' I was so proud of her, and it shut his mouth. But a man who's not too busy talking is a man with a busy mind. He got even more curious."

She stops the story as we pull into a station and the ambient noise in the car gets too loud to talk quietly. Most everyone gets out of the car, and only a few passengers get on.

"When do we get off?" she asks.

I check the map, then the station we're leaving. "Next stop."

"Good. Very good."

"So, Neil?"

"He chased me." She practically glows when she thinks about him.

Do I glow like that when I think of Dario? What I feel inside doesn't match Willa's serene expression.

"You ran?" I ask.

"I didn't need a man weighing me down, but he caught me, heart first. Now he lives in the house with me. I couldn't manage all the girls without him."

Willa's the most competent person I've ever met, and Colonia girls who run away are too much to manage alone. We're too broken and useless.

"We can't be that bad," I say, hoping she'll relieve either my guilt or shame. But she does neither.

"Honey, none of you are bad, but every one of you's been living in a shadow world. You're all ground down. The constant fear eats at the heart. Obedience destroys the mind."

"I don't feel destroyed."

"You're in good shape right out of the gate. But the only reason you can put two and two together on your own is because of who your father is. You had it easy. Comparatively."

The train rocks back and forth, speeding through the tunnel.

"Is that good or bad?"

"We'll find out." She smiles at me, but I'm not comforted.

Willa shows me how streets and avenues are counted, how to tell which direction you're going, and how addresses flow from one number to the next. It's so engaging, I don't recognize the block until we're halfway down it.

Home. I am ho... wait.

This isn't home. It's where I was taken against my will. It's where I was imprisoned and starved.

The last time I stood outside the lobby doors, I was carrying a bag of Quick Lick soup and a piece of candy. This building is where I learned to speak my mind. To say no. To say yes. To know the difference.

"We can go back in?" I'm frozen in front, remembering

how we sped out from the underground garage's emergency exit.

"According to Oria and Benny," Willa says, "we can go back starting tomorrow. But I have a few things to pick up from my apartment... if it's still there."

Of course it's still there. Unless she's wondering if we... *they* stole all her things.

The Colonia may be a lot of things. We're not *thieves*.

Or maybe they are.

CHAPTER 26

SARAH

Picking up a few things doesn't mean the same thing to me as it does to Willa.

Neil's kind eyes and wickedly handsome face are on her phone screen as she picks through the clothes she left when she first moved to the house with the button-rich kitchen. They're laughing at how skinny she was.

Are the clothes upstairs too small on me now? Or too big? I feel like I'm the same size.

Also, I'm hungry. Does Quick Lick go bad? Because I think there's still some up in Dario's apartment.

"Willa?" I interrupt.

"Yes, honey?"

"I'm going up to my old apartment."

She hands me the key that will get me to the restricted floors. "You stay away from that greenhouse."

"Okay."

"Be safe, Sarah," Neil says from his rectangle.

"I promise not to trip or stub my toe."

The elevator takes forever, so I take the stairs. I find myself slowing on the landing where Dario chose to lose his war rather than kidnap me again—and chose to die over separating from me.

It's a nice memory, but a violent one.

Which is why the distant scream doesn't shock me at first. I don't jump out of my skin. I stand there, waiting for another. When it doesn't come, I slowly and quietly climb the stairs, listening.

The top floor hallway is quiet, but subtly wrong. The suite door is closed, but the middle one is ajar. A bottle cap leans in against the corner jamb of the office's double doors. One of the bulbs in the recessed lighting is out.

I'm about to push open the middle door when I hear the scream again. My spine turns into an icicle and the surface of my skin tingles. I'm aware of the breath in my lungs and the pressure of the floor under my feet. A light splash-stain is almost hidden in the wallpaper pattern. The elevator cables churn in their shaft. More voices come through the walls. A slight echo. A crack far away. I turn slowly. The stairway door is still open, and the sounds I'm newly aware of are coming from there.

Instead of going into Dario's apartment, which I came to do, I go back into the stairwell. Instead of going back downstairs, which I should do, I head up to the greenhouse, toward the voices.

Halfway up, I realize Dario would not approve of this decision under any circumstances. The sounds coming out of that greenhouse are neither good nor wholesome. He's not here to protect me. I cannot protect myself. It's incredibly stupid, and if I don't stop, I'll be compromising the happiness we've been promising each other.

I stop, but don't know how to turn around. Footsteps creak above me.

One sentence rises above the others. It's a shriek. From a man. All throat.

"Whaddya want from me?"

The murmuring goes silent. The wind stops whistling in the shaft. The last footstep is taken.

"Your dick."

Two words. Concise. Unquestioning. Coldly confident.

Two words delivered as a message from the future. My future.

Two words in Dario's voice.

I take the stairs two at a time and burst into the greenhouse.

There are men. Half a dozen in varying states of boredom. One zip-tied to the steel shelving, bloody-faced, pants cut off from waist to thigh like reverse shorts and leaving his penis dangling like a sad caterpillar. One man with his back to me, shirt stretched over his shoulders, half untucked from his jeans, arms and knees bent in a state of readiness, fists flexing.

"Did you get it?" He sounds like a monster, and he is. He always was.

One of the bored ones clears his throat.

Dario looks over his shoulder, at me, and I am consumed by the power of his attention.

"Fuck!"

I have the sudden urge to kneel, but I don't. The effort to stay on my feet leaves me weak-willed, and I explain myself as quickly as possible. "Willa was taking me on the subway, and she wanted to get some things, so I came up to get I don't know those fuzzy socks or—"

"Why did I get you a fucking phone?" Dario shouts, now fully turned around, jaw clenched tightly, beautiful on fire. He could demand anything from me. He could tear me apart with his dick and I'd submit to him. But all he wants is the answer to a question.

Why did he get me a phone? To teach me something or to...?

What was it?

I can't think with him standing over me, shoulders forward, neck bulging with vein and muscle, hard and thick as his cock.

Why did he get me a fucking phone?

His eyes are on fire, burning my solid insides into the liquid pooling between my legs.

The things he can do to me with those arms, that mouth, that focused rage. The clatter of a man running up the steps releases his gaze from mine. He looks over my shoulder.

"I got it," says the voice behind me. The man who ran up the stairs passes Dario a knife with a curved blade, handle first. I recognize it from his kitchen. It's used for meat.

He got me a fucking phone to...

"In case I needed you," I say. "That's why you got me the phone. In case I needed you, and I didn't. When I need you, I'll call you."

One of the men standing around blurts out a laugh. Dario turns toward him and he goes silent.

The guy hanging from the shelving sobs, and in it is a name.

"Sarah?"

I recognize him.

"Shut the fuck up," Dario says, slapping him across the face. I've never seen anyone hit that hard.

"H-H-Henry?" I say when the echo of the slap dies down.

Henry was on the boys' side of the school. He was the best student. Prizes. Ribbons. I dig to find a specific memory of him, and they're all looking up at him on stage.

"I'll show the lady out." Connor comes toward me with his hand out.

I slap it away and point at Dario—this terrifying hulk of a man. "You promised me."

"Take her downstairs." He spins the knife on the heel of his hand and turns his attention on the sobbing, caterpillar-dick man hanging from zip-ties. Dario's intentions are obvious, and Henry is terrified.

"Come, lass." Connor takes my arm. "You don't need to see this."

"I do." I yank away from his grip and get in front of Dario. "I need to see you break your promise."

"Sarah." With grinding mouth and shut eyes, he utters my name as a warning.

"Go on." I ball my fists and set my feet apart. "Do it."

"I'll get her out of here." Again, Connor puts a hand on my arm.

"Let him take me, you coward." I pull toward Dario. His eyes open. His jaw loosens. "Let him drag me away. Take me somewhere I don't want to go and lock me up there. Let him do it because you're afraid I'll see your promises don't mean anything."

He spins the knife on the heel of his hand again, then on

the tip of his middle finger before gripping it in his fist and heading for Henry.

He's going to do it, and I'm going to remember it forever. I cringe so hard my eyes are nearly closed.

Dario's arm shoots forward.

I keep my eyes open. I need to see what he's done. Every time I open my legs for him, it will be for the man I love and this murderer, who I want so badly my skin is electric for his touch.

He plants the blade in a wooden table and faces me. "Come."

"Where?"

Dario isn't taking questions.

"When I say come." He grabs me by the back of the neck and pushes me in front of him. "You come."

He grips me tightly, keeping me in front of him for the trip down the stairs, into the hallway, through his apartment. He's taking me back to the suite via the chainsawed wall.

"I won't stay locked up." I make the pronouncement of control even as I let him control me. "And I won't forget it. I won't trust you ever again."

My last statement is the breaking point where I resist the forward pressure of his hand and he releases it. I find myself freed, and he finds I'm not where he wants me.

I push at him, punching whatever my fists can find, knowing it's not doing more than annoying him into greater waves of anger. He tries to hold me still, but I avoid his hands, slipping away to slap, scratch, punch whatever part of him I can reach.

The wind is knocked out of me. For a split second, I think

I've been thrown on the floor, but the pressure on my back is the wall outside my bedroom and gravity isn't what's keeping me there. It's his hand on my throat.

"You think I'm breaking a promise," he growls low in my ear. "I'm keeping a promise. The first one I ever made and the last one I'll ever break. To protect you."

"Pleeeeeaaaseeeee...." The wail comes from above—through the ceiling. It sounds like a plea made with a last breath of hope.

"Not like this," I manage to say. "He's innocent. Not like this."

He pulls back to look me in the eye, hand dropping to my upper chest. "Who's innocent?"

"The man in the greenhouse? Henry? He's really smart. He was doing long division in first grade. Is that his crime? Too smart for you?"

Dario takes his hand off me, shaking his head as if he's disappointed. It's not until then that I notice the smell. Sharp, like mothballs, and earthy like overcooked cabbage.

"You want to know how innocent he is?" Dario looks toward the door leading to my old bedroom, then back at me. "Go ahead."

He's not freeing me to do what I want, and he's not making me go in any direction. He's not stopping me from knowing something dangerous. Following the trail of my curiosity to the last question.

"Or," he says, "you can go back down to Willa's apartment and let her take you the fuck home. Right or left."

He's giving me a choice to go into my old bedroom or out the door. To know difficult things and trust him again, or not know them and always nurture suspicions.

I want to trust him, and I want to know. But I also want the trust to be easier. I want the knowledge to be comforting. I want simply remedied problems. I want to go back to yesterday's pancakes and syrup. His laugh. His care. I want the lion surveying his kingdom, not the lion of the bloody hunt.

He's less angry. He seems almost sorry that he can't give me the easily won safety I want.

"Right or left," he repeats. "There's no forward."

"Fine." Using my last threads of insolence for strength, I go right. Down the hall, where the strange smell is coming from. My bedroom.

I see it.

I see her.

The not-her.

Dario removes the pillowcase from her face, and I see her.

The formerly-her who was starting to teach me about magnets and chemicals. Who tried to ease me into my captivity. Who helped me get dressed in this very bedroom.

"Dafne," I whisper.

Why am I here? I don't want to be here. I start to turn, but Dario stops me. He's strong enough to keep me still by my jaw and shoulder, facing absolute horror, and I'm weak enough to feel safe in his hands.

"Whoever did this..." I start but can't finish.

"You know who did it." His lips are at my ear, feeding my mind what it already knows, but won't accept.

"I want to go home."

"Look at her," Dario whispers. "You need to know what they do to traitors. The women, they hollow them. She's taken apart and sewn up to give her a tight, dry hole. Look at her. Your friend Denise's Aunt Clara probably handed the doctor a scalpel. If they let her live, she would have been sold like livestock overseas. They murdered her instead. Dressed her first. Propped her up, then strangled her. Look. She got mutilated days ago. The bruises are fresh, but her stitches started to heal."

Strangled. That's why there are no other bloody wounds, just a blackened neck and red fabric.

"That's my dress."

He's not holding me still anymore. I'm looking not because I want to, but because that's what I have to do.

This is me.

"How else do I talk to people who send this kind of message?" Dario asks. "How else do I tell them that I'm going to protect you with my own life?" He puts back the pillowcase. "That piece of shit upstairs is not innocent."

"He did this?"

"He works in the clinic. He knows."

"What the ever loving..." Willa's voice comes from the doorway behind me, but I don't turn toward her. I'm afraid to stop looking at Dafne.

They do this at the clinic.

Denise's aunt works there. Did she ever confirm the stories were true? Or did she only use them to scare the girls?

"Jesus," Willa adds.

"You're taking her back with you," Dario says. He's not talking to me.

Are we all party to this? Even if we don't know specifically, what have we all chosen not to see? I don't have the luxury of that choice anymore.

"I'll meet you at St. Easy when this is over," he says to Willa, as if I'm not even there. "Just pack her up and go. Period. If I change my mind, shoot me."

"I'm not going." I go to the closet and slide open the linen drawer. The sheets are still folded and as crisp as the day I left, untouched by what happened here.

"Yes, you are," he says.

"Dario," Willa says gently. "I'm not going to shoot you, and I'm not taking her."

"Do it, Willa."

I choose a white flat sheet and close the door.

"No."

"Do you need a closer look at what they'd do to her?"

Holding a single corner, I let go of the rest of the sheet, and it unfolds.

"No," she replies. "I don't. I've watched you eat yourself alive for too many years. You've pushed everything in your life into a corner for this. Saving a few wasn't enough. Then killing a few wasn't enough. You needed more. You needed to rob their treasure. Desecrate her right in front of them. It wasn't enough. Now you want to do what? Kill them all? I don't know whether you'll do it or not, but I can tell you how this story ends. You'll never have enough revenge. Not until everything you love is burned dry. You can't even control yourself, and you want to control her. But this? What you're doing here... it's suicide. And I can't decide that for either of you. Have at it. If she wants to take a bullet for you, I can't stop her. She's a complete person. She can make her own choices."

I snap the sheet open and drape it over Dafne's body.

"I'll take her myself." He sounds as commanding and assured as ever, but he has no power over me.

When the wave of fabric settles, I fold my hands at my belly and confirm my decision.

"I'm staying."

CHAPTER 27

SARAH

"I'M STAYING." I SAY IT AGAIN, BUT FOR MYSELF BECAUSE WHEN I said it the first time, I sounded like someone else. A little like my grandmother, but more than anyone, I sounded like Willa. My voice didn't have her accent or her depth, but it had her certainty.

The sky is blue.

Rain falls downward.

Water is wet.

I'm staying.

The second recital is no different. It has been decided. I regret to inform you that no petitions for change will be accepted.

Even Dario has to take a pause before he tries to over-turn my decision. It's a moment I can wait through until his personal power overcomes mine or I experience, yet again, his ability to change plans with unexpected contingencies. It's a moment where I can melt, again, under his authority. I can fall into the safety and strength of his arms.

I want to. So much. Even when he breaks his promises. Even when he's more animal than man. Even when he's tearing my heart to shreds, he is everything to me.

But I don't use that moment to wait for my weakness to show itself.

"We're not separating." I meet Dario's gaze with a surety that matches my voice. "I'm not waiting for you to come for me. I'm not your slave or your burden. And I don't want you to think I'm disobeying for the sake of it. I'm not trying to show you that I have a mind of my own. You know I do. I'm staying for my own survival." Dario's between me and the way out of the room. I step close to him and put a palm on his chest. "If I stay, I may die, but I'll die by your side, where I'm meant to be. If I leave, I may stay alive, but I'll never love again. I'll never, ever feel safe without you."

"You don't know what you're choosing."

"I do." I glance at Dafne's shape under the sheet, then back at him. "I really do, and I wish I could say good luck and just get on a plane, but I'm not going to."

He takes the hand I've laid on his chest and kisses my knuckles before closing his eyes and resting his chin on them.

"You're going to make me crazy." He opens his eyes. "Let Connor drive you back to the safe house. Please. I'll be there when I'm done."

When he's done.

I know what that means, and I won't offer approval or condemnation.

I try to go around him, but he takes me by the wrist, stopping me. I don't fight him, because he won't trap me for long, and he won't hurt me. I know it from the love in his expression.

Staying with him doesn't mean being his shadow or witnessing his barbarity.

"What you do with Henry..." I shake my head and let my hand drop away from his. "That's up to you. But I think that greenhouse has seen more than enough suffering."

He grabs my wrist again before I'm out of reach. "I'll always do everything in my power to protect you. Always everything."

I nod instead of saying I'll always do everything in my power to stay with him.

Always. Everything.

Willa gets into the back seat with me, claiming she needs the lift. I don't believe her. Dario didn't ask her to watch me, but I guess he didn't need to.

"You okay?" she asks when we're on the road. Connor's in the front, and the car is so big he seems as if he's in another room, but she speaks quietly. "That was a lot."

"It was." I'm not sure if she means the condition of Dafne's body or seeing Henry zip-tied to a shelving unit. One would have been a lot. Both is overwhelming. "I don't know how he doesn't carry this around with him every day."

"He does." She doesn't have to ask who I'm talking about. "Trust me, he does."

"Do you think he'll ever stop?"

"I don't know if he can." She takes out her phone and looks at the lock screen for longer than it would take to check the time. "Dario and I could have been something. I couldn't do it until he let all that go, and he laughed at me. Literally laughed. He said, 'I'm not cutting off my dick for you.' There was no point arguing. If a man thinks his masculinity is eating nickels, you either leave him or learn to love digging money out of shit."

"No," I say decisively. "I don't agree."

She looks at me with a raised eyebrow. "With what?"

"I won't learn to love it. And I won't give up on him. He saved me, and I'm going to save him."

"Good luck." Shaking her head, she opens her phone. "If anyone can fix that hot mess, it's you."

There's not much confidence in her statement of confidence.

She's looking at her phone, so I take out mine.

There's a notification. When I open it, I find a message from Massimo's number.

—That day he took you, Grandma
said you'd never turn on us.
She's always right—

—Just please say you're safe—

<VOICE MSG>

Leaving Massimo's texts unanswered was easy, but now there's a voice message, which I don't know how to access. It's probably exactly what it sounds like, and more of the same.

Do I really not know how to access a voice message? Or do I not want to figure it out for myself?

Scroll. Select. Press OK.

That was easier than I thought it would be.

I press the triangle that means *play* on the kitchen stereo and put the phone to my ear. It works. My brother's voice comes through.

Hey, Goody. It's me. Massi. Listen. You have to hear this from me, in my voice. I want you to know that no matter what you think you saw on Armistice Night, it's not what it looked like. It was all a show for Lucari. We figured if we made like we didn't need you, he'd lose some of his leverage. You know? Like, if a man don't know the value of what he has, he doesn't really have it. And Dad said it'd come out in the wash after... (pause) *anyways, I can't stand that we made you think none of us care. We care, aright? We care a lot. Hang tight and when shit gets scary—hide.* (pause) *All right. I love you. We love you. Bye.*

"Sarah?" It's Willa. I forgot I was in the car with her. "Are you all right?"

I nod and close the phone. She swipes it from me before I can get it into my pocket.

"Hey!"

"What did he say to you?" she says, phone behind her back. "He's got a hurtful mouth on him, and I can teach you to make him wish he never opened it."

"No, it's... please give it back." I hold out my hand. "Please. I mean it."

Reluctantly, she places the phone in it.

"Don't you cry over him," she says. "I see tears coming and don't you deny it."

"I'm fine." I'm obviously anything but fine, and I should let her believe the message is from Dario and that he was careless and cruel. But just as Massimo couldn't let me think my family didn't care about me, I can't let Willa believe Dario caused the tears I'm holding back. "It's someone else."

"What is it then?"

I shoot a look toward the driver's seat, then the rearview mirror. Connor doesn't seem to be watching us, but he has ears.

I speak as softly as I can. "Do you think there will ever be a truce?"

She scoffs. "As soon as one side asks for a truce, the other side thinks they're winning. No one asks for peace when they're on top."

"I guess not." I look out the window, watching the world pass by.

"I've seen some smart, shrewd, strong women through this," Willa says. "Of all of them, you're the most dangerous. All the others wanted out. Worked for it. None of them had Dario's hands on them. None even spent more than an hour with him. None knew why we do this. But your circumstance means you know more and less than you think you do."

"I know everything now." I shudder, thinking of Dafne.

"You don't, but you know the stakes. You know what he's fighting for and against."

I nod, running my thumb over the edge of the phone.

I have to assume Massimo knows about Dafne. More than that, I have to assume he knows she was hollowed, and that it's real, and it's now. Not some ancient, forgotten practice. I want to call him back right now and ask him, but I also don't want to know. I want to keep loving my big brother.

"Sarah," Willa says sharply to direct my focus back to her, then drops her voice again. "Who messaged you?"

"No one." I cover the phone and its shameful truths.

"You said it wasn't Dario. Who is it?"

The secret of the texts is unbearable, and the voice message has made it harder to hold. I don't know what to do about any of it. I don't know how Massimo knows my number or what to make of his words.

"I wasn't messaging anyone." I put the phone on her lap. "They were messaging me. Massimo. My brother, Massimo."

Willa flips the phone open and navigates it with competent ease.

"You didn't erase these," she says of my brother's messages.

"I didn't realize I could."

I also didn't realize I should, because I'm a fool.

"You called first." She holds up the phone, showing me a list on the screen that I'm supposed to understand.

"I was just seeing if I still knew his number."

"You do, apparently." She listens to Massimo's message about how much he cares about what I think of him. How my family loves me. How it's not over, and I should hide. When it's done, she takes it from her ear. "Did you remember anybody else's number? This one?"

She holds up the phone again.

"Denise. My best friend."

She hands the phone back to me. "For your own safety, one of us needs to tell Dario, and I think it should be me."

"I'll do it."

"He may not take it well."

He won't. He'll be mad I was the first to call and mad that I didn't tell him about the messages.

"What can he do to me that he hasn't already done?"

"You want to find out?" She sighs and sits back. "Because I sure don't."

She's a sensible woman who's terrified of a wild animal. I'm confident I can talk reason to the hungry bear, maybe soothe it by stroking its fur. At the very least, I can submit and play dead while the savage rages and ravages.

"He should be mad," I say. "I should have told him. After everything that happened today, he has to be able to trust me."

She sighs, then says, "I should have come up here at the start of this whole plan. Taken you down to the island myself. First thing. But I let him talk me into waiting. Now it's too late."

We pass Tommy's Pizzeria, then pass the red brick church. FIND PEACE! has been replaced with DON'T CRY, COME BY! Connor makes the left into the sparser, darker part of town. We're going to be back soon, and I have things to get off my chest.

"I love him," I say into my lap. "I don't want to. I know it's wrong. I got lazy, but it's so hard, Willa. He makes me feel safe. He gave me a place in the world, and it's not just for convenience. I'm not an accident for him. He cleared a place in his heart for me. I'm his *choice*. And that changed me. It opened me. It broke my shell and I just poured out through the cracks." I pick up my head—vision splotched with bursts of color and light before it settles into crystal clarity. "I'm all these pieces and I'm everywhere."

I open my arms to indicate the mess I made of the whole wide world. She takes the opportunity to hug me.

"Dario cannot love you the way you love him."

"I know."

"I'm on your side, Sarah. And by that, I mean between you and Dario, I'm on both your sides, but I will stand by you."

"Once I tell him, he's going to kill Massimo."

"He might."

"I don't want him to."

"Then I'll say something I'll regret." She sits back and folds her hands in her lap. "We'll all have to explain ourselves to God. None of us have to explain ourselves to Dario Lucari. Whether or not you tell him about these texts is up to you. It's your choice."

When she offers me control, a burden lifts from my shoulders. All I have to do is not sink under the weight of everything else.

My phone vibrates. She hands it to me. I feel her eyes on me as I open it.

Massimo.

—You listened to it—

"He knows?" I show her the screen. "How?"

"It's in your settings." She takes the phone and pokes around. "I'll shut off read receipts."

"Does it ever stop?" I ask. "Because I want to throw this thing out a window."

"You get used to it. Come look." I lean over to watch what she's doing. "Press menu, then settings, scroll like this, here, here, to read receipts, and it looks like you can choose everyone or no one."

"No one then."

"Dario probably has it set up so he knows when you've read his messages. Play with that shit at your peril." She hands me the phone.

Will I play with that shit?

I will not.

I close the phone without changing the settings. Navigating the outside world isn't what I expected. There are too many trapdoors, and I'm blindfolded, hobbled, hands tied behind my back.

We pull through the gate and down the drive.

"Sarah," Willa says, "I want you to listen to me, one last time."

"Okay."

"You've been sheltered to the extreme your entire life. You can only do so much."

"And I'm a liar. To Dario. About Emo's messages."

"You can fix that."

"I will. I'm going to fix everything."

"Sarah..." Her tone is a warning. "No one can fix everything."

"But everyone should try."

She doesn't nod or say she agrees, but she does. I know she does.

The first thing I have to do is tell Dario.

Connor stops in front of the house and turns around to the back seat. "We're here, lassies."

"I need to go to JFK," Willa says. "You can take me there or drop me home. I'll get a cab."

"I'll take you." He gets out, leaving us alone.

"You're going?" I already knew she would leave, but the moment came sooner than I thought it would.

"You'll be fine." She squeezes my hand. "I promise. You have everything you need."

"But I don't know how to drive." I'm trying not to cry. "And I trust you, Willa. I never thought I'd trust my husband's ex-wife more than I trust myself but—"

She breaks out in laughter, and I join her.

"You are your husband's wife," Willa says, carefully wiping away a tear. "I never thought I'd say this to anyone, but Dario loves you. If anyone can change the trajectory of his life, it's you."

Connor opens my door and stands there.

I hug Willa a long time. Let him wait.

CHAPTER 28

DARIO

WHEN THINGS FALL APART, IT'S FROM THE CENTER. THE CHAOS spreads outward—out of control, out of reach. I know the pattern. We broke into Chuck Laraby's Central Park West townhouse with the perfect plan. Planned for all external contingencies. The center would hold if I kept mouths shut and held on to the take longer than I promised.

Our own mistakes almost got us killed. Peaches needed money, Shakey had a big mouth, and I was young.

Shakey became Tongueless, but no amount of retribution could undo the central collapse of trust. The inside weakened, and the unit broke.

The Colonia know—after tonight—how strong I am, but when I drag my bloodstained soul home, I don't feel strong. I feel tired. Bone-weary. Ready to explode.

The house is dark. She's waiting for me on the couch, watching the front windows like a dark angel. She knows who I am. She knew it when I took her. She's seen it for herself. Now she knows that I won't deny the truth or pretend that I can protect her from it. She has feared me, but now she will hate me as well, and I will fall apart from the inside.

I stand in the doorway, waiting for Sarah to do something I can't define. Once she does the indefinable, I'll go to her. I'll take her, or hold her, or destroy her in my arms. I have no plans because I can't predict the external contingencies.

And so I wait an eternity, held together with string and paper glue, knowing she can't hear the man's screams echoing in my head—but fearing she can sense them, and that they disgust her.

"Dario."

"I need you," I blurt out before she's done saying my name. I wait for her to finish—ask what she's been waiting hours to ask—but she's silent in the dark.

Need is not enough. She's right.

"He's alive," I say. It's so quiet I can hear her breathe. I step all the way into the house. "He's alive and I was never going to kill him. Does that help?"

She says nothing. Not enough.

"No. It doesn't. There's more than one way to kill someone. You know that." When I close the door, the room gets even darker. "Separating a man from his balls, that's death. So, yes, you see through that. You don't know how to do much in the world, but you know how to see through me."

I walk to the couch and stand before her, taller and yet diminished. Her eyes follow me. They don't judge me. They only invite me to judge myself.

"I need you," I say. "I had the knife right between his legs, where the skin changes. Danny had a hot iron to cauterize it. The guy, Henry, he'd pissed and shit himself. He stank like the sidewalk under a hydrant. He was dead already. Begging us to kill him instead. Even after we gagged him. He didn't even know what he was begging for. No. Maybe he knew. I didn't know. All I kept hearing was you saying you'd never trust me again."

My fingers brush along her cheek and her reaction is defined by what it's not.

She's not tilting her head into my touch.

She's not putting her hand over mine.

She's not asking a single question.

"But trust what?" I continue through her silence. "You saw what happened to Dafne. You saw the message they were sending. I'm supposed to pull this guy down and give him a token for the bus home? So you'd pat me on the head? For your version of trust? For keeping a promise I didn't want to make? No. That's not trust. Not to me. I need you to trust that I will take care of you. I will skin them. Leave muscle and bone and tan their hides. I will dismantle this city brick by brick. Level it to the bedrock. Nothing's going to stop me from taking care of you, and I need you to trust me."

Finally, she breaks her silence. "Did you give him the token?"

"We gave him a lift to 18th and Second." I stopped the story at the corner of the Colonia's clinic. She doesn't need to hear the condition we dumped him in, but she tilts her head a little. My version of trust will win out, but I need her, so I bend, for now. "What they took from Dafne, I took from him. Not his life. Just the pleasure of life. He'll still be able to piss without a head. Eventually. Maybe."

Still, silence.

The frustrating torment of her silence pushes me toward a panic I didn't know I was capable of. I can't swear I won't hurt anyone, ever. I won't lie outright. Unless I'm desperate.

"What do you want from me?" I sound desperate already.

"I want you to trust yourself." She reaches for my hands. "That you can be better. That you *are* better."

She tugs me down to her. I lean on the back of the couch, surrounding her with my arms, and kiss her face. My senses awaken to a chemical change. She smells of home, and fulfillment, and a warm femininity—all of it fleeting. Her mind is being reshaped, and her body is reacting to it. She is in transit. Destination unknown.

Or maybe I'm changing the way I experience her.

We wrap our bodies together on the couch. I trace the lines of her face, memorizing the eyes that see through my defenses, the lips that speak my name, the ears that listen for our shared truth.

Then something in her shifts. She looks away. Swallows hard. I try to deny the change by kissing her. Instinctively, my hips grind into where she's soft and warm.

"Dario." She backs up a little and fondles my lapel. "I have to tell you something."

"Tell me." I bite the base of her neck and suck the skin between my teeth. When she gasps, I let go.

So much has changed between the day I took her and today, but her vulnerability pries me apart just the same. Big brown eyes, warm as her body from the inside, express a shy hesitance I haven't seen since our first weeks—when I terrified her.

"Okay." She clears her throat. "Apparently, I don't know how a cell phone works."

"That's not really news."

"And so..." She pats my chest, flicking a button under her nail.

When she parts her lips to speak, a loud double-beep fills the room.

"What's that?" she asks.

"Someone's at the front gate." I get on my knees, pausing while she's beneath me, wide-eyed and needy. "Don't move."

In the kitchen, I release a panel above the microwave, revealing a security monitor with a split screen. One side shows the entry gate from above. The other is from a camera that points right inside the car. Oria's driving and she gives the signal that she's alone.

I press a button to open the gate.

"I really need to tell you something." She's moved to the kitchen doorway, heart protected by crossed arms.

"Let me see what she needs." I close the panel, then kiss my wife. "Stay here. I'll be right back."

Crickets. A faraway boat's horn. Sarah waits inside and I wait in front as the Toyota that came with Oria's place crunches its way down the drive, headlights softened by gathering autumn fog.

Oria pulls up to the house and gets out as if the car's on fire. "I talked to Nico."

She's shaking. I don't know how she drove here in a straight line.

"You sure?"

"It was video."

"How did he look? Where was he?" I ask.

"It was dark. I couldn't see anything behind him."

"So, what's the problem?"

"He didn't mention meeting me at Teterboro not one time, and you said he was. I made implications. I asked him about it. I brought that horse to water and got nothing."

Sarah and I were coming to an understanding, and I don't have the patience for the interruption of Oria's paranoia.

"Look, just show up. He'll be there."

"He said 'I'm sick of the junk all over this town.'"

Junktown.

I freeze, thinking of what that word means to us. That imaginary corner of peace and play that turned into a nightmare of freezing death.

"Junktown?" Sarah's whisper is a scream in my mind. She's at the top of the front steps, feet bare, arms crossed against the chill.

"Get inside," I tell her.

"That's the alley where your mother died."

"You don't even have shoes on!"

"Dario." Oria gets my attention. "It wasn't a mistake, was it? He was telling me something."

"You're meeting him at the airport in two days. I told you."

"How do you know they didn't find him instead?"

"Because they want *me*." I thrust my arm in Sarah's direction. "They want *her*. Their eyes aren't on *him*."

Oria and I are locked in a staring match, trying to read each other's determination, when a rhythmic buzzing comes from behind me.

A phone.

Oria breaks the gaze to look over my shoulder. I turn to find Sarah pulling her phone from her pocket. It lays in her palm, flashing and vibrating.

I step toward her. She's shaking, phone out like evidence of a crime. I'm aware that I'm intimidating her, but I can't stop doing it.

Someone's texting her, and it's not me.

"What did you do, Sarah?"

"It was an accident, and I don't know how it happened. I was seeing if I remembered his number. I hung up, then the texts started coming. I never replied."

"Who?" I ask in a low growl.

"Ma-Ma-Mass—" She doesn't have to finish. The puzzle comes together.

"Fuck!" I bark.

"Shit," Oria says under her breath.

"Why, Sarah? Why. Did. You. Do. That?"

"I don't understand how." She glances from me to Oria, looking for sympathy. "I didn't tell him my number."

The buzzing stops.

"You don't have to." I grab the phone and flip it open.

"I didn't say where we are. I didn't say anything."

"Cell tower pings," Oria says it to me as if I don't already know. "They can find us."

I scroll through the texts. Bullshit, bullshit, and more

brainwashing bullshit. She never answered him. I have no idea if that matters.

Sarah continues, "He says he misses me. He wouldn't hurt me."

She makes me want to laugh and embrace her and kill her at the same time. I can't do any of those things. None could express the depth of my fear. Only anger finds a voice.

"And who is this?" I point at another number on the list.

"Denise. Her house phone. She didn't pick up either."

"God. Fucking God, how can I love an incompetent this much? You don't even know how a fucking phone works!"

"I don't get it."

"You gave up your location," Oria says with more compassion than I'm able to work up right now.

Sarah's face twists as if she's been punched. Confusion in the squint of her eyes. Hurt in the tightness of her chin.

She should be all of those things. Just for putting herself in danger, she should be too hurt and terrified to repeat it.

I hate myself for thinking this is justice.

I don't want her to get hurt, but I especially don't want to be the one who does the hurting.

Not anymore. Not ever again.

Lying to myself is still lying. I'm going to have to hurt her over and over for reasons I can't predict.

"Fuck this." In a few taps, I connect the line. "Fuck the fuck out of this."

"Who are you calling?" Oria asks suspiciously.

I don't answer. She'll know soon enough.

"Goody?" Massimo Colonia's voice comes over the phone.

"You alone?" I bark.

"Who is this?"

"Your brother-in-law. Are you alone or are you in earshot of a bunch of savages?"

"Very funny, coming from you."

"Answer."

"I'm home. Alone. Where's Sarah?" he asks.

"On her knees, sucking my dick, as far as you're concerned."

"What do you want from me? You think you're gonna provoke me?"

"Don't call again. Don't try to contact her. Don't even let my wife cross your mind or I'm going to send you pieces of your sister, starting with her sweet cunt. In a box—"

"You're sick."

"—and we'll keep sending pieces."

"Until when? What do you *want*?"

I hang up.

"Fuck!" I shout my shame to a sky that doesn't hear me.

Oria starts, "Do you want me to—"

I toss her Sarah's phone. "Tamara's going to need the SIM card. Ask her what she can do." I turn my attention to Sarah. I know my look can wither every leaf in the forest, but I can't soften it. "You weren't ready for a phone."

Sarah spins on her bare heel and storms into the house.

CHAPTER 29

SARAH

Doing what you're told is an art form, and I was trained to love a life of utter obedience—first to my father, then to my husband.

But my father has rejected me, and I'm not married to my husband. So it's only me giving the orders here, and the man I love needs me. My bare feet storm through the dimly lit house with my mind narrowing on a single decision.

I'm staying with him, and he's staying with me.

He's going to fight it, and I'm going to fight back.

He's going to win. He's going to put me on a plane and send me away because I'm dangerous. I don't have the strength or knowledge to beat him. I don't have the skills. I have nothing but the force of my will and it's not enough.

At the back of the house, the sliding glass opens onto the dark forest. I hear him come in the front.

"Sarah?"

I'm not ready to talk yet. I need a minute to take stock of my value to him.

His walking shoes sit by the back door. Mine are in the front. So I stick my feet in his and step onto the deck, closing the glass behind me. Clopping in unlaced shoes five sizes too big, I walk into the darkness, arms crossed, sifting everything I know through the sieve of everything I think I know.

I don't know how the world works, but I know how the Colonia does.

No. It's been proven I don't know how the Colonia functions.

"I didn't mean those things," Dario's voice comes from behind me. When I turn, he's backlit by the glowing windows of the house. "They were just to upset him."

"I know you're not going to cut me in pieces."

"Good."

"But I'm not a prop for you. You can't move me around like I'm an object. Here. There. Now she's fine. Now she's cut up like a pizza."

"I told you I didn't mean that."

"But you thought it. You had it in your mind, because you think of me as something you can just send away."

"I should have sent you weeks ago."

I've never heard him sound so desperate, and it's then I realize that though he can force me to go, he won't. He wants my consent, even if he has to demand it.

What is the price of my agency? Does it have to be so expensive?

"I'm sorry about the phone," I say.

"You should have told me."

"I know."

"Why, Sarah? Why didn't you?"

"I kept thinking he'd stop if I didn't answer, and he

wasn't saying anything that I thought you needed to know." First reason stupid, second reason worse. The third has to be dug from the raw, core truth. "He's my brother, and he was never this nice to me."

Dario nods and looks away as if he can't deal with how pathetic I am. It's unbearable.

"I have value." I go toward him instead of running away.

"No." His denial is such a blow I feels my knees go weak under me, but he catches me by the waist. "You don't have value." He holds me when I try to wrestle away. "A value is a number. It's for a comparison to other numbers. Other things. A diamond has value. A piece of real estate. A bank account has value. Not you. You don't have some value I can measure. You're priceless."

All my strength goes into my arms as they snake around him and squeeze him so close, I can't dream of a world outside his love. His jacket is too thin to hide the warmth and shape of his body, and his bones and muscles cannot mask the beating of his heart.

"I'm so sorry, Dario."

"You just forced me to do what has to be done anyway. People... men will die. I might be one of them. But my brother's been sitting in the middle of it. If I turn tail and run, what does that make me?"

"A coward."

He's already started a response, but he stops, open-mouthed, before a sound comes out.

I take a deep breath, because of every stupid thing I've done, this is the most stupid.

"Let me go talk to Massimo. In person."

"Are you fucked in the head?"

"I can talk sense into him." My sense won't be sense the way Dario sees it. I have another few seconds to dump everything in my head. "We speak the same language. I know what's important to him. He might have objected to what happened to Dafne. He might not have believed the message—the dress—and if I just—"

"No."

"Or why can't I call him and talk to him? He might be an ally for us—"

"There is no us!"

He pushes me back against a tree, changing his angle to the house. With the light on one side of his face, I can see the fire in his eyes. It's not rage. Not lust. It's something I've never seen before.

"Let me help you," I say.

"No." He releases me and walks back to the house.

I chase him with those big, stupid shoes, tripping on the edge of the deck, hands out to break my fall. He starts to come back outside to help me up, but I launch myself at him, feet free, arms extended, pushing him back into the kitchen. We both land in a crouch, me leaning forward, Dario on his back foot, surprised... but not for long.

I get a hand under the seat of a chair and hurl it at him. He throws up his arms and catches it, but I've already thrown a vase.

"Why not?" The vase catches a chair leg and thuds to the floor. "Because I'm weak?" He uses the chair for a shield against the flying teakettle. "Because I'm stupid?" The flour canister sprays white powder. "Because I'm incompetent?" The salt and pepper shakers separate midair. One is deflected with the chair. The other hits his shoulder. "Because you're better off without me?" I'm going to throw every last damn thing this stupid kitchen hasn't hidden behind an invisible cabinet door.

"Stop!" He tosses the chair aside and grabs my arms before I fling the cast-iron pan at his head.

"Tell me why!"

"Because I'm scared!" The expression I couldn't define—the one that was neither rage nor lust—it's all over his face, clear as day, and it's terror. It doesn't melt away with the admission that it exists but intensifies into something red hot and feral. "You scare the *fuck* out of me. Anything that happens to you from now on—for the rest of your life—it's my fault. If I leave you here. Send you away. If your fucking plane crashes on the way to the island, it's my fault, because you would have been sitting home doing fucking needle-point if I hadn't taken you."

"I'm your wife. Your problems are my problems."

He lets me go and puts his hands in his pockets. "Shit." He takes a little blue box from his pocket and stares at it as if every accusation ever made against him—the true and untrue—is inside it. "*Shit!*"

He opens the box. I expect all of life's miseries to fly out like crows, followed by hope.

"Look! Do you see this? I didn't even ask you to marry me. I left you here without... shit!" His face crumples as he holds out one hand, palm up, to indicate some obvious point the diamond ring makes, even if it's not obvious to me. "I can't even do this. I ran off like a fucking..."

Without finishing, he falls onto a chair, postured like a dishrag with the box dangling from his fingertips. He runs his fingers through his hair, looking at the floor as if he wants to drill two holes into it.

I can't bear to see him like this. He wasn't built to coexist with fear. He's supposed to channel it into rage, and actions, and plans.

I kneel at his feet, looking up at his reddened face.

"You're Dario Lucari. You're my husband. You are not scared. I'm not sitting at home embroidering because you taught me more."

"I taught you *nothing*. You're overconfident. You're on a suicide mission. I'm more fucking terrified now than I was when I made you marry me."

"You didn't make me fall in love with you."

"Love doesn't matter. It's meaningless. Love's not going to save us."

He knows a lot more about the world than I do. He knows society. How people move and think. He knows about tools and technology. But he doesn't know anything about love, and he knows less about what's going to save me.

"Make me stop loving you then." I stand before him, and he looks up at me. Every dancing fire in his eyes flickers with life—a kaleidoscope of conflicting passions. "If it doesn't mean anything, make my love go away. You can't. Outside your family, you've never been loved past reason. Past hurt and harm. You were always alone, and now you're not, because I love you, and I'm going to fight for it. For us. I'm going to fight for you as hard as you fought for me."

One eye narrows. A newly ignited fire glints where despair had taken hold.

"That's not your job."

I take the box from him and pull the ring out of its slit.

"Saving you is my job." I slide off the snowflake ring and put it on the other hand.

I'm about to replace it with the new ring, but he stands and takes it for me.

"My job," he says, sliding the diamond ring past the scar and deep against the base of my finger. "Is to keep you safe from the world, and me."

"You'd never harm me."

His touch starts tender along my jaw, but gains force as he grabs the back of my neck.

"Are you sure I haven't already?" He tightens his fingers at the back of my head, pulling my hair until I'm looking straight up at him. He's himself again. Powerful. Arrogant. Fierce.

He's a king returning from a battle that nearly killed him, and I am grateful.

"You have, so much, and you love me."

"Tell me to stop." He takes my shirt by the neck and pulls hard, tearing it down the front. "Tell me I'd stop if I loved you." I can't move my head as he pulls up my bra.

The terror that filled his expression before is still there, but it's strapped down by a rigid control, bucking and bloating, stretching the limits of the harness. It will break free without a valve.

I am that valve.

This whole time—the rage, the violence, the controlling demands—all of it was fear.

"You love me. Don't stop."

"Love is a liability." By the hair, he drags me to the hall

and throws me up the staircase, pinning my lower back with his knee. "Tell me to stop."

"I'm not scared."

With one move, he yanks my pants down. "I made you reckless."

A burning sting explodes on my bare bottom. He's never hit me that hard.

"You made me see."

He smacks me again and pulls my pants all the way off. I twist onto my back, where the edge of the stairs digs into my spine. He pulls off the shreds of my shirt, pushing me to the top of the stairs at the same time as he wrestles off my bra. I'm naked, breathless, halfway up a flight of stairs.

"I love you," I say.

"Sure you do." Violently, he pulls my legs open, exposing me to a gaze that has its own pressure. "Say stop or say nothing."

"I love you."

"Enough." He unbuckles his belt. "I swear to God, your next word is stop or it's nothing."

"Nothing."

"Turn over." He slides the leather belt through the loops. "Hands and knees."

When I obey to put elbows on one step and knees three steps below, he cracks my ass with the belt.

"Nothing!" I cry.

"Crawl to the bedroom."

I do as I'm told. With each move forward, he tries to hurt me out of loving him, beating me on like a pack mule. He pulls me onto the bed, flips me onto my back, and opens my legs, brandishing the belt.

I cringe, waiting for him to hit me where I'm most sensitive.

"Tell me to stop."

"Nothing."

"Fucking Colonia."

He doesn't hit between my legs but uses the belt to strap my left elbow to my left knee. I cringe all over again when he gets another belt from his closet, but he doesn't hit my pussy with it. Instead, he ties my free elbow and knee together, leaving me splayed before him as he undoes his fly.

"I should lock you in the basement." His pants drop below his waist as he pulls off his shirt. "Let you wait until I come back."

"Nothing."

He steps out of his pants, naked now, hard-on raging. "You think I won't because I love you?"

"Nothing."

He slaps his palm between my legs. I jerk with pain, then burst pleasure. He slaps again, pauses, then again, so hard I grunt through my teeth.

"I can stop."

"Nothing," I cry through spit and tears.

He puts his hands inside my thighs, spreading me wide so he can see how sore and red I am. When his grip gets too tight to bear, I whimper, but he doesn't let up.

"If they catch you, they're going to put you in the staffa —with your arms strapped down this time—and when they find out I fucked you, they're going to let any aggrieved party fuck you. Then they're going to hollow you like they did to Dafne, but they won't kill you. They'll sew you back up so they can sell you as a virgin." He takes his hands away. "I won't let that happen."

When his cock touches my pussy, I'm so sore to the touch that I cringe and gasp, but I'm so wet he stretches the beaten skin and slides right in.

"Look at me," he says when he's buried to the root. "Look at this man who loves you and tell me to stop hurting you."

I haven't lied to him. What he's doing feels good and right. His pain, so carefully placed for my ecstasy, is what I never dared crave.

I challenged him to make me stop loving him, but at this moment, his response is somehow empty. I don't want to be punished out of love. I want to be cared for through every single thing. I want to be loved not despite my mistakes, but because of them. Because they're mine, and though I don't want to be defined by my imperfections, I want to be loved for them. I want less, and much, much more.

"Stop." My voice shakes, but he freezes. He's not even breathing. Instinctively, I know he's waiting for my confirmation, so I swallow, take a strong breath, and say two words with steady purpose. "Stop. Please."

He stops immediately and bends over me to kiss the space between my breasts.

"What do you want?" he murmurs into my skin, asking my heart for its deepest desire.

"I want you to love me."

After a pause, he kneels straight and unlashes my right elbow and knee.

"If that's what you want." He tosses the belt aside and goes to the other one. "That's what you'll have."

When the second belt is off, he gently lowers my knee. I caress his face, drawing the shape of his cheekbones with my thumbs, tracing the dark circles under his eyes. He rests his elbows on either side of my head and kisses every part of my face.

"Whatever you want."

"I want you to be mine as much as I'm yours," I say.

"I am."

He believes it, and months ago, when I was a different person, I might have believed it too. But I'm different, and so is he.

"You've given me every part of you that you're willing to give," I say.

A little voice in my head suggests that maybe I shouldn't be asking for anything. He's a man. I've been raised to do what he tells me. That voice is quiet. It makes statements in the form of a question and tells me to obey the strict harangues of my grandmother. It's afraid of punishment and consequences.

There's another voice, and it's not afraid. It's been waiting for its moment, and that moment is here.

"I want more." I wrap my legs around Dario and pull him close.

"Tell me how much more." With a shift, he's inside me again, gently rocking side to side. "It's yours."

"I want everything you're not willing to give me." I hold his face to mine, nose to nose, eye to eye. "I want your regrets."

"I regret everything I did to you. But nothing that brought me to you."

A halo of quiet euphoria ripples outward from our joined bodies, but I keep my eyes on his.

"I want your anger."

"No."

"Yes. Say yes. I don't need protection from you."

He doesn't look away. "I can't."

"I'll take it."

"Sarah." My name is a scold, a call, a declaration of love. The swell between my legs increases as if a rock was dropped in the exact same place in the pond.

"I want your fear."

"I'm always afraid, Sarah."

So deep in his eyes, I see it. His fear is small, but bright, and constant, and raw. It's the fire under everything else, and the rippling waters of my pleasure will never put it out.

"I want your love."

"You have it."

"Your trust."

"Yes. Look at me, Sarah." He moves slowly, with his mouth so close to mine that we share his words. "Look at me. You have it."

I want his respect and his joy. I want his tenderness in a way I've never been allowed to want anything. I want his very soul and no less, but I can't say it while locked in his gaze, with every syllable building in my throat turning into a single vowel of surrender.

From ten miles above, I hear his voice groaning "yes, yes, yes," as he joins me in heaven.

We don't say a word, lying there wrapped in each other. There's no vocabulary to define what just happened.

The effects of it are temporary, and the world intrudes.

A musical dinging comes from somewhere in the room. He groans and picks up his pants, reaching into the pocket for his phone.

"Tamara." He looks at me as he listens to the response, then presses his lips tight. "Let me get you on speaker." He touches a button and says, "Repeat that for Sarah."

"Hi, Sarah." She sounds as if she's speaking softly into a tin can.

"Hi." My reply is weak with the shock of Dario including me in a conversation about my own phone.

"I pulled the data delivery schedule for Sarah's carrier. The towers aren't delivering ping data in real time. They batch compressed folders on a schedule. Upside for the carrier is less stress on the network. Downside for law enforcement and their benefactors is that you can't get around the schedule."

"How long do we have?"

"Sixty-three hours, seventeen minutes."

"And the other number? Denise?"

"Landline. Data pings on the cell side are the same."

"Thank you." He's about to cut the call when Tamara pipes in again.

"I've changed her routing to a VOIP out of Siberia. Which I would have done in the first place if you'd told me."

"Next time." He kisses down the length of my arm with a reverence that turns rough inside the elbow.

"Next time." She hangs up.

He throws his phone aside and kisses my shoulders in earnest.

"I want my phone back."

"I'm getting you a new one."

235

"What if Denise calls that number?"

He backs up to look me in the eye.

"You're very smart, Sarah Colonia." He leans back. "And very brave."

"What does that mean?" I sit up. "Yes or no?"

"It means yes, even with a new phone number, you'll get the call. You can still jump into danger for your friend."

"And you still trust me. Even after me doing a stupid thing."

One eye narrows a tiny bit. I expect him to say he has yet to punish me for calling Massimo, and just to prove he can —he will.

Instead, he takes my right hand, where I put the snowflake ring.

"When I put this on your finger..." He removes the old ring. "I stole you. I didn't care about anyone or anything. I didn't earn the right to have you, so I took you. You're not a stolen thing anymore. You're not my prize. I said a lot of things before, and for some of them, I'm sorry." He kisses the base of each of my fingers, back and front. My palms are damp again, but he doesn't seem to care. "But you are dangerous. You're too well-intentioned. You're a pain in the ass, and you might get me killed. Whether you agree to marry me or not, I'll die a better man because of you."

"You won't die."

"I know I'm a terrible person." He lifts my left hand and kisses it around the new diamond. "Will you marry me anyway?"

"Yes."

"Thank you." He kisses my lips.

I hold the diamond up to the moonlight. It's not just fire. It's electric. It's a sky full of falling stars.

This ring is a "yes."

Yes, I will marry him.

I will stand beside him, with him, and for him.

I will sin in his name.

I will not leave him behind.

CHAPTER 30

SARAH

At first, I pretend to sleep to make sure he drops off. He needs the rest. But it's hard not to relax in his arms, and the pretending turns real.

Of course, he's not next to me when I get up.

Putting on a robe, I look out the window. The garage door is open. I pad down there.

The Audi is still there, and the cover's been removed from the other car to reveal its shining black paint and white pinstriping. It's lifted from the floor and Dario's legs stick out from the underside as he makes metal-on-metal noises. I assume he doesn't know I'm standing here. I'm wrong.

"Can you get me the socket wrench?" he says from under the car. His grease-streaked hand sticks out from under the chassis, palm up expectantly.

I can only see him from the waist down, lying on a big sheet of cardboard. Greasy jeans. Black boots. T-shirt riding up just enough to reveal a tease of hair between his navel and his belt.

Stepping over him to the cloth where he's laid out the parts and tools, I only take a moment to admire the promise of what's under his jeans. "Which one is that?"

"The silver one that clicks."

There are three, so I take a guess, handing him one that looks like an undersized lollipop on one side and a six-sided tube on the other. It must be right because I get no complaints, just the clicking noise he warned me about.

"Calipers." His hand is out again. "Looks like a crocodile head."

I try to pick up the tool, but it's flatter than the wrench.

"Thank you."

"What are you doing?"

"Been meaning to swap out the brakes for awhile."

"I mean... why are you doing this *now*?"

"You can't drive it with manual brakes."

"I'm driving?" I say with both fear and excitement.

"Can you get me the light?" I give him the little flash-light. "'Ank-oo."

Kneeling, I look under the car. It's raised about a foot, still leaving very little headroom. Dario's laid a bright light on the end of an extension cord near his crown, making a near-blinding halo around his head. It's obviously still not enough. He's got the flashlight in his mouth, trying to see around a corner.

I slide in next to him and take the flashlight from between his lips. At first, he's disconcerted to find me there. Then I put the light on the calipers, and he turns his attention back to his work.

"I can't teach you to drive before you go. There's not enough time for that." He takes a little sliver of metal from his chest pocket, jams it between two other pieces of metal I have no name for, and measures with the calipers. "But I can get you started."

"I could drive the other one. The Audi?"

"This one's cooler. Light me here."

I move the flashlight where he wants. "What are you going to do now?"

"About?"

"The war. Or peace."

"You're not supposed to ask questions."

"Rule one was always stupid," I say. He turns his head in the tight space to look at me. The extension cord light is so bright, long eyelash shadows reach across his cheek. "They were all stupid actually. All the rules."

"Keep it up. You're going to get yourself punished." The promise of his hurt makes my thighs tingle.

"Obedience? Cross that off the list." I swipe the air with my finger. "The truth?" I swipe again.

"You want permission to lie?"

"I don't need permission," I say, leaning into him. "But making it a rule just made me want to get around it. Same with loyalty. You had to earn that."

"Rule five is forever. Your orgasms are still mine, prima."

"You can keep that one. But..." I pause to make sure I want to say this, and decide I feel safe enough to. "I think you need permission to be at war with my family."

He turns toward me again. This time, the shadows reveal deeply concerned lines across his brow. I want to sketch the story they tell.

"Do I?"

"If you want me to help you." I shrug as much as I can in

that position. "I can get past doors in the church and the clinic. The rectory. All kinds of places."

"So can I. Brute force. Pick the locks. Shoot them."

"What if I got you in with a boop?" I press my thumb to his nose. "Like that."

He looks away but doesn't touch the brake. I can tell he wants to know more, but he won't ask.

"I have thumbprint entry into my father's office," I add before he can tell me all the reasons why I shouldn't be asking questions and he shouldn't be asking permission. "Maybe you want to get into the fourth floor, or maybe the basement. You'll be shooting every lock in the place. You'll wish you had a set of keys, and I think you don't."

That's not entirely true. I don't know what to think, so I made a wild and improbable bet on his inability to do a thing. He doesn't tell me I'm wrong. He doesn't say anything. I feel my opportunity slipping away in the silence.

I continue, "You need me, and I'll help you if I know your plan. I can get in so quick."

He smiles. "Let me tell you about this quick job we did and how not quick it was." He fidgets with the mechanics of the brakes. "Before I turned twenty, I learned petty shit doesn't pay. There's less chance of getting caught doing one big hit a year than a hundred poor assholes who'll kill you before letting go of what little they have. If the job's big enough to spread the take between a few guys, you'll find some underpaid security guard with a sick kid and no insurance."

He stops. Fidgets. Asks for the light at a different angle. I have a hundred questions already, but I don't prod him. He trusts me or he wouldn't tell me any of this.

"The Metropolitan Museum, on Fifth," he says. "You know it?"

"We went once with class."

"Really big, right?"

"Seems to be. We only went to the part with the coats of armor and swords."

"Two and a quarter million square feet holds eight percent of the actual collection. There's a public warehouse on Madison with a ton of shit and that's the end of what they have... if you're not looking. But if you know the right people, you know there's another storage facility in Newark the size of a city block. Four stories high. Billions in art any schmuck can fence because the Met barely knows what they have in there."

He goes silent again, but this time, I'm not so patient.

"You robbed that?"

"Nah. Wouldn't touch it. But the one in Astoria? Where they hide the shit they picked up from a bunch of worthless Nazis and Blackshirts? They haven't added a single thing to that warehouse since the sixties, and nothing's come out. The weekend security guy showed me the sign-in books."

"Did he have a sick kid and no insurance?"

"He puts his daughter through three years of college. Then his wife gets sick. Can't work. They made too much the year before to get more aid, so..." He waves away the details I barely understand, and I'm grateful. For one, I can't figure out how you can make too much to afford something, but I'm also not used to a father allowing a daughter to go to college, much less pay for it. Dario continues before I get too lost in the weeds. "He told a friend, and it got to Nico, who brought Samir to me. He'd let us in for a cut. No-brainer. We grab small shit. In and out. Quick."

"I get it. If I help you, it won't be a quick thing because of this other quick thing that wasn't quick."

"No. It was. Boom, boom. In and out. Done."

"That's good, right?"

Dario will not be rushed to a judgment of how good or bad it was.

"Some of it was garbage. Some was worth a fortune. We fenced it all. But Nico, he hadn't aged out of the system. He had these foster parents on the Upper West Side. Lawyers, and loaded. He saw everything money could buy, and he was greedy. I was too, but for him, because I missed him. So he told them he was staying with me for the weekend, and we went again. Same plan with Samir, but just me and Nico. It went perfectly. We were in. But when we tried to get out, Samir wasn't sitting in his little box watching *Shark Tank*. I knew it had gone bad as soon as I saw Lester Holt on the TV. So we backed up into the warehouse, and we hid."

"What happened to Samir?"

He shrugs. "We'd left our phones behind so we couldn't be tracked. It was the smart thing. The safe thing. But without them... for all we knew, Samir was dead or fired. Maybe he'd set us up. All we could do was crawl under a rack and wait. We counted the shift changes by when the weekend guards came around with their flashlights." He wipes the shiny disk. "We decided that if we died rich and never got revenge on the Colonia, that would be a failure. From then on, it wasn't about money, but the next day, we weren't even sure if we'd get out alive at all."

"How long was it?"

"Friday night to Samir's next shift on Monday night. There was no water, so we stopped pissing ourselves after the first day. We couldn't even make spit. Nico went into that warehouse a little bitch and came out a grown man." He hand-tightens a bolt that doesn't budge. "I don't want that for you. You're already a woman."

"Look, whatever happened, it won't happen again. You're smarter now. You can predict what can go wrong."

"No, Sarah. Samir's wife needed him. He got a replacement for three hours and figured he'd be back, but she ended up in the hospital and it took all night. It was too risky to show up on a day he wasn't working, so he showed up when he was supposed to. When my brother didn't come back on Sunday, his fosters went batshit. They didn't let me see him for two years."

"That, you should have known was going to happen."

"Once the unexpected happens, Sarah, the consequences get predictable... and they're all bad."

"Nonsense." In this cramped space, overreach seems within bounds. There's no room for polite little dishonesties. I'm just saying what's on my mind. "All of that was preventable."

He leans back as far as he can, as if he needs to see me from farther away to figure out if I'm serious.

"Isn't there a way to carry a phone you can't track?" I say. "Like shutting it off or something? And you knew Samir's wife had health issues. You didn't ask if he was in the habit of leaving his post? Or if she tended to call with problems in the middle of the night? And you had no extra men, no lookouts... no one for just-in-case who could have been like, 'Hey,

Samir, please don't just leave without pulling out Dario and Nico, because they have no water and didn't even pack a granola bar.' I mean, what did you expect when you were so reckless?" When he doesn't answer, but stares at me under the glare of the light bulb, I can't help myself. "And as far as Nico's parents go, I don't care if they were foster or not, they were responsible for him. I promise you, our children are not coming and going as they please. Spending the weekend with *who*?" I scoff. "How old were you, Dario? Out of your teens, even? Barely a man. My God, money couldn't buy them good sense. What did they think you two were up to?"

He blinks so slowly that for a split second, I think he fell asleep under the car. But he opens his eyes, grips the edge of the chassis, braces his arms, and slides out. I start to wriggle myself in that direction but stop squirming when I feel him grip my ankles. He slides me out along the cardboard, and when I'm out, he helps me up.

"You're staying here. So you're safe, yeah. But also." Reaching into the engine, he removes a cap. "I don't want you to have weight on you. I'd rather you hate me than drag around guilt you had a part in something you didn't want to happen." He pops a yellow top from a jug of blue liquid. "So no thumbprint. Not a single boop." He pours the liquid from the jug into the hole he uncapped, silent, deep in his thoughts until the container is empty. Still pensive, he screws the cap back on. "And we can't wait any longer. I'm going to kill your father."

He waits for me to object, but I do not.

"I can get you the keys to everything." My hesitation comes from wondering if I should hesitate, but there's no need to. Dario and I have to win this if we want to live in peace. "If it's useful to not shoot your way in and out."

"It could be." He's not exactly distrustful—but managing his expectations. He tosses the jug into the trash can. "Tell me."

"Can you get into the church again? You probably won't be able to go the same way as last time."

"There's another way." He steps toward me with his shoulders at an angle, as if he's not ready to believe I can deliver what I promise. "The skylight over the back stairs."

I try to imagine the safest pathway through, but I need to engage my eyes and hands. There's a thick, square pencil on the tool bench. I stick it behind my ear. "Let me think."

I leave the garage and pace to the living room with my mind in the halls and rooms of my youth. I feel them. The thick air, the smell of mildew in one place, and the constantly changing smell of food cooking in another. The broken and the repaired. The old and the new. I am physically present in my mind and mentally detached from my body.

Grabbing the arm of the couch, I pull it away from the wall.

Dario's behind me. If he touches me, or speaks, the spell will be broken.

Sliding the pencil from my ear, I make a line. Then another. I narrate what I draw. Here are stairs. Here is a hallway. This is a door that's behind a thumbprint, and here's one waiting for a key or clever hand.

"This..." I make an X then a circle around it. "Is a maintenance room, and next to it is the site director's office, which is a thumbprint lock on a steel door. There's a cabinet on this wall." Tap tap... then I draw another X. "The keys to everything are inside it."

"What does everything mean?"

"Once, I forgot the keys to our apartment. I got sent down here for the spare set."

"Your personal apartment? With your father?"

"Yes."

"Do you know what else is in there?"

"No. Can I finish?"

"Go on."

"So the cabinet has a combination lock. But there's a bathroom back here." My cheek's pressed to the plaster as I tap the boxes I drew. I switch my focus from the pencil to the man leaning his shoulder on the wall. "But it's from the original construction, and every wall cabinet in that building is connected to another in the adjoining room, separated by a tin sheet." I push off the wall and stand straight. "So if you go into the bathroom, the medicine cabinet's on the other side. Unscrew the back with one of those fancy tools you have." I toss the pencil on the table. "Take the keys. Do what you have to do."

He comes to me, hands out, and holds my face still while he breathes me in from chin to temple.

"You'd do this for me?" He's still long enough for me to look into his dark-webbed eyes.

"I'm doing it for me."

"This can't be undone." His whisper is a warning.

"I'll wait for you here."

"First you drive, then you wait."

I nod, leaning even closer to him. Our lips meet, and with a kiss, I betray my family and my father.

———

Dario takes the car out to make sure the brakes work the way they're supposed to, but before he gets out of the garage, he winds up stopping so short the tires stretch to ovals.

I rush over to his window. "Are you all right?"

"Perfect. Let me get the fluid going."

I watch, closing my sweater around me as he takes the car around the driveway a couple of times, stopping and starting until he's satisfied. Finally, he parks in front of me.

Putting my hand on the top of the door, I lean into his open window. "Is the fluid going?"

He opens the door but doesn't get out. "Let's do this." He spreads his legs and pats the leather seat between them. "Come on."

After a moment of suspicion, I let him guide me into the front seat with him. It's set back far enough to let me lean comfortably into his chest and take in the dials and levers around the steering wheel. He takes my hands and places them on the top of the steering wheel.

"Is this how everyone learns?"

"The wheel is a clock. Hands at ten and two."

"You hold the wheel by the bottom." I put my hands where he does.

"Forget what I do." He moves my hands where he wants them.

"Sometimes you don't even use both."

"Put your feet on top of mine."

Arguing about the steering is getting me nowhere, so I

find his feet with my own. We're attached everywhere with pressure at the extremities.

"Okay," I say. "What now?"

"Relax."

"I am relaxed."

"Relax more." He kisses the back of my neck. "Close your eyes."

"What? How—"

"Do it."

"Fine."

"Now breathe so deep I feel it."

I do it, taking in air until my back presses against him, then I exhale.

"Do you feel me?" he asks softly.

I do feel him. Over my hands. Under my feet. Breathing against my neck. I feel his growing attention at my lower back.

"I feel you." I wiggle against him. "There."

"That's for later." He moves my foot with his. "This is stop. This is go. Gear shift is here."

"Remember that time I drove already?"

"The time you almost killed someone? Yes." He puts my hand on the knob-ended stick behind the wheel. "The car is locked when it's in park. Push stop."

My foot sinks on the stop pedal.

"Then you can go from park." He clicks down. "To reverse." The car jolts. "Neutral is the same as park without the lock, and finally, drive." The car jerks in the other direction.

"Drive is after reverse," I note. "That makes no sense."

I feel, more than hear, his laugh. "Open your eyes."

I do. The world looks the same, but he's with me, making sure I don't fail.

"Now, go."

This time, obeying him is easy. He guides my turns, my stops, my feet on the pedals. His touch starts out hard and controlling but softens to the power of a feather floating down to the ground.

I'm doing it—actually doing it—and it's fantastic.

CHAPTER 31

DARIO

WHEN WE'VE GONE AROUND THE DRIVEWAY SO MANY TIMES SHE'S gotten it down to a science, I tell her to park by the front door. She's breathless, eyes bright as stars, a smile wider than an ocean. I don't tell her she's not ready to back into the garage without putting the car into the kitchen.

We're barely in the house, and I have to press her against the wall, feeling her breaths move her chest against mine.

"I have to have you." I grind my erection against her.

"Can't you control yourself?" She hitches up her leg to wrap around my waist.

"I cannot control how I feel about you."

"I mean long enough to get upstairs."

I kiss her with unrestrained affection, demanding nothing else, leading her inside. We are languid together, undressing up the stairs. Without urgency down the hall. It doesn't take any control to be here, in this bed, tasting her, feeling her moan into my mouth. I demand nothing from it, and she only offers a moment that we stretch into minutes.

"You're a master of control," she says.

"I've proven that a dozen times already."

"You have." She touches the edge of my mouth, gazing up at me with her rich brown eyes. "But I have nothing to prove."

I trace my thumb along her neck.

Tomorrow, I may live in a world where I am separated from this collarbone. This throat. This chin.

If only happiness stuck to a soul for as long as anger does.

Instead of saying that, I kiss her, opening my mouth to get the sting of doubt off my tongue.

I worship her body with my lips, prizing the difference between where she's soft and where she's rough. Her fingers run through my hair, gripping it when I suck on her nipple.

She pushes me away and, with a wanton grin, runs her hands and lips over my body. I let her taste the drop that's formed at the tip of my dick.

I pull her up before I let loose in her mouth. She's above me, hair falling over her face, knees on either side of my hips. I push her back so she's up on her knees as I finger her cunt.

"Oh, Dario."

"What is it?" My view of her writhing body is perfect from below.

"That's so good."

"I want you to fuck me now." I hook two fingers in her pussy and draw her forward. "Sit on my cock, sweet prima."

Up on her knees, she hovers above my cock. I point it upward with one hand and push her down with the other, watching my body disappear into hers.

We twist together, in no rush to start or finish. I angle myself to stimulate her nub, and she takes the cue, moving with me.

"You love to fuck," I say, getting off on this sweet thing doing the fucking. "Don't you?"

My big hands squeeze her tits, run over her face, defacing the beauty they touch.

"I love to fuck," she says, and I stick two fingers in her mouth. She sucks them, still beautiful, even when I destroy her.

"Keep fucking."

She *mms* against my fingers, her movements losing control and stability.

"You want to come?"

She nods. I take my fingers from her mouth and put my hands on her throat.

"Please. Please let me."

"Stay still. I have it."

Holding her in one spot, I fuck her deep and hard until she stiffens, pulsing around my cock. When I explode inside her, it's like coming home... together.

"What's the first thing you want to do on St. Easy?" I ask. Her head rests on my chest and my legs are twined around hers.

"Is there surfing?"

I'm feeling the pressure of all the preparation I need to do, but I can't leave her just yet.

I am preparing to kill her father, after all.

"The waves are too small." I run my thumbnail over her arm, and I draw the pad of my thumb in the opposite direction. Feeling a field of goose bumps, I reach behind her and pull the throw blanket over us. "I can teach you to snorkel."

"Are there sharks?"

"Yes."

"I saw a thing on television. A woman went under the ocean in a cage to take pictures of them."

"Sharks?"

"She had on a suit and a mask and a tank of air," she says.

"You don't have to wear all that. And you don't have to go into the ocean if you don't want. I'll make them teach you to snorkel in the pool."

"Can you get me one of those cages though? And the whole outfit with the tank on the back?"

"You want to swim with sharks?"

"I want to see them. She was so close she could see stuff —like meat—stuck between its teeth. She patted its nose just like this." She taps and strokes my forehead, then yawns, putting her head back on my chest. "It didn't attack her."

"It was full from the last guy who went down in a cage."

"I want to do it." Her voice has a soft, breathy wetness against me, and the rise and fall of her body is getting shallow and even.

"Pet a shark?"

"Mm-hm."

Of course, I'm not going to let her near a fucking shark, but I might be too dead to keep her from getting in that cage. And if I live, she'll see me as the man who locked her in a house and left her behind. She'll walk away from me if she has any sense, then I'll have to watch helplessly as she swims with sharks.

"You're a dangerous woman, you know that?"

I wait for her to answer, but she doesn't wake up enough to admit it.

When I'm sure she's deeply asleep, I slip out of bed to continue the work of surviving long enough to join her in paradise.

I make a call while I get in the car. Connor finally picks up.

"Boss?" The music behind him says he's at a party or club. Lucky guy, but I'm luckier.

"I need to get a signal to Massimo. Do we have an open channel?"

"Yeah. Live one though. Face to face. It's dangerous."

"Remo's got cheeks like a baby. They won't hurt him."

"What message do you want him to deliver?"

"Peace." I start the car and head down the drive.

"Peace?"

"I'm thinking about peace. Meet me in an hour and I'll tell you about the war that we'll fight before it."

Since the Hell's Kitchen headquarters is permanently soiled, we've moved operations to a vacant restaurant in Washington Heights. Our equipment is less corporate now. There are no conference tables or filing cabinets. My team has lined the stainless steel surfaces of the kitchen with guns, and the shelves are stacked with ammunition.

They're all watching me intently, waiting for the details.

"I put out an offer for peace negotiations." Someone sucks in a breath. Someone else clears his throat. "It went to Massimo. Asked him to keep it quiet. Kid's a soft touch. No?"

They all nod. Good.

"He'll meet me. He won't keep it quiet, and he won't be alone. But while half his guys are watching us—"

"And trying to kill you," Oliver says.

I nod to his concerns but continue. "Connor's team is going to slip into Precious Blood and get us the keys to the kingdom. The interior access points. Possibly Peter Colonia's apartment."

There are some nods, but enough bafflement that I know someone's seen the hole in the plan.

"The building parking lot under Precious Blood has biometric authentication," one of the older guys says. "Ever since the wedding, it's locked up. Unless we want to blow off the doors?"

Good man.

"There's a soft spot on the roof and a clear line to custodial. What I'm looking for is the keys to Peter Colonia's life. His bathroom. His car. Anything. Once we have them, we'll know how to finish him."

Remo, the youngest of the DiLustro loaners, runs in, panting.

"He said... he said..." He leans on the table to keep from collapsing after his lungs burst.

"Take it easy, kid," Connor says.

"Massimo," Remo says after he gets a slap on the back. "He said yes. He'll meet you on the north platform of St. Nicholas. Three hours."

I laugh. That's three in the morning.

"If he wants to meet that far past his bedtime, I'll be there."

———

On any New York City sidewalk, a person may walk over thick, silver-dollar-sized glass disks embedded in the concrete. Under those disks are passages where deliveries flow from business to business, keeping trucks from blocking the main roads.

Behind papered windows and padlocked doors, down creaky wooden steps and past an open, walk-in refrigerator, Connor points a flashlight down one of those tunnels.

"St. Nicholas Station is three lefts and two rights. Not in that order," Connor jokes. I know the way. "We'll have it cleared from the north platform. Just don't let him follow you back."

I trust it'll be cleared, but I walk it with him anyway.

"You okay to get the keys?" I ask.

"Just keep the little prince occupied."

"Then Monday. That's the big job."

"Been chomping at the bit to get this started for a long time now."

"Things can go really fucking sideways."

"That's what they say."

We turn a corner and step through a broken wall. The graffiti on the walls of this tiny room is twenty years old. The smell of humanity is long gone.

"Listen." I take Connor's arm to stop him. "After this, no matter how it goes, I'm out."

"Out?"

"I'm leaving with Sarah. Going to the island."

"You can't." He's two heartbeats from pissed off. "Not until every last one of them is dead."

"I have to. I can't protect Sarah here, and I can't leave her. She's the priority and—" He starts to cut me off, but I hold my hand up to buy another few words. "And you need to take over. Do it any way you want."

"Come on, mate. There's no way."

"I'll leave you everything you need. The property's yours to use. The money's in the bank. Everyone will fall into line behind you."

He looks away, into his own mind and his own potential.

"I don't like it," he says. "You're putting the mozz on this whole thing."

"Do I have to ask what that means?"

"No." He opens a steel door that leads to another dark tunnel. "Just don't cark it when you meet with Massimo."

I know what cark it means, and I have no intention of dying before Sarah and I fly the fuck out of here.

CHAPTER 32

SARAH

Dario and I lie on train tracks between the two rails. Shoulder to shoulder. I face him, but he's faced forward, nose to the ground. The train is coming. I hear its shattering clatter. I call his name. *It's me. I'm over here.* He does not turn. *Here. Here. Here. Come to me here.* The train comes as he starts to face me, and I wake with the deep sense that I didn't just have a dream, but a memory.

The early morning light is muted by thick, dark clouds. It's still raining, and a new round of thunder rolls.

Before he left, he gave me a new phone. It's so much sleeker and flatter than my old one, that when it's in my back pocket—not ringing—I almost forget it's there.

He warned me that he wouldn't call until he knew it was safe to do so. He was clear that I shouldn't call him unless it was an emergency. I needed to be patient and I needed to get ready.

I said I could and promised I would.

My rolling suitcase—rescued from the irrelevance of the closet—is spread open on the bed, a wide, empty mouth with rows of zipper teeth.

Part of me doesn't believe we're going away together. He's lied before. He could be lying now just to get me to go. The moon could be made of green cheese.

There's no harm in being ready, so I pack.

I don't have much to put in there.

Before I met Dario, I'd never needed a packed bag in my life, and I've now had two in... how long has it been? A full month? How long ago was a lifetime?

I have one valuable thing. My pencil box. I pack that.

When it's nestled against my pajamas, I remember the rings on my fingers. A snowflake on the right and a solitaire on the left.

Two more valuable things.

I take the bag downstairs myself. It doesn't weigh enough to ask for help.

"Can I help you with that, *signora*?" Benny asks at the foot of the stairs.

"Sure." I let him take it. "Maybe put it in the trunk of the big car in the garage. The Buick."

"Good. You should know you're protected," he says. "There are men all around the perimeter."

"Thank you."

"I'm at the front gate. I'll head out there from the garage. Unless there's something else you need?"

"I'm good."

He nods and takes away my suitcase.

The thunderstorm doesn't take a breath. The weather

lady says it'll keep up like this through the night. I sit on the couch with a sketch pad. The gray day turns smoke gray, then wedding gown satin, and all the while, my page stays blank white. The storm's flashing, and the banging sounds like a war being waged in the sky. The lighthouse flicks a beam against the cloud cover every ten seconds.

It rains with the intensity of an outraged father, then continues as if the sky is trying to break the earth.

Is Dario really going to kill my father? Did I really help him do that?

This house is a way station between ignorance and panic. I have no map for guilt or regret because I feel none. If killing Peter Colonia—my father—makes the world safer for Dario and me to be together, then Peter Colonia must die.

I'm so deep in thought that when the phone rings, I jump.

I check the number. It's not Dario. It's not any of the handful of numbers I know off the top of my head.

I should let it ring, then call Dario. But he said not to unless it was an emergency.

Is getting a call from an unknown number an emergency?

Obviously, it doesn't matter if I answer or not. Whatever harm's been done has been done and Dario knows that. But maybe it's him. Maybe he lost his phone and he needs me.

I answer. "Hello?"

"Sarah?" My name comes through wet sobs. It's a woman.

"Who is—" I'm interrupted by a deep, snotty snort. "Denise?"

She may be in trouble. She may be on a Manhattan street corner, terrified and alone.

I can call Dario and he can go get her on the way back from killing my father.

I stop myself from laughing out loud. I'm so naïve.

"It's me," she says. "I can't believe it's you. This number was in his phone, and I hoped you'd pick up." Snort. "Are you mad?"

"Of course not!" I speak for myself, because Dario won't be happy. "Are you all right?"

"Yes, I'm... oh Sarah. It was so good to see you. I miss you so much. You looked beautiful. In that gross bathroom... you glowed." A cracking boom comes from her side of the line. Thunder. "And I know you didn't have anything to do with what happened to Henry."

That's not completely true. He still has some of his dick left because of me.

"Where are you?"

"On the rectory phone. I can't talk long. It got weird here today."

"Tell me you're all right."

"He found the video," she says through chattering teeth. "Found the phone and then the video and..."

"Who?"

"Marco." She sniffles. "And he wanted to know where it came from, and I tried not to tell him. I really did. But he did the thing where he hurts me, and Marco Jr. and Dahlia were in the next room."

"It's fine. Denise. It's okay."

Dario may not think it's okay, but I'm not him.

"He's the one who did a bad thing. In that greenhouse, it was him and he was being a disgusting animal. Why is he blaming me?"

"Can you run away?"

"And it's not like I asked you to meet me in a park bathroom."

This is my fault. All my fault. She's in the rain, crying, telling me how her husband beat her, and he did it because of me.

"Run," I say. "Right now. Just get on the bus."

To where? I can't tell her to come to me. But Denise doesn't want directions.

"I can't," she says. "What about the kids?"

What can I promise her? What can I say that's true?

"Give me time," I say. "I'll figure something out."

"I don't know if you can."

"I will. Dario's been rescuing Colonia women for years. He has this..." I'm about to tell her about the island. How much she'd love it. How Willa's girls are so happy, and how I'll be there and we can be friends forever. I stop myself. She doesn't need to know that. "... organization. He's done it before. He'll do it for you."

"You don't know?" Thunder cracks on her end again, while lightning flashes on mine.

"Know what?"

"It's a rumor, I guess, but they're saying that Lucari was meeting with Massimo in the subway..."

He was?

Why? Was that part of the plan? Have I been alone in the house enough hours for the world to change that much?

"When?" I ask.

"I guess, I've been trying to get alone with a phone for, like, an hour and a bit... and anyway the good news is Lucari jumped in front of a train and—"

"No. He didn't." The denial comes from a place in my body so deep, no knife could reach it.

"Maybe he slipped, I don't know. But you're free! He's—"

"Shut up, Denise. I'm warning you."

She shuts up while I turn into Black Widow, midair, flexed, nothing beneath me, nothing above, anchorless and suspended in the timelessness of a held breath.

Lightning splits shadow from sight, and thunder follows before the burst finishes freezing time. Denise snorts, and the spell is broken.

"He's dead," she says. "You can come home now."

"I'm not coming home."

"Please come home."

"Good-bye, Denise." I hang up.

The rain is harder. The lightning is sharper. The thunder cracks like a bone.

Now things are different. This, now, begins my life after he died. There was before he drove the car at my wedding. And there was after. Now the after is before, and I'm living a new after.

Maybe.

Denise probably heard some messy story fourth-hand, and Dario will show up in the driveway asking for dinner.

Hand shaking, I end the embargo and call him. I have to do it twice before my fingers get the shape right.

He does not answer. After twelve rings, it hangs up on me.

There's nothing I can do to help a dead man, and if he's alive, he said not to call.

Am I being obedient or sensible? I can't tell. This couch in this dark room is becoming a new prison. This space before actual despair stretches like dough. It will break, and so will I.

But there's Benny. I know how to get him.

I rush to the kitchen and find the blue button he showed me when I first arrived, but nothing happens. I press it again, harder this time.

Is he dead too?

"Hello?" It's Benny.

"Thank God."

"Mrs. Lucari?"

"Benny. I'm sorry to ask and I'm sorry I don't know. Have you heard from Dario?"

"I have not. Do you need something?"

"If he... if something happened... would you hear about it?"

He pauses, making *mm* and *ahh* sounds that a man makes when he's thinking.

"What kind of thing happens?" is his answer.

"If he died."

He laughs. "If Mr. Lucari died, we'd all hear him battling the devil for control of hell." He clears his throat. "Sorry. Yes. We'd know."

"Thank you."

Deciding I can live with that, I prep for the next day's meals.

265

The rain stops and turns to mist, but the sun stays hidden behind a steel curtain of clouds.

Then I think, how would Benny know what he'd hear and what he wouldn't? Dario's never died before.

They must have paths of communication.

What if they're broken?

By the time the sun is a glowing ball through a filter of rainclouds at the top of the sky, I've decided the rumor Denise heard is too specific to be false.

Dario still hasn't called. I know he's dead.

Grandma always said the chores don't care about your troubles. I start with the laundry, but when I load everything from the hamper into a basket, I'm overcome with the smell of burned popcorn. It's him. This beautiful bite of something wonderful popped and charred is his and his alone. Washing these clothes will wash him away forever.

I crouch in front of the hamper, bury my face in one of his shirts, and try to weep. Inhaling the scent, I dig deep for sadness. I try to find despair. But I don't have anything but love, and hope, and a fierce need to hold my collapse at bay until the minute I know for sure he's gone.

Standing, I shove the clothes back in the hamper. There will be no laundry yet. I will not erase him from my senses before I see a body.

This is hope. I'll decide when to let it go.

From downstairs, the phone rings. I run to it. It's face down on the couch.

Dario telling me he's alive. Someone else telling me he's dead.

I flip it over. The numbers are a blur. Why?

At some point, my eyes released tears, and blinking them away only makes more.

I press the green button because green is for go. Time to start a new after.

"Hello." My voice cracks like thunder, breaking the word into two parts. I clear my throat and try again. "Hello?"

"Prima. You called me?"

Only then do I cry for real.

CHAPTER 33

DARIO

ON FIRST INSPECTION, THE KEYS WERE, IN FACT, NOT USEFUL. Anyplace important was behind biometric locks, and for those that were also unlocked with a key, the key had probably been moved to a cabinet with a real back. All this was probably caused by us breaking into the church, shooting up the place, dragging the boss's daughter in front of a priest, and forcibly marrying her.

Four of us—the ones who don't sleep—have got them laid out on the stainless surface in Dasano's kitchen, a block from where Massimo threw me on the tracks, as we all read the handwritten tags.

I should go home. The keys will be missed in the next hour or day or week, but at some point, they'll be missed. We have to hit Peter now.

Daddy likes boiled eggs and toast in the morning.

I want to go home and wipe away Sarah's history with that man. Bring out her sweetness. The soft innocence of her face in sleep. I want to take her for another drive. Maybe a little parallel parking. If there's alternate side parking for the street sweeper, there won't be any cars parked on one side of the whole block.

I take out my phone. She called, but the thought about alternate side parking won't stop nagging. Which side will be empty?

He eats breakfast and lunch in his office, and we eat in the kitchen.

It doesn't matter where I can park, but I can't let it go. On east-west streets, the north side of the street is empty on Tuesday, Thursday, and Saturday, but I parked on Sunday and...

"It's Monday?" I already know the answer, but I'm confirming while I think.

It's easier if we all work together, and I have the biggest kitchen, so...

"At sunrise, it is," Connor says, pushing a little ring over to Oliver. "Teacher's closet."

"After midnight," Oliver replies as he sorts the keys. "That's when it became Monday."

They take the dough home to bake.

"There's no bread on Mondays," I say. They all look at me. "That's what my wife told me. She has the biggest kitchen. The women came to her apartment to knead dough to bake at home."

I'm never done cooking on Mondays.

"Does this say main 3?" Danny shows Oliver a tag.

"Maint. Short for maintenance. Third floor." He grabs another set before addressing me. "They're probably going to the second-biggest kitchen now."

"No." I rifle through the newly tagged keys. "According

to Aunt Clara, last Monday, Denise was going to flush herself into the sewer on Thirteenth Street." I find the set I'm looking for. "The church has a commercial kitchen on the garden level. All the women are there tomorrow."

"You mean today?" says Oliver.

Ignoring the quip, I hold up the keyring. "Water main. We're going to cause fucking chaos."

The keys give us access to hatches and circuit boards you don't really see when you're walking by. We get to enough of them from the parking lot and the roof. How the Colonia got the key to the phone box on the street is just the Colonia being the Colonia.

At 1:55 p.m., fifteen minutes before Peter Colonia heads to the shitter to read his *New York Post*, the electricity cuts out. The sewer pipes get backed up, spitting shit everywhere.

While security tries to figure out what's happening and a dozen or so women walk around with dough on their hands that they can't wash off, Peter and one bodyguard go out in the rain to the donut shop on the corner. They order coffee and bear claws, commandeer a table, and Peter goes in the back to sit on a borrowed throne.

And that's where we get him.

With the thunder crashing, we drop down from the roofs to the back alley. I hit the fire alarm. Connor locks the back door, sending everyone out the front. Danny takes out the bodyguard. I push open the bathroom door, snapping the hook and eye in one push.

"What the—" Peter Colonia, the king of a secret fiefdom, rests his newspaper on his bare thighs. "You."

The task doesn't lend itself to unnecessary risk, so I don't hesitate to put the knife in his gut, where it's soft enough to penetrate fully. Shocked, he gropes for me, making guttural hiccups.

With the fire alarm whooping, I lean into him, smelling the last whiffs of the morning's aftershave and the after-noon rot of a half-day's worth of evil done, to give myself the right angle between knife and father.

"Die knowing I love her." I yank the blade upward with all my strength. The stink of shit fills the tiny bathroom. "And she loves me."

I crouch in front of him to look up at his popping eyes as he spits blood, making *ka-ka-ka* sounds, as if he wants to tell me something. His arms flail, the left hitting his right breast repeatedly.

"She was a gift to you." I put the heel of my hand on the base of the knife handle. "And now she's my partner. If you'd valued her even a little bit, she wouldn't be with me, making my shitty life worthwhile." I place my second heel behind the first. Peter keeps tapping his right chest. "Thank you, Pop."

With the power of my legs, I push forward and up. He makes a *hunh*.

"Thank you." I push again, burying the blade in his heart.

I step away so he won't knock me over when his ass slides forward on the toilet. His jacket opens, revealing a taut rectangle in his jacket lining. He was tapping the phone in his pocket.

"Come on!" Connor barks.

I remove my knife, then take the phone.

When we get outside, the rain has stopped.

And that is that.

I thought it would be sweeter.

Our car trudges uptown, tires splashing water from curb to pedestrians. In the back seat, I listen to Connor and Danny joking about the difference between guts being emptied *into* the toilet and *onto* the toilet. I try to hide the fact that I'm shaking. It could be the complexity of the job, the identity of the man my knife cut into, the end of an era, or the beginning of a new one.

Whichever it is, something inside me rattles for attention. I need to talk to her. She's already called me, and I put it out of my mind to execute this plan in time. I called Benny before we started the job and he said everything was fine. How long has passed?

We're still in the city. A good forty minutes from privacy, maybe more if there's any flooding on the east side. I don't have that long to make sure she's all right.

She answers. Thank God.

"Prima." I try to keep it down, but my guys stop joking. It's now too quiet. "You called me."

I was so relieved to hear her voice I didn't notice she's sobbing. I slap Danny in the back of the head and point to the side. He pulls up to a space in front of a hydrant.

"What's going on, prima?" I get out of the car and jump

a puddle to the nearest storefront—a smoke shop lit up in purple and red.

"I'm so happy."

She didn't just call me, tonight of all nights, to tell me she ate a cookie or saw a good movie.

"Why?" Leaning against the glass, I turn my face away from the street to the display of pipes and hookahs.

"You're alive." In the mirror behind a two-foot-tall glass bong, a wild-eyed man stares back at me. He has a smear of blood across his neck and a thick drop above his left eyebrow.

"Of course I'm alive. Did you think I wasn't?"

"I knew." She breaks down into sobs of joy, broken only by bursts of laughter. She's hysterical, and I don't have time for it. Not now.

"Prima! Please." When I lift my hand to rub away the drop of blood, I see the reflection of darkened fingernails. It's not dirt under them.

"Denise called."

"Finally."

"They're all saying Massimo threw you under a train. She said you were dead, and I should come home."

Never. She's never going back there. Denise misses her friend, or the Colonia planted the call.

"And I knew." She makes her last straggling sniffles. "I just knew."

"Did you tell her where you are?"

"No. But Dario. Before we leave, we have to go get her. Marco's—"

"No. Sarah. Listen to me. I'm moving Benny to the house. You... just..." I don't know what to instruct her.

There's nothing concrete to command. "Please. Just hold it together. I'm coming. Soon. Okay? Just hold steady."

"Okay." She swallows her panic.

"Don't pick up the phone unless you know who it is."

"Got it."

"I love you." I say that to her after I made sure her father knew it. With his blood under my nails, I said that, and I have more to say. "I love you and we're going to be swimming with sharks together really soon. Okay?"

"I love you too."

"Hang up so I can send Benny over."

She hangs up. The center cannot hold. She's not ready to be in my life, and I'll never be ready to be separated from her. I have to get the both of us out of here.

Once in the car, I text Benny a quick note to go to the house and keep his eyes on my wife until the new guys arrive. He gives me a thumbs-up. I put Oliver in charge of sending anyone he can spare from Dasano's, which is closer to where she is.

Good. Done. Secured.

We're going. For sure. There are sharks waiting.

Sarah will meet Nico. See what Oria's like when she's not panicked and stricken. Sarah can take a job in our operation, or work with Willa, or spend the days and nights getting fucked.

Something in my pocket make a sharp, electronic sound I don't recognize.

"Which one of you left fucking sounds on?" Connor barks.

"Peter Colonia." I take out the dead man's phone.

"Amateur," Connor grumbles. "That's what happens when you have it too good."

It's not a call. It's an invitation to a live feed. I have the sense to be alarmed.

I just spoke to Sarah. It was really her and she was really all right. She wasn't faking it.

I accept the feed.

"What's that gutted fucker's kink?" Connor turns to ask me from the front seat.

"Underground garage porn." I hold up the phone to show him the video feed of a generic concrete lot. Two spaces—boundaried by worn-out white lines—are taken up with black Mercedes sedans. Connor squints at the screen.

"The tow away sign." He stretches to get closer. "Monument Towing. That's ours."

The towing of illegally parked cars in my buildings is managed by Monument, which is owned by—once you get through the Russian doll structure—me.

I turn the screen back to me, and the sign, right there, promises that if you park illegally, and your car is gone, you should call Monument. Then I recognize the scribble of graffiti on one of the pillars. And the way the number two painted in front of one spot has a smeared top hook.

"It's the lot on 116th and Lex," I say as a truck pulls into frame, knocking the clearance beam.

"The sound's on? How the fuck—?"

"Danny," I call. "Get us there."

"Got it, boss."

There's only one reason this would be on Peter's phone. Bad things are about to happen.

Connor doesn't need to be told this is serious. He unbuckles and climbs in the back seat.

The truck rumbles hard, brakes squeaking when it turns right. It's going to hit the low crossbeam if it goes too far.

"Call Oliver. Everyone who isn't with Sarah needs to head over there right now."

"Done."

Big letters are printed on the side of the truck.

KING PENGUIN

COLD SOLUTIONS

A penguin in a red hat and scarf stands in front of the black letters, giving an impossible thumbs-up.

The rain stopped like God's tap, but the traffic hasn't caught up. I calculate how long it'll take to get there.

The truck head-in parks between two Mercedes. A man gets out of one and points at the camera I'm watching through. His voice is muffled, but it's a question.

This is for Peter's eyes. They have to know he was murdered twenty minutes ago.

A Suburban pulls in and Sergio Agosti gets out with three other men. He looks at the camera and holds up a middle finger.

They know. My fingers go cold.

Sergio takes a pair of glasses from his pocket and puts them on, smiling, squinting, postured like a guy who sits in front of computers all day.

They're Nico's glasses.

"Connor." I speak too low for the devil to hear. "Tell Benny the plan's changed. He needs to send everyone down. Every last man except him needs to be at 116th and Lex immediately."

That truck's cargo isn't a peace offering.

CHAPTER 34

SARAH

The teapot whistles over the flameless, heatless burner. I move it away from the magnets and listen to it hiss, wondering where Benny is.

Dario's alive. He's on his way back. He told me so, but he also told me Benny was coming to the house. He should have been here already.

A noise from the yard snaps me out of it. A high-pitched scrape of metal on stone.

I look out the sliding glass doors. A deer is dragging an aluminum chair backward across the patio. It's stuck in his antlers. He shakes, whipping it around, then folds under its weight.

I run outside to calm an eight-hundred-pound beast.

The idiocy of this plan doesn't hit me until I'm barefoot on the patio stones, face to face with a terrified animal huffing clouds of cold breath. I put out my hands, which does nothing. He's not afraid of me in particular. The antlers are so entangled in the four legs of the chair,

I'm not sure anything less than sawing them off will help.

"Benny?" I say in a normal voice so I don't scare the deer, but of course he wouldn't hear me unless he were already close enough to see this, which he's not.

The deer gets up on his hind legs, makes a distressed honking noise, and drops down with a *clop* that shakes me. He twists his head as if he's trying to screw and unscrew it, but now the chair's even tighter.

There's nothing I can do alone. I back up slowly, hands raised in surrender to and readiness for an enemy I can't beat. When I get in the house and slide the glass door closed, the distance and safety clarify the size of the animal.

"Cripes."

I need help. My phone's upstairs. I'll call Dario and he'll either send someone or I'll find out he's still here somewhere. On the way there, I pass the door under the stairs that leads to the security center. Maybe the video will show where Benny is. My thumbprint opens the door.

"I remember you!" someone exclaims from inside.

I know the voice. Even though it's coming from a speaker, it's hollow and echoing, almost drowned out by a loud rumble, but it's him.

Sergio. My never-to-be husband.

I go into the room. All the monitors are flickering between dead scenes. Gates. Lobbies. Alleys. An underground parking garage. That one is full of men in dark jackets. Guns. Wide stances. A face-off of some kind. A man turns with his arm out like a host welcoming holiday guests.

Sergio, standing in a puddle made by the tailpipe drip of a white box truck.

KING PENGUIN

COLD SOLUTIONS

I scan the men, looking for Dario, but I don't see him.

Does that mean he's somewhere safe?

Was this his plan?

Is this how he feels every time he can't protect me? It's awful, and he's competent and capable. If he wasn't, I'd put him in a box and lock it to keep him safe.

"Whassup, dickhead?" Sergio asks playfully. "Long time."

Through the opposite line of men, Dario emerges.

His image is no more than a flickering mass of glowing dots. Step by step. Not rushing. Head high. Shoulders straight. At peace with his darkness. In full control of untold power.

A king this mighty doesn't need a crown.

"What are you doing here?" he asks as if Sergio's question, his insult, and his observation are all meaningless buzzing.

"Who put you in charge of stupid questions?"

My father used to reply with that when I asked about his business. I didn't have a response until I was about thirteen. It was "You," and he didn't like it. Not one bit.

Dario answers with his own question. "What do you want?"

I can't discern anyone's expression in the mud of blobs

and shadows, but I don't like it. I want to tell Dario to duck, or run, or just shoot at everything.

"Wanna show you something really fucking cool." Sergio pulls down the metal rod that runs vertically along the back of the truck. "You came to my wedding, which didn't come off exactly, but what stood out to me, was you forgot to introduce me to your family." He snaps another lock.

I'm going to see something I don't want to, and I'm powerless to stop it or look away.

"Or maybe." Sergio shrugs. "Your brother fell out of your pocket when you were running away."

Sergio opens the double doors. Bright light shines from the back, momentarily blinding the camera. When it adjusts, the contents of the refrigerated truck pinch into view.

A man in a room behind a glass door that's frosted with water crystals at the corners. His blue lips are working a mile a minute, and his clothes are strewn all over the bare floor, leaving his skin icy white and his shrunken penis retreating into the warmth of his gut.

This must be Nico.

"You're an animal," Dario roars with the full force of his rage.

"It's an old truck," Sergio says. "The thermostat's shot. He got hypothermic quicker than we thought."

"What do you *want*?!"

"I mean, my dad wants a bite of the LES and Peter wanted his daughter back but—"

"He threw her away twice."

"And now he's dead in a donut shop and I got a popsicle for my trouble. Kinda sucks for everybody."

"You can't have her." Dario's trying to sound calm, and maybe he's succeeding, but through the security speakers, his words are a tremor.

"How you doin' in there, pal?" Sergio knocks on the window to get Nico's attention.

"*Don't need no car to get to junktown.*" Nico sings what sounds like a childhood jingle.

"I can negotiate the Lower East Side!" Dario shouts.

"*No train, no boat, no bicycle.*"

"For a popsicle? Sure. But now you gotta make the Colonia whole too. You did just kill the Big Daddy."

"*Just two feet and some snacks for the ride.*"

Silence from everyone but Nico, who keeps singing and singing. No deal is being made, but nothing's being denied.

"*Ladder, stairs, and fences riding hard going...*"

"Take him out now," Dario demands. "As a show of good faith."

"*... where no buffalo roam, just big iron beasts.*"

"Why?" Sergio asks as if it's a completely legitimate question. "He's got a good six minutes left in that song." He bangs on the frost-crackled plexiglass. "Don't you, buddy?"

"*With big toothy buckets, yeah, going...*"

Dario says something I can't hear, then reaches under his jacket. Every man in the lot draws their gun. Dario holds up a hand, then lowers it. His men lower their weapons.

"What are you doing?" I ask the screen.

"*Home, home, home to junktown.*"

Dario removes his gun from the holster and holds it with fingertips pinching the handle.

"Take me," he says, louder this time.

"No," I tell him from miles and miles away in my safe house. "No!"

"Let him go." He puts the gun on the ground and holds up his hands. "Forget Sarah. Just take me."

"No!" I scream, elongating the vowel in a forever denial, as two men drag Dario out of the frame and the parking lot erupts into gunfire.

When I have no breath, the scream continues.

I tap keys, trying to find the next camera. I need to see where they've taken him. If I lose sight, I don't know what they'll do to him. But there's a ramp. An office. A safe.

And still, my scream continues.

The deer in the woods, knocking his antlers into a tree to untangle the chair. The back gate at the end of the service road.

The scream.

The front gate.

On the other side—a man standing next to an idling car.

And inside the gate—Benny, face down in the mud.

The scream isn't mine. It's not even a scream. It's the beep of the front gate intercom. The man has his back to me. He's pushing it over and over.

Who is it?

"Who is it?" I ask, but he can't hear me from this tiny room.

It doesn't matter. I don't care who it is. I care about Dario. The only man who's ever loved me for who I am and who I can become.

Sobbing, I try to bring back the underground parking lot, but I can't.

A door.

A stairwell.

The deer.

The front gate again.

Benny hasn't moved, but the man has turned.

It's Massimo.

I freeze. The far away danger to Dario has become very personal and very close.

Run. I'm going to run. That, I can do. I run out of that terrible room, through the kitchen, to the garage. When I thumb the pad, the light goes from red to green, but the door won't open. I jerk it back and forth, but the rain has swelled the wood to a near-impossible size. I ram my shoulder against it.

"Ow!"

Can I go around? Or just walk down the driveway?

No. Enough is enough. This is the best way, and I can get through. I throw my shoulder against the door even harder, and it pops open with a squeak.

The loud beeping is nonstop, even here in the garage.

The Audi is gone, but the Buick shines, uncovered and ready. Dario keeps the keys in the cabinet. It opens without a trick or delay. No fingerprint required because every second counts. Keys in the door, guns on the rack. I open the garage door with the button on the wall and take the keys with the MET 5th AVE keychain.

I can't save Dario from here, but I can get to him. I take a rifle that looks like one I saw on television. Is it the same kind? Holding one end, I slide the wood tube on the bottom against the black barrel on top. It clicks.

Right. Slide, shoot, slide, shoot.

I realize I can't run. The outer gates won't open for me. My access was set up to protect me and now it's trapping me.

But the back gate. Maybe it's stuck. Maybe it got left open on garbage day. And anyway, if I can't open it, I'll shoot it open. Drive out the back while Massimo's in the front, waiting to bring me home so I can fulfill a trade my husband would never make.

I'll find Dario. I'll get him. We will swim with sharks together.

I put the rifle in the trunk and get into the car. My ears are relieved from the constant screeching when the door closes.

The car starts.

"Okay," I say to myself. "I know how."

I push the brake and put the car into drive. Ease up on the brake. I go out to the turn and stop.

Getting to the back is easy. Left around the house, then follow the road. Should be right around there.

But Massimo's in the front, trying to take me away. He can chase me.

More importantly, he has value.

I can use him to get Dario back.

I go straight, to the front, so slowly it seems like forever before the gate comes into view. But there it is, with Massimo's car pulled right up to it, and my brother pushing the intercom button enough to wake the dead.

I stop before hitting Benny's body. Massimo sees me and takes pressure off the button to wave with both hands. I get out.

"Goody!" He grips the bars of the gate as though he's

jailed. "You're okay! We tracked your number from that call and..."

He's smiling. How can he be happy?

"... now I can take you where it's safe."

"I'm not going with you." I walk around to the back of the Buick and open the trunk.

"Everything's going to absolute shit," he says. "You have to come with me. It's..."

When I slap the trunk closed, I have the rifle over my shoulder.

His eyes go wide. "What are you doing?"

"Where are they taking him?"

"Put that down before you hurt someone."

I point it in his direction. I don't know if I'm aiming right, but I imitate what I saw on television, putting it at my hip, not in front of my face. I'll figure out if I'm doing it right once Massimo tells me where they took my husband.

"Where is he?" I demand.

"Who?"

"Emo!" The tops of my lungs empty until all I have left are sobs. "Tell! Me!"

"What happened to you?"

I pull the trigger. Get thrown back a step as the bullet goes who-knows-where.

"Jesus fuck!" Massimo cries. "Are you serious?"

I get both feet under me and the muzzle back up. I'm panting so hard I don't know if I'll even get that close to hitting a target again.

I don't want to.

I can't possibly shoot him, but when I slide the bottom

of the gun against the top, the loud click is enough to scare the hell out of a grown man—and I feel the power in that.

"You're not gonna shoot me, Goody. Unless you aim for Hoboken or something."

He's trying to make me laugh so I'll calm down and not shoot him by accident, because I'm crying too hard to shoot him on purpose.

"Can you just put that down for a minute?" He holds out his hands. He hasn't taken out his own gun yet. He trusts me too much.

"I won't trade myself for Dario," I say through tears. "And don't lie. You'll never let him go. Not for me. Not for someone you don't value more."

"You're not making any sense."

He's talking as if I'm a toddler or a crazy person. But I'm just a woman, sob-racked, breathing through snot, shoulders shaking too much to aim this gun at the side of a barn.

Useless. Valueless.

They'll only give Dario up for someone they value more, and that isn't me.

My tears dry up like a drop of water on a hot pan. I sniffle. Take my hand off the gun long enough to wipe my nose with my cuff.

"That's better," Massimo says.

"Is it?" I put both hands back on the gun, stalling, while I look for the place where the gate's power meets its motor. "Is it really?"

Dario said he'd shoot out the locks in Precious Blood, but I don't know what to shoot to get out of here.

"Just open the gate," he says, with no understanding of the situation. All he knows how to do is give orders.

By force of will, I quell my shaking shoulders. I won't be able to shoot this gate open or drive away if I'm trembling like a child.

"If you say so." I shoot at the lock at the center, where the two gates are joined.

They pop loose. Massimo ducks.

"Jesus fucking Christ!"

"Open them!" I bark while sliding and clicking the gun mechanism. I get in the car without even seeing if he obeys me. I put it in drive and look up to find Massimo pushing the gates open.

I don't have time to be shocked or pleased. All I have time for is letting up on the brake, letting the car roll forward, next to Massimo's, where I stop.

"Massi."

He leans into my window and says, "I need you to come with me." Massimo speaks like a brother whose sister has always done what she was told. "I'm in charge now. They got Dad."

"In a donut shop," I murmur, completing the sentence. *Now all I got is a popsicle.*

"So, you know." Massimo taps his fist on the top of the door. "Murdered him on the fucking toilet."

He expects me to feel something. A delicate feminine sadness. Maybe a gun-toting, murderous rage. What I feel is nothing.

"If Dad's dead," I say, "and you're in charge now, that makes you really valuable for a trade."

"A what?" He shakes his head to get out the last of his sister's nonsense. "Goody. Wake up. Our father was stabbed to death."

He still thinks I want to go see Daddy's body and weep behind a black veil.

"It's a good idea, and no one gets hurt. Please do it, Emo. It's no skin off your back at all. You'll just go be in charge like you were always meant to be. I'll get Dario back and we—he and I—we'll go away. I swear, we'll never set foot in New York again. You'll forget I even existed. Just let me trade you."

"You're talking crazy." He opens the Buick's door but doesn't grab for me. "Let's go. Right now. Come on." He backs up, takes five steps to his car, and opens the door to get in. "And leave the gun before you hurt someone."

I take the rifle and stand with the barrel to him. "You know I know how to shoot this thing!"

"You got lucky half the times you've used it."

"Don't make me shoot you."

"Okay, fine." He puts his hands up and comes to me, smirking.

"You drive." I step aside.

"You really had a time of it, didn't you?" Instead of going straight to the driver's seat, he leans in my direction, and his intention to grab the gun is the clearest thing I've ever known.

I shoot him.

He falls, holding his leg, screaming.

"I'm sorry, Massimo," I say too quietly for him to hear as I toss the rifle into the passenger seat. "I was aiming for your shoulder."

He's bleeding. He could die. He's useless dead.

I push the front seat forward and yank my brother up.

"Why?" he screams.

"Just don't die." I put his arm around my shoulder.

"Why did you do it?" He follows with a string of curses through his teeth.

"Because what I value is important. Lean on me and your good foot. Come on."

"What you value? What are you talking ab—?" He's past screaming, but grunts, red-faced, when the pain is too much.

"Easy does it. One more." I let him use me as a crutch to get into the back seat, then I slap the door shut.

Okay.

I have this.

I'm not smart enough or experienced enough to execute this plan. Dario would be ashamed of how little I've thought it out, but I'm brave enough and more than desperate enough to get killed trying it.

First, I'm going to drive this car.

TO BE CONTINUED

BREAK ME is the last book in the series.
Get it everywhere.

If you're looking for something to tide you over until book three is out, I recommend *The DiLustro Arrangement*...a complete mafia romance trilogy.

When he forced me to marry him, I cried for love I'd never know.
When he locked me away, I cried for the freedom I lost forever.

Every other tear I've shed is for my soul, because I'm falling for the devil himself.

Mafia Bride | Mafia King | Mafia Queen

You can start it now with *MAFIA BRIDE*!

Keep in touch!

I've got a really cool Facebook group, a Twitter feed that's 78% political rage-outs, and a TikTok that I've been told is hilarious and that I use to feed my Instagram.

If you're not into social media (and who can blame you?), sign up for my mailing list.

ACKNOWLEDGMENTS

1. When I was 19, I had a 1970 Buick Skylark. 350 V8. Cherry red with white interior and convertible top. Manual steering and brakes. One of the first US-manufactured catalytic converters. It was the most baller thing I've ever owned in my life. After driving it for a few months (I was fucking fabulous), my dad sent it to the mechanic for power brakes. I pulled it out of the parking spot and—because my muscle memory was used to the manual braking—proceeded to stop at the corner with an ear-splitting screech. I almost had a makeout session with the windshield. The rubber I laid down on that day is still there.

2. The kind of estate Dario's set up for the safe house probably exists in Yonkers, but it may or may not be in view of the light from the Executioner's Lighthouse. I couldn't figure out how to know that without going there myself. As much as I'd love a research trip home, actually flying across the country to check for lighthouse flashes seemed overkill.

3. I'm intrigued by the idea of illegal trade in post

WWII artifacts, so you'll probably see more stuff from *partigiani* and Italian Blackshirts as I build up this world.

4. This book—in particular—took a village of professionals, including but not limited to: Lyric Audiobooks for coordinating a perfect audio version in the nick of time, Laurelin Paige, who had the balls to be dead honest about the "final" draft, Cassie from Joy Editing who bent over backwards to get the job done, and Amy Vox Libris who made sure my left foot wasn't up my ass. No word on the whereabouts of the right foot, however.

PAIGE PRESS

Paige Press isn't just Laurelin Paige anymore...

Laurelin Paige has expanded her publishing company to bring readers even more hot romances.

Sign up for our newsletter to get the latest news about our releases and receive a free book from one of our amazing authors:

Laurelin Paige
Stella Gray
CD Reiss
Jenna Scott
Raven Jayne
JD Hawkins
Poppy Dunne
Lia Hunt
Sadie Black

ALSO BY CD REISS

THE DILUSTRO ARRANGEMENT

Some girls dream of marrying a prince. I never imagined I'd be sold to a king.

Mafia Bride | Mafia King | Mafia Queen

THE GAMES DUET

Adam Steinbeck will give his wife a divorce on one condition. She join him in a remote cabin for 30 days, submitting to his sexual dominance.

Marriage Games | Separation Games

THE EDGE SERIES

Rough Edge | On The Edge | Broken Edge | Over the Edge

THE SUBMISSION SERIES

One Night With Him | One Year With Him | One Life With Him

Made in the USA
Monee, IL
13 November 2022

17660731R00177